D0671367

Elsie's Widowhood

Elsie's Widowhood

Book Seven of
The Original Elsie Classics

Martha Finley

CUMBERLAND HOUSE
NASHVILLE, TENNESSEE

Elsie's Widowhood
by Martha Finley

Any unique characteristics of this edition:
Copyright © 2000 by Cumberland House Publishing, Inc.

Published by Cumberland House Publishing, Inc.,
431 Harding Industrial Drive, Nashville, Tennessee 37211.

Cover design by Bruce Gore, Gore Studios, Inc.
Photography by Dean Dixon Photography
Hair and Makeup by Calene Rader
Text design by Heather Armstrong

Printed in the United States of America
1 2 3 4 5 6 7 8 — 04 03 02 01 00

PREFACE

IT WAS NOT IN MY HEART to give my favorite child, Elsie, the sorrows of widowhood. But the public made the title and demanded the book; and the public, I am told, is autocratic.

So what could I do but write the story and try to show how the love of Christ in the heart can make life happy even under sore bereavement? The apostle says, "I am filled with comfort, I am exceeding joyful in all our tribulation;" and since trouble, trial, and affliction are the lot of all in this world of sin and sorrow, what greater kindness could I do you, dear reader, than to show you where to go for relief and consolation? That this little book may teach the sweet lesson to many a tired and burdened soul, is the earnest prayer of your friend,

—M.F.

CHAPTER FIRST

All love is sweet,
Given or returned. Common as light is love,
And its familiar voice wearies not ever.

—*S*HELLEY

"COME IN, VI, DARLING," said Mrs. Travilla's sweet voice, "we will be glad to have you with us."

Violet, finding the door of her mother's dressing room ajar, had stepped in, then drawn hastily back, fearing to intrude upon what seemed like a private interview between her and her namesake daughter. Elsie was seated on a cushion at her mamma's feet, her face half-hidden on her lap, while mamma's soft white hand gently caressed her hair and cheek.

"I feared my presence might not be quite desirable just now, mamma," Violet said merrily, coming forward as she spoke. "But what is the matter?" she asked in alarm, perceiving that tears were trembling in the soft, hazel eyes that were lifted to hers. "Dear mamma, are you ill? Or is Elsie? Is anything wrong with her?"

"She shall answer for herself," the mother said with a sort of tremulous gaiety of tone and manner. "Come, bonny lassie, lift your head and tell your sister of the calamity that has befallen you."

There was a whispered word or two of reply and Elsie rose hastily and glided from the room.

"Mamma, is she sick?" asked Violet, surprised and troubled.

"No, dear child. It is—the old story." And the mother sighed involuntarily. "We cannot keep her always; someone wants to take her from us."

"Someone! Oh who, mamma? Who would dare? But you and papa will never allow it!"

"Ah, my child, we cannot refuse; and I understand now, as I never did before, why my father looked so sad when yours asked him for his daughter."

Light flashed upon Violet. "Ah, mamma, is that it? And who—but I think I know. It is Lester Leland, is it not?"

Her mother's smile told her that her conjecture was correct.

Violet sighed as she took the seat just vacated by her sister, folded her arms on her mother's lap, and looked up with loving eyes into her face.

"Dear mamma, I am so sorry for you! For papa, too, and for myself. What shall I do without my sister? How can you and papa do without her? How can she? I'm sure no one in the world can ever be so dear to me as my own precious father and mother. And I wish—I wish Lester Leland had never seen her."

"No, darling, we should not wish that. These things must be. God in His infinite wisdom and goodness has so ordered it. I am sad at the thought of parting with my dear child, yet how could I be so selfish as to wish her to miss the great happiness that I have found in the love of husband and children?"

Violet replied with a doubtful "Yes, mamma, but —"

"Well, dear?" her mother asked with a smile, after waiting in vain for the conclusion of the sentence.

"I am sure there is not another man in all the world like papa—not one half so dear and good and kind and lovable."

"Ah, you may change your mind about that some day. It is precisely what I used to think and say of my dear father before I quite learned the worth of yours."

"Ah, yes, I forgot grandpa! He is—almost as nice and dear as papa. But there can't be another one. I'm very, very sure of that. Lester Leland is not half so nice. Oh, I don't see how Elsie can!"

"How Elsie can what?" asker her father, coming in at that moment and regarding her with a quizzical look and smile.

"Leave you and mamma for somebody else, you dear, dear, dearest father!" returned Vi, springing up and running to him to put her arms about his neck and half smother him with kisses.

"Then we may hope to keep you for a good while yet?" he said interrogatively, holding her close and returning her caresses in a most tender, fatherly fashion, the mother watching them with beaming eyes.

"Yes, indeed—till you grow quite tired of me, papa!"

"And that will never be, my dear. Ah, little wife, how rich we are in our children! Yet we are not rich enough to part with one without a pang of regret. But we will not trouble about that yet, since the evil day is not very near."

"Oh, isn't it?" cried Violet joyously.

"No, Lester goes to Italy in a few weeks, and it will be one, two, or maybe three years before he returns to claim his bride."

"Then it is not time to fret about it yet!" gleefully cried Vi, smiles chasing away the clouds from her brow.

At her age a year seems a long while in anticipation.

"No, daughter, nor ever will be," her father responded with gentle gravity. "I hope my little girl will never allow herself to indulge in so useless and sinful a thing as fretting over either what can or what cannot be helped."

"Ah, you don't mean to let me fret at all, I see, you dear, wise, old papa," she returned with a merry laugh. "Now I must find Elsie and pass the lesson on to her. For I shrewdly suspect she's fretting over Lester's expected departure."

"Away with you then!" was the laughing rejoinder and she went dancing and singing from the room.

"The dear, merry, light-hearted child," her father said looking after her. "Would that I could keep her always thus."

"Would you if you could, my husband?" Mrs. Travilla asked with a tender smile, a look of loving reverence, as he sat down by her side.

"No, sweet wife, I would not," he answered emphatically, "for as Rutherford says, 'grace groweth best in winter' and the Master says, 'As many as I love, I rebuke and chasten.'"

"Yes, and 'we must through much tribulation enter into the kingdom of God.' Ah, we could never choose for our precious children exemption from such trials and afflictions as He may see necessary to fit them for an eternity of joy and bliss at His right hand!"

"No, nor for ourselves, nor for each other, my darling. But how well it is that the choice is not for us! How could I ever choose a single pang for you, beloved? You are the vein of my heart, my life, my light, my joy!"

"Or I for you, my dear, dear husband!" she softly whispered as he drew her head to a resting-place upon his chest and pressed a long kiss of most ardent affection on her pure white brow. "Ah, Edward, I sometimes fear that I lean on you too much, love you too dearly! What would I ever do without you—husband, friend, counselor, guide— everything in one?"

Violet went very softly into her sister's dressing room and stood for several minutes watching her with a mixture of curiosity, interest, and amusement, before Elsie became aware of her presence.

She sat with her elbow on the window seat, her cheek in her hand, eyes fixed on some distant point in the landscape, but evidently with thoughts intent upon something quite foreign to it. The color came and went on the soft cheeks with every breath and conscious smiles played about the full, red lips.

At last turning her head and catching her young sister's eye, she crimsoned to the very forehead.

"Oh, Elsie, don't mind me!" Violet said, springing to her side and putting her arms around her. "Are you so very happy? You look so and I am glad for you; but—but I simply do not understand it in the least bit."

"What, Vi?" Elsie asked, half-hiding her blushing face on her sister's shoulder.

"How you can love anybody better than our own dear, darling, precious papa and mamma?"

"Yes. I—I don't wonder, Vi," blushing more deeply than before, "but they are not angry—dear, dear mamma and papa—it seems to me I never loved them half so dearly before—and they say it is quite natural and right."

"Then it must be, of course; but—I wish it was somebody else's sister and not mine. I can't feel as if a stranger has as much right to my own sister as I have. And I don't know how to do without you. Oh, Elsie, can't you be content to live on always in just the way we have ever since we were little bits of things?"

Elsie answered with an ardent embrace and a murmured "Darling Vi, don't be vexed with me. I'm sure you wouldn't if you knew how dearly, dearly I love you."

"Well, I suppose you can't help it!" sighed Violet, returning the embrace.

"Can't help loving you? No, indeed! Who could?" Elsie returned laughingly. "You wouldn't wish it surely? You value my affection?"

"Oh, you dear, old goose!" laughed Violet. "But that was a willful misunderstanding. There are none so stupid as those who won't comprehend. Now I'll run away and leave you to your pleasant thoughts. May I tell Molly?"

"Yes," Elsie answered with some hesitation, "she'll have to know soon. Mamma thinks it should not be kept secret, though it must be so long before—"

"Ah, that reminds me that I was to pass on to you the lesson papa just gave me—that fretting is never wise or right. I leave you to make the application," and she ran merrily away.

So joyous of heart, so full of youthful life and animation was she that she seldom moved with sedateness and sobriety in the privacy of home, but went tripping and dancing from room to room, often filling the house with birdlike warbling or silvery laughter.

Molly Percival sat in her own cheery, pleasant room, pen in hand and surrounded by books and papers over which she seemed very intent. Now and then she lifted her head and sent a sweeping glance through the open window. She was drinking in with delight the beauties of a panorama of hill and dale—sparkling river, cultivated field, and wild woodland, to which the shifting of lights and shadows as now and again a fleecy, wind-swept cloud partially obscured the brightness of the sun, lent the charm of endless variety.

Molly's face was bright with intelligence and good humor. She enjoyed her work and her increasing success. And she had still another happiness in the change that had come over her mother.

Still feeble in intellect, Enna Johnson had become as remarkable for gentleness and docility as she had formerly been for pride, arrogance, and self-will.

She had grown very fond of Molly, too, very proud of her attainments and her growing fame. She asked no greater privilege than to sit in the room with her, watching her at her work, and ever ready to wait upon her and do her errands.

And so she, too, had her home at Ion, made always welcome by its large-hearted, generous master and mistress.

"Busy, as usual, I see," remarked Violet as she came tripping in. "Molly you are the busiest bee and richly deserve to have your hive full of the finest honey. I'm the bearer of a bit of news very interesting to Elsie and me; in fact, I suppose I might say to all the family. Have you time to hear it?"

"Yes, indeed, and to thank you for your kindness in bringing it," Molly answered, laying down her pen and leaning back in a restful attitude. "But sit down first, won't you?"

"Thank you, no; it's time to dress for dinner. I must just state the fact and run away," said Violet, pulling out a tiny, gold watch set with brilliants. "It is that Elsie and Lester Leland are engaged."

"And your father and mother approve?" asked Molly in some surprise.

"Yes, of course. Elsie would never think of engaging herself to anybody without their approval. But why should they be expected to object?"

"I don't know, only — he's poor and most wealthy people would consider that a very great objection."

Violet laughed lightly. "What an odd idea! If there is wealth on one side, there's less need of it on the other, I should think. And he is intelligent, sensible, talented, amiable and good — rather handsome, too, if I do say."

"And so you are pleased, Vi?"

"Yes, no, I don't know," and the bright face clouded slightly. "I wish — but if people must marry, he'll do as well as another to rob me of my sister, I suppose."

She tripped away and Molly, dropping her head upon her folded arms on her work table, sighed quite deeply.

Someone touched her on her shoulder and her mother's voice asked, "What's the matter, Molly? You don't envy her that poor artist fellow, do you? You needn't. There'll be a better one coming along for you one of these days."

"No, no, not for me! Not for me!" gasped the girl. "I've nothing to do with love or marriage, except to picture it for others. It's like mixing delicious drinks for other lips, while I — I may not taste them — may not have a single drop to cool my parched tongue or quench my burning thirst."

At the moment life seemed to stretch out before her as a dreary waste, unbrightened by a single flower—a long, toilsome road to be trod in loneliness and pain. Her heart uttered the old plaint: "They seem to have everything and I nothing."

Then her cheek burned with shame and penitent tears filled her eyes as better thoughts came crowding into her mind.

Had she not a better than an earthly love to cheer, comfort, and sustain her on her way? Hadn't she a love that would never fail, a Friend who would never leave nor forsake her, whose sympathy was perfect, who was always touched with the feeling of her infirmities, and into whose ear she could ever whisper her every sorrow, perplexity, anxiety, certain of help—for His love and power were infinite.

And the minor blessings of her lot were innumerable: the love of kindred and friends, and the ability to do some good and give pleasure by the exercise of her God-given talents, not the least.

CHAPTER SECOND

Marriage is a matter of more worth
Than to be dealt in by attorneyship.

—*S*HAKESPEARE

LESTER LELAND WOULD SAIL in a few weeks for Europe. He was going to Italy to study the great masters and with the determination to spare no effort to so perfect himself in his art that his fame as the first of American sculptors should constitute a prize worthy to lay at the feet of his peerless Elsie.

Their engagement was presently made known to all the connection, and with no pledge or request of secrecy, her parents deeming such a course wisest to all parties. Elsie had many suitors and it was but just to them to let it be understood that her selection was made.

The communication was made by note to each family, which note contained also an invitation to a family dinner at Ion, given in honor of the newly affianced pair.

Of course the matter called forth more or less of discussion in each household, everyone feeling privileged to express an opinion in regard to the suitableness of the proposed match.

It created some surprise at the Oaks, but as Lester was liked and his genius admired by them all, there were no unfavorable comments.

At Ashlands the news was received in much the same way, Herbert remarking, "Well, as it isn't Vi, I don't care a pin."

Of, course everyone at Fairview was delighted. At Pinegrove it was pronounced "an odd affair, but just like the Travillas—in choosing their friends and associates they never seemed to look upon wealth as a recommendation or the want of it as an objection."

It was at breakfast time that the note of invitation, addressed to old Mr. Dinsmore, reached Roselands. He glanced over it, then read it aloud.

"My great-granddaughter engaged to be married!" he remarked as he laid it down. "I may well feel myself an aged patriarch! Though 'few and evil have the days of the years of my life been,'" he added, low and musingly, ending with a heavy sigh.

"No such thing, father!" said Mrs. Conly, in a quick, impatient tone. "I'm not going to hear you talk about yourself. You have always been an honorable, upright, polished gentleman."

"But what a wretched misalliance is this!" she commented, with covert delight, taking up the note and glancing over its contents. "A poor artist, destitute of fame and money alike, to mate with an heiress to hundreds of thousands! Why, poor as I and my children are, I should have rejected overtures from him for one of my girls with scorn and indignation."

"Which would have been a decided mistake, I think, mother," remarked Calhoun, respectfully. "Leland is a fine fellow, of good family, and very talented. He'll make his mark someday and you may live to take pride in saying that the wife of the famous sculptor Leland is a niece of yours."

"A half grandniece," she corrected, bridling. "But I shall be an ancient dame indeed before that comes to pass."

"I have found him a gentlemanly and intelligent fellow," remarked Arthur, "and as for money, Elsie is likely to have enough for both."

"So she is," said the grandfather.

"And he is thoroughly good and will make a kind and appreciative husband," added Isadore.

Virginia looked scornful and contemptuous. "He's too goody-goody for me," she said, "but just like the Travillas in that, so will fit in exactly, I presume. Well, if people like to make fools of themselves, I don't see that we need be unhappy about it. We'll accept the invitation, of course, mamma?" turning to her mother. "And the next question is what shall we wear?"

"We must wear handsome dinner attire, of course," was the reply, "for though none but relatives and connections are to be present, it will be a large company."

"Yes, and I've no fancy for being outshone by anybody. Aunt Rose is sure to be very elegantly attired, Cousin Ross Lacey and Cousin Horace's wife no less so. Talk of my fondness for dress—it's small compared to theirs!"

"It is principally the doing of the husbands," said Isadore. "Both—or I might say all three, for Uncle Horace is no exception—are very fond of seeing their wives well dressed."

"An excellent trait in gentlemen—the determination that his nearest female relatives shall make a good appearance," remarked Mrs. Conly, furtively glancing from father to sons.

"But the ability to bring it about is not always commensurate with the desire, mother," replied Isadore softly.

"Thank you, Isa," said Calhoun, following her from the room, for she had risen from the table with her last words. "My mother does not seem to comprehend the difference between my circumstances and those of some of our relatives, and I am sure has no idea of the pain her words sometimes give to grandpa, Art, and myself."

"No, Cal, or she could never be so cruel," Isa answered, laying her hand affectionately on his arm and looking lovingly into his eyes. "I know that my brothers deny themselves many an innocent gratification for the sake of their mother and sisters. And Cal, I do appreciate it."

"I know you do, Isa. Now tell me what you will want for this—"

"Nothing," she interrupted, with an arch smile up into his face. "Do you suspect me of praising your generosity for a purpose? I have everything I want for the occasion. I do assure you. But, Cal, what do you suppose Uncle Horace will think of Elsie's choice?"

"He will not object on the score of Leland's lack of wealth, unless I am greatly mistaken. But here he comes to speak for himself," he added as a horseman was seen coming up the avenue at a brisk canter.

They were standing in the hall, but now stepped out on the veranda to greet Mr. Dinsmore as he alighted. He gave his horse in charge to a young man who came eagerly forward to the service quite sure that he would be suitably rewarded.

It was the lad's firm conviction that "Massa Horace" possessed an inexhaustible supply of small coins, some of which were apt to be transferred to the pockets of those who waited upon him.

Greetings were exchanged and Mr. Dinsmore said, "I am on my way to Ion. Suppose you order your pony, Isa, and ride over with me. They will be glad to see you. I want a few moments chat with my father, and that will give you time to don your hat and habit."

Isadore was not loath and within half an hour they were on their way.

"You have heard the news?" her uncle remarked inquiringly of her.

"Of Elsie's engagement? Yes, you were discussing it with grandpa and mamma, were you not?"

"Yes," and he smiled slightly.

"You don't think as she does about it, uncle?"

"No, I am fully satisfied—that the young man is well-bred, good, amiable, honest, intelligent, educated, talented, and industrious seems to me quite sufficient. My only objection is that the engagement seems likely to be a long one. And yet, that has the advantage of leaving the dear child longer in her father's house."

"Of which I for one am very glad," said Isa. "What a sweet girl she is, uncle!"

"Yes, she strongly resembles her mother in person and character. She has always seemed to me a sort of second edition of her."

They found the Travillas, old and young, all out on the veranda enjoying a family chat before scattering to their various employments for the day.

Grandpa, though seldom a day passed without a visit from him to Ion, was welcomed with all the effusion and delight that might reasonably have been expected if he had not been seen for a month. His daughter's eyes shone with filial love and pleasure as they exchanged their accustomed affectionate greeting. And, as he took possession of the comfortable armchair Mr. Travilla hastened to offer, his grandchildren clustered about him—the little ones climbing his knees with the freedom and fearlessness of those who doubted neither their right nor their welcome.

But in the meantime Isadore was not forgotten or overlooked. She too was quite at home at Ion and always made to feel that her visits were esteemed both welcome and a pleasure.

There was a slight timidity of manner, a sweet half-shyness about the younger Elsie this morning that was very charming. Her eyes drooped under her grandfather's questioning look and smile and the color came and went on her fair cheeks.

He said nothing to her, however, until the younger ones had been summoned away to their studies, then turned to her with the remark, "I must congratulate Lester Leland when next I see him. Well, my dear child, I trust you have not made a hasty choice?"

"I think not, grandpa. We have known each other quite intimately for several years," she answered, casting down her eyes and blushing deeply. "You do not disapprove?"

"I've no right to object if your parents are satisfied," he said. "But there, do not look uncomfortable. I really think Lester a fine fellow and am quite willing to number him among my grandchildren."

She gave him a bright, grateful look, then she and Isa stole away together for a little, girlish confidence, leaving the older people to a more businesslike discussion of the matter.

On every subject of grave importance Mr. Dinsmore was taken into the counsels of his daughter and her husband. His approval on this occasion, though they had scarcely doubted it, was gratifying to both.

There were no declinations of the invitation to the family dinner party, and at the appointed time the whole connection gathered at Ion—a large and goodly troop—the adults in the drawing room and parlors, the little ones in the nursery.

There was the Roselands branch, consisting of the old grandfather, with his daughter, Mrs. Conley, and her numerous progeny.

From the Oaks came Mr. Horace Dinsmore, Sr., and Mr. Horace Dinsmore, Jr., with their wives and a bright, beautiful, rollicking, year-old boy, who the proud, young father styled Horace III. There were also Molly's half-brother and sister, Bob and Betty Johnson, to whom their aunt and uncle still gave a home and parental care and affection.

All the Howards of Pinegrove were there, too—three generations, two of the sons bringing wives and little ones with them.

The Carringtons, of Ashlands, were also present; for, though not actually related to the Travillas, the old and close friendship and the fact that they were of Mrs. Rose Dinsmore's near kindred, seemed to place them on the footing of relationship.

Mrs. Travilla's sister Rose was also there. She was now Mrs. Lacey, of the Laurels—a handsome place some four miles from Ion—and mother of a fine son, who she and her husband brought with them to the family gathering and exhibited to the assembled company with no little joy and pride.

It remains only to mention Lester Leland and his relatives of Fairview, who were all there, received and treated as honored guests by their entertainers and with urbane politeness by the others except Mrs. Conly and Virginia, who saw fit to appear almost oblivious of their existence.

They, however, took a sensible view of the situation and were quite indifferent as to the opinions and behavior toward them of the two haughty women.

No one else seemed to notice it. All was apparent harmony and good will. And Lester felt himself welcomed into the family with at least a show of cordiality from most of the relatives of his beloved.

She behaved very sweetly, conducting herself with a half-shy, modest grace that disarmed even Aunt Conly's criticism.

A few happy weeks followed, weeks rosy and blissful with love's young dream. Then, Lester tore himself away and left his Elsie mourning, for half the brightness and bloom of life seemed to have gone with him.

Father and mother were very patient with her, very tender and sympathizing, very solicitous to amuse and entertain and help her to renew her old zest for simple home pleasures and employments —the old enjoyment of their love and that of her brothers and sisters.

Ah! In later days she recalled it all—especially the gentle, tender persuasiveness of her father's looks and tones, the caressing touch of his hand, the loving expression of his eye—with a strange mixture of gladness and bitter sorrow. There was an unavailing, remorseful regret that she had not responded more readily and heartily to these manifestations of his strong fatherly affection. There came a time when a caress from him was coveted more than those of her absent lover.

❦❦❦❦❦❦❦

CHAPTER THIRD

*Faith is exceedingly charitable and
believeth no evil of God.*

—RUTHERFORD

DELICIOUS SEPTEMBER DAYS had come; the air was soft and balmy. A mellow haze filled the woods, just beginning to show the touch of the Frost King's fingers.

The children could not content themselves within doors and the wisely indulgent mother had given them a holiday to spend the morning with them on the banks of the lakelet, floating over its bright surface in their pretty, pleasure boat.

Returned to the house, she was now resting in her boudoir, lying back in a large easy chair with a book in her hand. Suddenly it dropped into her lap. She started up erect in her chair and seemed to listen intently.

Was that her husband's step coming slowly along the hall? It was like and yet unlike it—lacking the firm, elastic tread.

The door opened and she sprang to her feet. "Edward! You are ill!" for there was a deathly pallor on his face.

"Do not be alarmed, little wife; it is nothing—a strange pain, a sudden faintness," he said, trying to smile, but tottered and would have fallen had she not hastened to give him the support of her arm.

She helped him to a couch, placed a pillow beneath his head, and rang for assistance. Then she brought him a glass of cold water, cologne, and smelling salts from her dressing table. She was doing all with a deft quickness free from flurry, though her heart almost stood still with a terrible fear and dread.

What meant this sudden seizure, this anguish so great that it bowed in a moment the strength of a strong man? She had never known him to be seriously ill before. He had seemed in usual health when he left her for his accustomed round over the plantation only a few hours ago and now he was nearly helpless with suffering.

Servants were instantly dispatched in different directions — one to Roselands to summon Dr. Arthur Conly, another to the Oaks for her father, to whom she instinctively turned in time of trouble and who was ever ready to obey the call.

Both arrived speedily to find Mr. Travilla in an agony of pain, bearing it without a murmur, almost without a moan or groan, but with cold beads of perspiration standing on his brow. Elsie was beside him, calm, quiet, alert to anticipate every wish, but pale as a marble statue and with a look of anguish in her beautiful eyes. It was so hard to stand by and see the suffering endured by him who was dearer than her own life.

She watched Arthur's face as he examined and questioned his patient and saw it grow white to the very lips.

Was her husband's doom then sealed?

But Arthur drew her and Mr. Dinsmore aside. "The case is a bad one, but not hopeless," he said. "I am unwilling to take the responsibility alone, but must call in Dr. Barton and also send to the city for the best advice to be had there."

"We have great confidence in your skill, Arthur," Elsie said, "but let nothing be left undone. God alone can heal, but He works by means."

"And in the multitude of counselors there is safety," added Mr. Dinsmore. "Dear daughter, 'be strong and of a good courage.' There shall no evil befall you, for your heavenly Father knows, and will do what is best."

"Yes, papa, I know. I believe it," she answered with emotion. "Ah, pray for me, that strength may be given me according to my day and to him, my dear, dear husband. No murmuring thoughts arise in either of our hearts."

The news had flown through the house that its master and head had been stricken down with sudden, severe illness. Great were the consternation and distress among both children and servants, so beloved was he. So strange a thing did it seem for him to be ill, for he seldom had a day's sickness in all the years that they had known him.

Elsie, Edward, and Violet hastened to the door of the sick-room, begging that they might be admitted, that they might share in the work of nursing the dear invalid.

Their mother came to them, her sweet face vary pale, but calm. "No darlings," she said in her gentle, tender tones. "It will not do to have so many in the room while your dear father is suffering so much. Your grandpa, mammy, and I must be his only nurses for the present; though after a time, your services may be needed."

"Oh, mamma, it is very hard to have to stay away from him," sobbed Violet.

"I know it, dearest," her mother said. "And my heart aches for you and all my darlings; but I am sure you all love your dear father too well to unwillingly sacrifice your own feelings when to indulge them might injure him or only increase his pain."

"Oh, mamma, yes, yes, indeed!" they all cried.

"Well then, dears, go away now. Look after the younger ones and the servants—I trust them all to your care. And when the doctors say it will do, you shall see and speak to your father, and do anything for him that you can."

So with a loving, motherly caress bestowed upon each, she dismissed them to the duties she had pointed out and returned to her station beside her husband's couch.

Mr. Dinsmore, Arthur Conly, and Aunt Chloe were gathered about it engaged in efforts to relieve the torturing pain. His features were convulsed with it but his eyes wandered restlessly around the room as if in search of something. As Elsie drew near they fixed themselves upon her face and his was lighted up with a faint smile.

"Darling, precious, little wife," he murmured, drawing her down to him till their lips met in a long, loving kiss, "don't leave me for a moment. Nothing helps me bear this agony like the sight of your sweet face."

"Ah, beloved, if I might bear it for you," she sighed, her eyes filling with tears while her soft, white hand was laid tenderly upon his brow.

"No, no!" he said. "That would be far worse, much far worse!"

Her tears were falling fast.

"Ah, do not be so distressed; it is not unendurable," he hastened to say with a loving, tender look and an effort to smile in the midst of his agony. "And He, He is with me, the Lord, my Savior! 'I know that my Redeemer liveth,' and the sense of His love is very sweet, never so sweet before."

"Thank God that it is so! Ah, He is faithful to His promises!" she said.

Then kneeling by his side, she repeated one sweet and precious promise after another, the blessed words and loved tones seeming to have a greater power to soothe and relieve than anything else.

The other physicians arrived, examined, consulted and used such remedies as were known to them. Everything was done that science and human skill could do, but without avail. They could give temporary relief by the use of opiates and anesthetics, but were powerless to remove the disease that was fast hurrying its victim to the grave.

Both Mr. Travilla and Elsie desired to know the truth and it was not concealed from them. On Mr. Dinsmore fell the sad task of imparting it.

It was in the afternoon of the second day. The doctors had held a final consultation and communicated their verdict to him. Moved to his very heart's core at the thought of parting with his lifelong bosom friend, and more for the far sorer bereavement awaiting his almost idolized child, he waited a little to recover his composure, then entered the sick-room and drew silently near the bed.

Elsie sat close at her husband's side, one hand clasped in his, while the other she gently fanned him or wiped the death damp from his brow. Did she know it was that? Her face was colorless, but quite calm.

Mr. Edward Travilla was at the moment entirely conscious, and his eyes were gazing full into hers with an expression of unutterable love and the most tender compassion.

At length they turned from her face for an instant and were uplifted to that of her father, as he stood close beside her, regarding them both with features working with emotion.

The dying man understood its cause. "Is it so, Dinsmore?" he said feebly but with perfect composure. "Elsie, little wife," and he drew her to him, both tone and gesture full of exceeding tenderness. "Oh love, darling, precious one, must we part? I go to glory and bliss of heaven, but you, my dear—" His voice broke.

Her heart seemed broken in twain, but she must comfort him. One bursting sob as she hid her face upon his chest, one silent agonized cry to heaven for help, and lifting her head, she gave him a long look of love, then laid her cheek to his and put her arm about his neck.

"My darling, my dear, dear husband," she said in her sweetest tones, "do not fear for me or for the children. The Lord, even Jesus, will be our keeper. Do not let the thought of us disturb you now or damp the glad anticipation of the wondrous glory and bliss to which you go. Soon you will be with Him, 'forever with the Lord.' And how glad our darling Lily will be to see her beloved father, dear mother to recover her son, and what a little, little while it will seem till we all shall join you there, never, never to part again."

"And neither she, my dear daughter, nor her children, shall want for a father's love and care while I live, my dear friend," said Mr. Dinsmore, his voice tremulous with emotion.

"I know it, I know it, and God be thanked that I leave them is such good and loving hands," Mr. Travilla answered, looking gratefully at his friend.

"You trusted your darling child to me," he went on low and feebly and with frequent pauses for breath, "and I give her back to you. Oh, she has been a dear, dear wife to me!" he exclaimed, softly stroking her hair. "God bless you, my darling! God bless you for your faithful, unselfish love! You have been the sunshine of my heart and home."

"And you, my beloved, oh, what a husband you have been to me!" she sobbed, covering his face with kisses. "Never one unkind or impatient word, look, or tone—nothing but the tenderest love and care have I had from you since the hour we gave ourselves to each other. And I thought, oh, I thought we had many more years to live and love together! But God's will be done!"

"Yes," he said, "His will be done with me and also with mine. Darling, He will never leave nor forsake you; and though I am almost done with time, we shall have all the ages of eternity to live and love together."

Silent caresses were all that passed between them for some moments; then Mr. Dinsmore inquired if his friend had any final directions to give about any of his affairs.

"No," he said, "all that was attended to long since. Elsie knows where to find all my papers and understands everything in regard to the property and my business matters as well as I do.

"And my peace is made with God," he continued after a pause, speaking in a sweetly solemn tone. "His presence is with me. I feel the everlasting arms underneath and around me. All my hope and trust are in the blood and righteousness of Christ, my crucified and risen Savior. All is peace. I am a sinner saved by grace.

"Let me see my children and give them a father's blessing and I shall have nothing more to do but fall asleep in Jesus."

Elsie and Vi were together in a room across the hall from that in which their father lay, sitting clasped in each other's arms, waiting, hoping for the promised summons to go to him when he should be sufficiently relieved to bear their presence.

Ah, there was in each young heart an unspoken fear that he would never rise from that couch of pain, for they had seemed to read his doom in the grave, anxious faces of grandfather and physicians. But, oh, it was too terrible a fear for either to put into words even to her own consciousness! How could life go on without the father who had thus far constituted so large a part of it to them?

A shuffling step drew near and Aunt Chloe appeared before them, her face swollen with weeping, her eyes filled with tears.

"You's to come now, chillens."

"Oh, is papa better?" they cried, starting up in eager haste to obey the summons.

The old nurse shook her head, tears bursting forth afresh. "He's mos' dar, chillens, mos' dar whar dey don' hab no mo' pain, no mo' sickness, no mo' dyin'. I see de glory shinin' in his face. He's mos' dar."

Then as their sobs and tears burst forth, "Oh, my mistis, my bressed young mistis," she cried, throwing her apron over her head. "Yo' ole mammy'd die to keep massa here for yo' sake. But de Lord's will mus' be done, an' He neber makes no mistakes."

※※※※※※※※

CHAPTER FOURTH

Death is another life.

—BAILEY

"OH, ELSIE, ELSIE, what shall we do? But it can't be true!" sobbed Violet, clinging to her sister in a heart-breaking paroxysm of grief. "Oh, it will kill mamma and we shall lose her, too!"

"No, no, honey, not so," said Aunt Chloe. "My bressed young missus will lib for yo' sake, for her chillens' sake. An' you ain't gwine to lose massa — he's only gwine home a little while 'fore de rest."

"Dear Vi, we must try to be composed for both their sakes," whispered Elsie, scarcely able to speak for weeping.

"Dear bressed Lord, help dem both, help dese po' chillens!" exclaimed Aunt Chloe. "Come, chillens, we's losing precious time."

They wiped away their tears, checked their sobs by a determined effort and hand in hand followed her to the sickroom.

Perfect ease had taken the place of the agonizing pain which for many hours had racked Mr. Travilla's frame, but it was the relief afforded not by returning health but by approaching dissolution. Death's seal was on his brow. Even his children could read it as they gathered, weeping, about his death bed.

He had a few words of fatherly counsel, of tender, loving farewell for each—Elsie, Violet, Edward: to the last saying, "My son, I commit your mother to your tender care. You have almost reached man's estate. Take your father's place and let her lean on your young, vigorous arm; yet, fail not in filial reverence and obedience. Be ever ready to yield to her wise, gentle guidance."

"I will, father, I will, I promise," returned the lad in a choking voice.

"And may not I, too, and Herbert, papa?" sobbed young Harold.

"Yes, dear son, and all of you, love and cherish mamma and try to fill my place to her. And love and obey your kind grandpa as you have always loved and obeyed me."

One after another had received a last caress, a special parting word, till it had come to the turn of the youngest darling of all—little Walter.

They lifted him on to the bed, and creeping close to his father, he softly stroked the dying face, and kissing the lips, the cheeks, and the brow—cooed in sweet baby accents, "Me so glad to see my dear papa. Papa doin' det well now. Isn't you, papa?"

"Yes, papa's dear child, I'm going where sickness and pain can never come. My little boy must love the dear Savior and trust in Him; and then one day he shall follow me to that blessed land. Ah, little son, you are too young to remember your father. He will soon be forgotten!"

"No, no, dearest," said his weeping wife, "not so; your pictured face and our constant mention of you shall keep you in remembrance even with him."

"Thank you, my dearest wife," he said, turning a loving gaze on her. "It is a pleasant thought that my name will not be a forgotten sound among all of the dear ones left behind. We shall meet again, beloved wife, meet again beyond the river. I shall be waiting for you on the farther shore. I am passing through the waters, but He is with me, He who hath washed me from my sins in His own blood. And you, dearest wife—does He sustain you in this hour?"

"Yes," she said, "His grace is sufficient for me. Dear husband, do not fear to leave me to His care."

Tears were coursing down her white cheeks, but the low, sweet tones of her voice were calm and even. She was resolutely putting aside all thought of self and the sore bereavement that awaited her and her children that she might smooth his passage to the tomb. She would not that he should be disturbed by one anxious thought of them.

He forgot none of his household. Molly and her mother were brought in for a gentle, loving farewell word, then each of the servants.

He lingered still for some hours, but his wife never left him for an instant; her hand was clasped in his when the messenger came. His last look of love was for her, his last whisper, "Precious little wife, eternity is ours!"

Friends carried him to his quiet, resting-place beside the little daughter who had preceded him to the better land. Widow and children returned without him to the home hitherto made so bright and happy by his loved presence.

Elsie, leaning on her father's arm, slowly ascended the steps of the veranda, but on the threshold drew back with a shudder and a low, gasping sob.

Her father drew her to himself. "My darling, do not go in. Come with us to the Oaks. Let us take you all there for a time."

"No, dear papa, 'twould be putting off the evil day—the trial that must be borne sooner or later," she said in trembling, tearful tones. "But—if you will stay with me—"

"Surely, dearest, as long as you will. I could not leave you now, my poor stricken one! Let me assist you to your room. You are completely worn out, and must take some rest."

"My poor children—" she faltered.

"For their sakes you must take care of yourself," he said. "Your mamma is here. She and I will take charge of everything until you are able to resume your duties as mother and mistress."

He led her to her apartments, made her lie down on a couch, darkened the room, and sitting down beside her, took her hand in his.

"Papa, papa!" she cried, starting up in a sudden burst of grief. "Take me in your arms and hold me close as you used to do, as he has done every day that he lived since you gave me to him!"

"My poor darling, my poor darling!" he said straining her to himself. "God comfort you! May He be the strength of your heart and your portion forever! Remember that Jesus still lives and that your beloved one is with Him, rejoicing with joy unspeakable and full of glory."

"Yes, yes, but oh, the learning to live without him!" she moaned. "How can I? How can I?"

"'When thou passest through the waters, I will be with thee; and through the rivers, they shall not overflow thee. When thou walkest through the fire, thou shalt not be burned; neither shall the flame kindle upon thee. For I am the Lord thy God, the Holy One of Israel, thy Savior,'" he repeated in low, moved tones. "'Behold I have refined thee, not with silver; I have chosen thee in the furnace of affliction.' Dear daughter, my heart bleeds for you, and yet I know that He who has sent this sorrow loves you far better than I do, and He means it for good. 'Faith is the better of the free air and of the sharp winter storm in its face. Grace withereth without adversity.'"

"Yes, yes," she whispered, clinging to him. "Go on, dear papa, you bring me comfort."

"What is so comforting is the love of Christ!" he went on. "The assurance that 'in all our afflictions He is afflicted?' My darling, 'the weightiest end of the cross of Christ, which is laid upon you, lieth upon your strong Savior!'"

"And He will never let me sink," she said. "Oh, what love is His! And how unworthy am I!"

Never very strong, Elsie was, as her father plainly perceived, greatly exhausted by the combined influence of the fatigue of nursing, overwhelming sorrow, and the constraint she had put upon herself to control its manifestations while her husband lived.

She must have rest from every responsibility and care, must be shielded from all annoyances, and as far as possible, must be kept from every fresh reminder of her loss.

For several days he watched over her with unceasing care and solicitude, doing all in his power to soothe, to comfort and console, allowing only short visits with Rose and the children, and keeping everyone else away except her dear, old mammy.

Never had father and daughter seemed nearer and dearer to each other than in these sorrowful days. To lay her weary head upon him while his arms folded her close to his heart gave some relief—more than could anything else—for the unutterable longing to feel the clasp of those other arms whose loving embrace she could never know again on earth.

But her nature was too unselfish and affectionate to allow a long indulgence in this life of inactivity and nursing her grief. She could not resist the anxious, pleading looks of her children. She, their only remaining parent, must now devote herself to them even more entirely than had been her wont. Grandma Rose was kind as kind could be, but mamma's dear place could be filled by no one but herself.

"Dear papa," she said when three days had passed, "I am rested now, and you must please let me go back to my duties. My dear little ones need me, the older ones, too. I cannot deprive them of their mother any longer."

"Would it not be well to give yourself one more day of rest?" he asked, gazing sadly at the wan cheeks and the mournful eyes that looked so unnaturally large. "I do not think you are strong enough yet for anything like exertion."

"I think the sweet work of comforting and caring for my darlings—his children as well as mine," she said with a tremble in her voice, "will do me good."

"It is partly for their sakes that I want you to take care of yourself," he said, putting his arm about her, while her head dropped on his shoulder. "Would it not have been his wish? Were you not always his first care?"

She gave a silent assent, the tears coursing down her cheeks.

"And he gave you back to me, making you doubly mine—my own darling, precious child! And your life, health, and happiness must be my special charge," he said with exceeding tenderness.

"My happiness? Then, papa, you will not try to keep me from my darlings. My dear, dear father, do not think I am ungrateful for your loving care. Ah, it is very sweet and restful to lean upon you and feel the strong, tender clasp of your arm! But I must rouse myself and become a prop for others to lean upon."

"Yes, to some extent—when you are quite rested. But you must bear no burdens, dear daughter, that your father can bear for you."

She looked her gratitude out of her tear-dimmed and swollen eyes.

"God has been very good to me, in sparing me, my father," she said, "and to my children, my seven darlings—all good and loving. How rich I ought to feel! How rich I do feel, though so sorely bereaved."

The tears burst forth afresh.

"You will let me go to them?" she said when she could speak again.

"Tomorrow, if you will try to rest and gain strength today. I am quite sure it is what he would have wished—that you should rest a little longer. The children can come to you for an hour today."

She yielded for that time and the next day he withdrew his opposition and he himself led her down to the breakfast parlor, where all were gathered to partake of the morning meal.

CHAPTER FIFTH

Weep not for him that dieth
For he hath ceased from tears.

—MRS. NORTON

THERE WAS MUCH UNSELFISH love for their mamma and for each other displayed by the young Travillas in those sad days immediately following the death of their dearly loved father.

Every heart ached sorely with its own burden of grief — excepting for that of little Walter, who was too young to understand or realize his loss. Yet, he was most solicitous to assuage that of the brothers and sisters, but especially to comfort and help "poor, dear, dear mamma."

They were filled with alarm as they saw their grandfather almost carry her to her room, then close the door upon them.

"Oh," cried Violet, clinging to her older sister and giving way to a burst of terrified weeping, "I knew it would be so! Mamma will die, too! Oh, mamma, mamma, mamma!"

"Dear child, no!" said Rose, laying a caressing hand on the young weeper's arm. "Do not be alarmed; your dear mother is worn out with grief and nursing — she has scarcely slept for several days and nights — but is not ill otherwise. I trust that rest and the consolation of God will still restore her to her usual health and cheerfulness."

"Oh, grandma," sobbed Elsie, "do you think mamma can ever be cheerful and happy again? I am sure she can never forget papa."

"No, she will never forget him, never cease to miss the delight of his companionship; but she can learn to be happy in the thought of his eternal blessedness and the same reunion that awaits them when God shall call her home. She will find happiness in the love of Jesus and of her dear children, too."

Rose had thrown one arm about Elsie's waist, the other round Violet, and drawn them to a seat, while Edward and the younger children grouped themselves about her—Rosie and Walter leaning on her lap.

They all loved her and now hung upon her words, finding comfort in them, though listening with many tears and sobs.

She went on to speak at length of the glory and bliss of heaven, of the joy of being with Christ and free from sin, of being done with sorrow and sighing, pain and sickness and death. She spoke of the delight with which their sister Lily, their Grandmother Travilla, and other dear ones gone before must have welcomed the coming of their father. She told of the glad greeting that he would give to each of them when they too should reach the gate of the Celestial City.

"Yes, grandma, papa told us all to come," said Rosie.

"I know he did, dear child; and do you know the way there, my dear?"

"Yes, grandma, Jesus said, 'I am the way.' He died to save sinners, and He will save all who love

Him and trust Him alone, not thinking anything they can do is going to help to save them."

"Save them from what, darling?"

"From their sins, grandma, and from going to live with Satan and his wicked angels and wicked people that die and go there."

"Yes, that is all so, and oh, what love it was that led the dear Savior to suffer and die upon the cross that we might live! Dear children, it was His death that bought eternal life for your beloved father and has purchased it for us all if we will but take it as His free, unmerited gift."

"But, grandma," sobbed Harold, "why didn't He let our dear papa stay with us a little longer? Oh, I don't know how we can ever live without him!"

This called forth a fresh burst of grief from all. Even little Walter cried piteously, "I want my papa! I want my own dear papa!"

Rose lifted him gently to her lap and caressed him tenderly, her own tears falling fast.

"Dear children," she said, as the storm of grief subsided a little, "we must not be selfish in our sorrow. We must try to rejoice that your beloved father is far, far happier than he could ever be here. I think the dear Savior took him home because He loved him so much that He could no longer spare him out of heaven. And Jesus will be your Father now even more than He was before. 'A father of the fatherless and a judge of the widows is God in His holy habitation.'"

"I'm very glad the Bible tells us that," remarked Herbert, checking his sobs. "I have heard and read the words often, but they never seemed half so sweet before."

"No," said Harold, putting his arm about him, as the two were almost inseparable.

"And we have grandpa, too. Papa said he would be a father to us."

"And he will, dear children," said Rose. "I do not think he could love you much more than he does if he were your own father, as he is your dear mamma's papa."

"And God will help you if you ask Him," said Rose, "help you to be a great comfort and assistance to your mother and younger brothers and sisters."

"Ah, if we might only go to mamma!" sighed Violet, when she and Elsie had withdrawn to the privacy of their own apartment. "Do you think we might venture now?"

"Not yet awhile, I think — I hope she is resting; and grandpa will let us know when it will not disturb her to see us."

"Oh, Elsie, can we ever be happy again?" cried Violet, throwing herself into her sister's arms. "Where, where shall we go for comfort?"

"To Jesus and His word, dear Vi. Let us kneel together and ask Him to bless us all and help us to say with our hearts, 'Thy will be done,' all of us children and our dear precious mamma."

"Oh, we can't pray for papa anymore!" cried Vi, in an agony of grief.

"No, dear Vi, but he no longer needs our prayers. He is so close to the Master, so happy in being forever with Him, that nothing could add to his bliss."

Violet hushed her sobs and with arms about each other they knelt, while in low, pleading tones Elsie poured out their grief and their petitions into the ear of the ever compassionate, loving Savior.

Fortunately for them in this hour of sore affliction, they were no strangers to prayer or to the Scriptures, and knew where to turn to find the many, sweet, and precious promises suited to their needs.

Some time was given to this, and then Elsie, mindful of the duty and privilege of filling — to the best of her ability — her mother's place to the little ones, went in search of them.

The tea hour brought them all together again — all the children — but father and mother were missing. Oh, this gathering about the table was almost the hardest thing of all! It had been customarily a time of glad, free, cheerful, often mirthful exchange between parents and children. There was no rude and noisy hilarity, but the most enjoyable social conversation and exchange of thought and feeling, while showing the perfect respect and deference to their parents and unselfish consideration for each other. They were not under galling constraints but might ask questions and give free expression to their opinions if they wished, and were indeed encouraged to do so.

But what a change had a few days brought! There was an empty chair that would never again be filled by him to whom one and all had looked up with the tenderest filial love and reverence. All eyes turned toward it, then were suffused with tears, while one and another vainly strove to suppress the bursting sobs.

They could not sit down to the table. They drew close together in a little weeping group.

The grandparents came in and Mr. Dinsmore, trying to gather them all in his arms, caressed them in turn, saying in broken, tender tones, "My dear children, my poor dear children! I will be a father to you. I cannot supply his place, but will do so as nearly as I can. You know, my darlings, my sweet Elsie's children, that I have a father's love for you."

"Yes, grandpa, we know it." "Dear grandpa, we're glad we have you left to us," sobbed one and another of them.

"And mamma, dear, precious mamma! Oh, grandpa, is she sick?"

"Not exactly sick, my darlings," he said, "but very much worn out. We must let her rest."

"Can't we see her? Can't we go to her?"

"Not now, not tonight, I think. I left her sleeping and hope she will not wake for some hours."

At that the little ones seemed nearly heartbroken. How could they go to their beds without seeing their mamma.

But Elsie comforted them. She would help mammy put them to bed. And, oh, it was the best of news that dear mamma was sleeping! Because if she did not she would soon be quite ill.

Molly Percival, because of her crippled condition, making locomotion so difficult, seldom joined the family at the table, but took her meals in her own room. A servant waited upon her and her mother, who, in her new devotion to poor Molly, preferred to eat with her.

The appointments of their table were quite as dainty as those of the others, the fare never any less luxurious than theirs.

A very tempting repast was spread before them tonight, but Molly could not eat for weeping.

Her mother, tasting one dish after another with evident enjoyment, at length thought fit to talk with her.

"Molly, why do you cry so? I do wish you would stop it and eat your supper."

"I'm not hungry, mother."

"That's only because you're fretting so; and what's the use? Mr. Travilla's better off, and besides he was nothing to you."

"Nothing to me! Oh, mother, he was so good, so kind to me, to Dick, to everybody about him! He treated me like a daughter, and I loved him as well as if he had been my own father. He did not forget you or me when he was dying, mother."

"No, and it was good of him. Still, crying doesn't do any good. And you'll get weak and sick if you don't eat."

Molly's only answer was a burst of grief. Oh, poor, poor Cousin Elsie! Her heart must be quite broken, for she idolized her husband. And the girls and all of them—how they did love their father!"

The servants came in with a plate of hot cakes and a slender girlish figure presently stole after, without knocking, for the door stood open, and went to the side of Molly's chair. It was Violet, looking oh so sad and sweet, so fair and spiritual in her deep mourning dress.

In an instant she and Molly were locked in each other's arms mingling their sobs and tears together.

"I'm afraid we have seemed to have neglected you, Molly dear," Violet said when she could speak, "but—"

"No, no, you have never done that!" cried Molly, weeping afresh. "And how could I expect you to think of me at such a time! Oh, Vi, Vi!"

"Mamma cannot come up, for she is not—not able to leave her room, and—and, oh, Molly, I'm afraid she's going to be sick!"

Molly tried to comfort and reassure her. "Aunt Rose was in for a while this afternoon," she said, "and she thinks it is not really sickness, only that she needs rest and — and comfort. And, Vi, the Lord will comfort her. Remember those sweet words in Isaiah — 'As one whom his mother comforteth, so will I comfort you; and ye shall be comforted.'"

Violet had come up to see Molly, lest the poor afflicted cousin should feel neglected, while Elsie was engaged with the little ones — taking mamma's place in seeing them to bed with a little loving talk on some profitable theme.

Tonight it was the glory and bliss of heaven, leaving in their young minds — instead of gloomy and dreadful thoughts of death and the cold, dark grave — bright visions of angelic choirs, of white robes and palms of victory, of golden crowns and harps, of the river of the water of life and the beautiful trees on its banks bearing twelve manner of fruits. They were left with thoughts of papa with sweet Lily by his side, both casting their crowns at Jesus' feet and singing with glad voices, "Worthy is the Lamb that was slain."

Leaving them at length to their slumbers, she joined Violet and Molly for a few moments. Then Edward came to say that their mother was awake and grandpa had given permission for them to go to her and just bid her goodnight if they could be quite composed.

They thought they could; they would all try so very earnestly to remain so.

She was in her dressing room, reclining in an easy chair, looking so wan and sorrowful.

She embraced each in turn, holding them to her heart with a whispered word or two of tender mother love. "God bless you, my dear, dear children! He will be a father to the fatherless and never leave nor forsake you."

Violet dared not trust herself to speak. Elsie only murmured, "Dear, dearest mamma!" and Edward, "Darling, precious mother, don't grieve too sorely."

"The consolations of God are not small, my dear son!" was all she said in reply, and they withdrew softly and silently as they had come.

The next morning and each following day they were allowed a few minutes with her, until four days had passed.

On the fifth, she came down to the breakfast room leaning on her father's arm.

As they neared the door, she paused, trembling like a leaf in the breeze, and turned up to him a white and anguished face.

He knew what it meant. She had not been in that room, had not taken her place at that table, since the morning of the day on which her husband was taken ill. He was with her then, in apparently perfect health. Now — the places which had known him on earth would know him no more forever.

Her head dropped on her father's shoulder, a low moan escaping her pale lips.

"Dear child," he said, drawing her to him and tenderly kissing her brow, "think how perfectly happy, how blest he is. You would not call him back here?"

"Oh, no, no!" came from the quivering lips. "'The spirit is willing, but the flesh is weak.'"

"Lean on your strong Savior," he said, "and His grace will be sufficient for you."

She sent up a silent petition, then lifting her head, "I can bear it now — He will help me," she said and suffered him to lead her in.

Her children gathered about her with joy that was a cordial to her spirit; their love was very sweet.

But how her heart yearned over them because they were fatherless—all the more so that she found her father's love so precious and sustaining in this time of sorrow and bereavement.

He led her to her accustomed seat, bent over her with a whispered word of love and encouragement, then took the one opposite—once her husband's, now his no more.

Perhaps it was not quite so hard as to have seen it empty, but it cost a heroic effort to restrain a burst of anguish.

❦❦❦❦❦❦❦❦

CHAPTER SIXTH

Happy be
With such a mother!
Faith in womankind
Beats with his blood, and trust in all things high
Comes easy to him,
and though he trip and fall
He shall not bind his soul with clay.

—*TENNYSON*

LIFE AT ION MOVED ON in its accustomed quiet course. Mr. Travilla's removal seeming, to outsiders, to have made very little change except that Mr. and Mrs. Dinsmore now took up their abode there for the greater part of the time, leaving the younger Horace and his wife in charge at the Oaks.

An arrangement for which Elsie was very thankful, for her father's presence and his love were as a balm to her wounded spirit.

Her strongest support in this, as in every trial of her life, was in her almighty Savior. On Him she leaned every hour with a simple childlike faith and confidence in His unerring wisdom and infinite love. But it was very sweet to lean somewhat on the strength and wisdom of the earthly father also, and to feel that the shield of his care and protection were interposed between her and the cold world.

Both his and Rose's companionship had ever been delightful to her, and were now a great solace and pleasure.

She gave no indulgence to a spirit of repining because her chief earthly treasure had been taken from her for the remainder of her life in this world, but was filled with gratitude for those blessings that were left, ever deeming God's goodness to her far beyond her deserts.

And her own sorrow was often half forgotten in tender compassion for her fatherless children. For their sakes, as well as because such was her Christian duty, she strove after a constant abiding cheerfulness—and not without success.

But it was not sought in forgetfulness of the dear one gone. They talked freely and tenderly of him— his looks, his words, his ways, his present happiness and the joy of the coming reunion with him. He was not dead to them, but living in the blessed land where death could never enter, a land that grew more real and attractive because he was there.

Elsie found great comfort in her children—dear as her own offspring, and dearer still because they were his also. They were very good and obedient, loving her so devotedly that the very thought of grieving her was painful.

Her abiding, unselfish love seemed to call forth its counterpart in them. They vied with each other in earnest efforts to make up to her for her loss of their father's love and ever-watchful tender care.

They were very fond of their grandfather, too, always yielded a ready obedience to his commands or directions.

He never had shown to them the sternness that had been one of the trials of their mother's youthful days, but was patient and gentle, as well as firm and decided. Mr. Travilla's example as a father had not been wasted on him.

He was accustomed to saying: he had three good reasons for loving them—that they were the children of his friend, Elsie's children, and his own grandchildren.

It was very evident that they were very dear to him, and they loved him dearly in return.

Mr. Travilla had left no debts, no entanglements in his affairs. His will was short, plainly expressed, and its conditions such as there was no difficulty in carrying out.

Elsie and her father were joint executors and were associated in the guardianship of the children, also. The estate was left to her during her natural life, to Edward after her death.

Hitherto the education of all the sons and daughters was to be carried on at home, but now Edward was to go to college.

It had been his father's decision, and his wishes and opinions were sacred. So, neither the lad nor anyone else raised an objection, though all felt the prospect of parting sorely just at this time.

There had been some talk of sending Harold and Herbert away also to a preparatory school, but to save them and their mother the pain of separation, Mr. Dinsmore offered to prepare them himself to enter college.

Elsie was in fact herself competent to the task, but gladly accepted her father's offered assistance desiring to increase as much as possible his good influence over the boys—hoping that they would so learn to emulate all that was admirable in his fine and gentlemanly character.

They were, of course, leading a very quiet and retired life at Ion. But with her household cares and the superintendence of the education of her younger children to attend to in addition to other and less pressing duties, Elsie was in no danger of finding time hanging heavy on her hands.

One of the numerous demands upon her maternal responsibilities and affection was found in the call to cheer, comfort, and console her namesake daughter. She was under the trial of separation from her betrothed, delay in hearing from him, and a morbid remorse on account of having, as she expressed it, "troubled poor, dear papa by grieving and fretting over Lester's departure."

"Dear child," the mother said, "he sympathized with but did not blame you and would not have you blame yourself so severely now and embitter your life with unavailing regrets. He loved you very, very dearly, and has often said to me, 'Elsie has been nothing but a blessing to us since the hour of her birth.'"

"Oh, mamma, how sweet! Thank you for telling me," exclaimed the daughter, tears of mingled joy and sorrow filling her eyes. "He said it once to me, when I was quite a little girl—at the time grandpa—your grandpa—and Aunt Enna were hurt and you went to Roselands to nurse her, leaving me at home to try to fill your place. Oh, I shall never forget how dear and kind he was when he came home from taking you there! He took me in his arms and said those very words. Mamma, I cannot recall one cross word ever spoken by him to me, or to anyone."

"No, daughter, nor can I. He was most kind, patient, forbearing, loving, as husband, father, master—in all the relations of life. What a privilege to have been his cherished wife for so many years!"

The sweet voice was very tremulous, and unbidden tears stole over the fair cheeks that had not quite recovered their bloom—for scarce a month had passed since the angel of death had come between her beloved and herself.

"Dear mamma, you made him very happy," whispered Elsie, clasping her close with loving daughterly caresses.

"Yes, we were happy together, I believe, as happy as it is possible for any to be in this world of sin and sorrow. I bless God that he was spared to me so long, and for the blessedness that now is his, and the sure hope that this separation is only but for a season."

"Mamma, it is that sweet hope that keeps you from sinking."

"Yes, my dearest, that and the sweet love and sympathy of Jesus. My father's and my dear children's love does greatly help me, also. Ah, how great is the goodness of my heavenly Father in sparing me all these! And He keeps me from poverty, too. How many a poor widow has the added pang of seeing her children suffering sore privations or scattered among strangers because she lacks the ability to provide them with food and clothing?"

"Mamma, how dreadful," cried Elsie. "I would never have thought of that. How thankful we ought to be that we do not have to be separated from you or from each other. To be sure, Edward is going away for a time," she added with a sigh and a tear, "but it is not to toil for a livelihood or endure any privations whatsoever."

"No, but to avail himself of opportunities for mental culture for which we should be grateful as still another of the many blessings God has given us. He will be exposed to temptations such as would never assail him at home; but these he must meet, and if he does so looking to God for strength, he will overcome and be all the stronger for the conflict. And we, daughter, must follow him constantly with our prayers. Thank God that we can do that!"

To Edward himself she spoke in the same strain in a last private talk had with him the night before he went away.

"I know that you have a very strong will of your own, my dear boy," she added, "and are not easily led. I believe it to be your earnest desire and purpose to walk in the way of God's commands, and that is a comfort to me."

"You are right in regard to both, mother," he said with emotion. "And oh, I could sooner cut off my right hand than do aught to grieve you and dishonor the memory of—of my sainted father!"

"I believe it, my son, but do not trust in your own strength. 'Be strong in the Lord, and in the power of His might.'"

"Yes, mother, I know; I feel that otherwise I shall fail. 'But I can do all things through Christ which strengtheneth me.' Mother," he added, turning over the leaves of his Bible (for they had been reading together), "in storing my memory with the teachings of this blessed Book, you have given me the best possible preparation for meeting the temptations and snares of life."

"Yes," she said, "'Thy word is a lamp unto my feet and a light unto my path.' 'Thy testimonies also are my delight and my counselors.' Let them ever be yours, my son. In doubt and perplexity go ever to them for directions—not forgetting prayer for the teachings of the Holy Spirit—and you cannot go far astray. Make the Bible your rule of faith and practice; bring everything to the test of Scripture. 'To the law and to the testimony if they speak not according to this Word, it is because there is no light in them.'"

"Mother," he said, "I think I have a pretty clear idea of some of the temptations of college life. Doubtless there are always a good many idle, profane, drinking, dissolute fellows among the students; but it does not seem possible that I shall ever find pleasure in the society of such."

"I hope not indeed!" she answered with emphasis. 'It would be a sore grief to me. But I hardly fear it. I believe my boy is a Christian and loves purity. He loves study, too, for its own sake. What I most fear for you is that the pride of intellect may lead you to listen to the arguments of skeptics and to examine their works. My son, if you should, you will probably regret it to your dying day. It can do nothing but harm. If you fill your mind with such things your spiritual foes will take advantage of it to harass you with doubts and fears. 'Blessed is the man that walketh not in the counsel of the ungodly, nor standeth in the way of sinners, nor sitteth in the seat of the scornful.' He who would rob you of your faith in God and His holy Word is your greatest enemy. Study the evidences of Christianity and be ever ready to give a reason for the hope that is in you."

"Mother," he said, taking her hand in his, "I will heed your counsel, but it seems to me that having seen Christianity so beautifully exemplified in your life and my father's that I can never doubt its truth and power."

Then after a pause in which tears of mingled joy and sorrow fell freely from her eyes, "Dear mother, you have given me a very liberal allowance. Can you spare it? I do not know; I have never known the amount of your income."

"I can spare it perfectly well, my dear son," she answered with a tender smile, pleased at this proof of his thoughtful love. "It is the sum your father thought best to give you—for we had consulted together about these matters. I do not wish you to feel stinted, but at the same time would have you avoid waste and extravagance, remembering that they are inconsistent with our Savior's teachings, and that money is one of those talents for whose use or abuse we must render an account at the last."

CHAPTER SEVENTH

But O! for the touch of a vanished hand,
And the sound of a voice that is still.

—TENNYSON

IT WAS A CHILLY NOVEMBER day, a day of lowering clouds, wind, rain, sleet, and snow.

Arthur Conley, coming into the drawing room at Ion and finding its mistress there alone, remarked as he shook hands with her, "The beginning of winter, Cousin Elsie! It is setting in early. It froze hard last night, and the wind today is cutting."

"Yes," she said, "even papa and my two big, hardy boys found a short walk quite sufficient to satisfy them today. But you poor doctors can seldom consult your own comfort in regard to facing wind and storm. Take this easy chair beside the fire."

"Thank you, no, I shall find it quite warm enough on the sofa beside you. I am glad to have found you alone, for I want to have a little semi-confidential chat with you."

She gave him an inquiring look.

"I am a little uneasy about grandpa," he went on. "He seems feeble and has a troublesome cough, and I think should have a warmer climate through the coming winter. I think, too, cousin, that such a change would be by no means hurtful to you or your children," he continued, regarding her grave, professional air. "You are a trifle thin and pale and need something to rouse and stimulate you."

"What is it you wish, Arthur?" she asked, with a slight tremble in her voice.

"I should be glad if you would go to Viamede for the winter and take our grandfather with you."

He paused for an answer.

Her face was turned toward a window looking out upon the grounds. Her eyes rested with mournful gaze upon a low mound of earth within a little enclosure not many yards away.

Arthur read her thoughts and laying a gentle hand on hers said in low compassionate tones, "He is not there, cousin, and his spirit will be near you in your Lily's birthplace, and your own, as much as here. Is not that home also full of pleasant memories of him?"

She gave silent assent.

"And you can take all your other dear ones with you as well."

"Except Edward."

"Yes, but in his case, it will only involve a delay in receiving letters. I am certain your father and Aunt Rose will go with you. And our grandpa—"

"Is a dear old grandpa and must not suffer anything I can save him from," she interrupted. "Yes, Arthur, I will go, if—if my father approves and will accompany us, of which I have no doubt."

He thanked her warmly. "It may be the saving of grandpa's life," he said.

"He is getting very old, Arthur."

"Yes, past eighty, but with care he may live to be a hundred. He has a naturally vigorous constitution.

And how he mellows with age, Elsie! He has become simply a very lovely Christian, as humble and simple-hearted as a little child."

"Yes," she said, turning toward him eyes filling with glad tears, "and he has become very dear to me. I think he loves us all—especially papa—and for that we shall have a happy winter together."

"I don't doubt it; in fact, I quite envy you the prospect of wintering at Viamede."

"Oh, could you not go with us to stay at least a few weeks? We should all be very glad to have you."

"Quite impossible," he said shaking his head rather ruefully. "I'm greatly obliged and should be delighted to accept your invitation, but it isn't often a busy doctor can venture to take such a holiday."

"I'm very sorry. But you think there is no doubt that grandpa will be willing to go?"

"He'll not hesitate a moment if he hears Uncle Horace is to go. He clings to him now more than to any other earthly creature."

"Papa is in the library. Shall we join him and hear what he thinks of your little plan?" said Elsie as she got up.

"By all means," returned Arthur, and they did so.

Mr. Dinsmore highly approved, as did Rose, also, on being called in to the conference.

"How soon do you think of starting?" she asked, looking at Elsie, then at her husband.

"Papa should decide that," Elsie answered, a slight tremble in her voice, thinking of the absent one to whom that question should have been referred were his dear presence still with them.

She caught a look of tenderest love and sympathy from her father. How well he understood her! How ever thoughtful of her feelings he was!

"I think the decision should rest with you, Elsie," he said, "though I suppose the sooner the better."

"Yes," said Arthur, "for grandpa especially."

"I presume no great amount of preparation will be needful, since it is but a change from one home to another," suggested Rose.

"No," said Elsie, "and I think a week will suffice for mine. Papa, can business matters be arranged in that time?"

"Oh, yes! So we will say this day next week."

The door had opened very quietly a few moments before, admitting little Rose and Walter, and stealing softly to their mother's side they were now leaning on her lap, looking from one to another of their elders and listening with some curiosity to their conversation."

"What is it, mamma?" asked Rosie.

"We are talking of going to Viamede, dear."

"Oh, that will be nice!"

"But we tan't doe wis-out papa," prattled Walter, "tan we, mamma? I wish my dear papa wood jus tum back quick."

Rosie saw the pain in mamma's dear face, the tears in her eyes as she pressed a silent kiss on the brow of the innocent questioner, and with ready, loving tact she seized the little fellow's hand, and drew him away. "Come, Walter," she said, "let us go and tell the rest about it."

They ran together and Arthur rose to take leave.

"Am I imposing upon your unselfish kindness of heart, my dear cousin?" he asked in an undertone, taking Elsie's hand in his. "Is it too great a sacrifice of your own feelings and inclinations?"

She answered with a verse, as was not unusual with her, "'Even Christ pleased not Himself.'"

Mr. and Mrs. Dinsmore were conversing apart at the moment.

"Perhaps," returned Arthur musingly, "we might make some other arrangement. Grandpa might be willing to go without—"

"No, no," she interrupted, "I could not think of giving him the pain of separation from papa, nor could I bear it myself. But do not trouble about me. There will be much pleasure mingled with the pain—pleasure in ministering to the comfort and happiness of the dear old grandfather, and in seeing Viamede and the old servants. I have always loved both the place and them."

Her father had caught a part of her words.

"Separation from me?" he said, turning toward her. "Who talks of that nonsense? It shall not be with my consent."

"No, papa, nor with mine, for either grandpa or myself," she said with a look of affection and a slight smile. "Arthur, will you carry a message from me to Isa?"

"With pleasure."

"Tell her I should be very glad to have her spend the winter at Viamede with us, if she feels that she would enjoy the trip and the quiet life we shall lead there. There will, of course, be no partying to tempt a young girl."

"Thank you," he said, his eyes shining. "I have not the slightest doubt that she will be delighted to accept the invitation. And, now I think of it, Aunt Enna and Molly will of course find a home with us at Roselands while you are away."

"No, no, they will go with us," returned Elsie quickly, "unless indeed they prefer to be left behind at Roselands."

Arthur suggested that they would be a great charge, especially upon the journey; but the objection was promptly overruled by Mr. Dinsmore, Rose, and Elsie.

Molly must go, they all said. She would be sure to enjoy the change greatly—the poor child had so few pleasures. And the same was true of Enna, also. She had never seen Viamede, and could not fail to be delighted with its loveliness. Nor would it do to part her from Molly, who was now her chief happiness.

"I trust they will appreciate your kindness. Molly will, I am sure," Arthur said as he went away.

As the door closed on him, Elsie glided to the window and stood in a pensive attitude gazing out upon that lowly mound, only faintly discernable now in the gathering darkness, for night was closing in early by reason of the heavy clouds that obscured the sky.

A yearning importunate cry was going up from her almost breaking heart. "My husband, oh my husband, how can I live without you? Oh, to hear once more the sound of your voice, to feel once again the clasp of your arm, the touch of your hand upon mine!"

A sense of utter loneliness was upon her.

But in another moment she felt herself enfolded in a strong yet tender embrace, a gentle caressing hand smoothing her hair.

"My darling, my precious one, my own beloved child!" murmured her father's voice in its most endearing accents as he drew her head to its usual resting-place on his shoulder.

She let it lie there, her tears falling fast.

"I fear this going away is to be too great a trial for you," he said.

"No, papa, but I am very weak. Forgive my selfish indulgence of my sorrow."

"My darling, I can sympathize in it, at least to some extent. I remember even yet the anguish of the first months of my mourning for your mother."

"Papa, I feel that my wound can never heal; it is too deep—deep as the roots of my love for him that had been striking farther and farther into the soil of everyone on the many days and years that we lived and loved together."

"I fear it may be so," he answered with tender compassion, "yet time will dull the edge of your sorrow. You will learn to dwell less upon the pain of separation and more upon his present happiness and the bliss of the reunion that will be drawing nearer and nearer with each passing day. Dear one, this aching pain will not last forever. As Rutherford says, 'Sorrow and the saints are not married together; or suppose it were so, Heaven would make a divorce.'"

"They are very sweet words," she murmured, "and sweeter still is the assurance given us in the Scriptures that 'our light affliction, which is but for a moment, worketh for us a far more exceeding and eternal weight of glory.'"

"Yes," said Rose, coming to her other side and speaking in low, tender tones, "dear Elsie, let those words comfort you, and these others also, 'Whom the Lord loveth he chasteneth and scourgeth every son whom He receiveth.' But for that and similar verses I should wonder much that trial of any kind was ever permitted to come nigh one who has been a loving disciple of our Lord Jesus since her very early years."

"Was it that I loved my husband too well?" Elsie queried in tremulous tones. "I do not think I made an idol of him, for inexpressibly dear as he was, the Master was dearer still."

"If that be so, then you did not love him—your husband—too well," her father answered.

"I hear my children's voices. I must not let them see their mother giving way to grief like this," she said, lifting her head and wiping away her tears.

They came in—the whole six—preceded by a servant bearing lights.

There was a subdued eagerness about the younger ones as they hastened to their mother asking, "Mamma, is it really so—that we are really going to Viamede?"

"Yes, dears, I believe it is quite settled. Grandpa approves and I hope you all are pleased."

"Oh, yes, yes!"

"If you are, mamma," the older girls said, noticing with affectionate concern the traces of tears on her face. "If not, we prefer to stay here."

"Thank you, my darlings," she answered, smiling affectionately upon them. "For several reasons I shall be glad to go, the principal being that our poor old grandfather needs the warm climate he will find there, and, of course, we could not think of letting him go alone."

"Oh, no!" they said. "He could not do without grandpa, and neither could we."

"And neither could grandpa go without his eldest daughter, or her children," added Mr. Dinsmore playfully, sitting down and taking Walter upon one knee, Rosie upon the other. "So, we will all go together, and I trust will have a happy time in that lovely land of fruits and flowers."

They had not seen it for several years, not since Walter was a babe and Rosie so young that she remembered but little about it. Both were delighted with the prospect before them and plied their grandpa with many eager questions, while their mother looked on with growing cheerfulness, resolutely putting aside her grief that she might not mar their pleasure.

The other four had gathered about her — Vi on a cushion at her feet, Elsie seated close on one side, Herbert standing on the other, and Harold at the back of her chair, leaning fondly over her, now touching his lips to her cheek, now softly smoothing her shining hair.

"My dear mamma, how beautiful you are!" he whispered in her ear.

"You might as well say it out loud," remarked Herbert, overhearing the words, "because everybody knows it and nobody would want to contradict you in the least."

"We are very apt to think those beautiful whom we love," their mother said with a pleased smile, "and the love of my children is very sweet to me."

"Yes, mamma, but you are beautiful," insisted Harold. "It isn't only my love that makes you look so to me, though I do love you dearly — dearly."

"Mamma knows we all do," said Violet. "We should be monsters of ingratitude if we did not."

"As I should be if I were not filled with thankfulness to God that He has blessed me with such dutiful and affectionate children," added the mother.

"Mamma, how soon will we go to Viamede?" asked Violet. That question being answered, another quickly followed. "We will not leave Molly behind?"

"No, certainly not, nor Aunt Enna, if they will kindly consent to go with us."

"Consent, mamma! I'm sure they cannot help being delighted to go. May I run and tell them?"

"Yes, my child, I know you always enjoy being the bearer of pleasant news."

Molly heard it with great pleasure and gratitude to her cousin, Enna with even childish delight. Neither had a thought of declining.

Isadore Conly, also, was very much pleased and sure she should vastly enjoy the winter with her relations, in spite of many an envious prognostication to the contrary on the part of her mother and Virginia. They would not go on any account they averred, and were glad they had been overlooked in the invitation—mean as it was of Elsie not to include them—for life at Viamede could not fail to be a very dull affair for that winter at least.

But Elsie, of course, heard none of these unkind remarks, and seeing the happiness she was conferring not only upon more distant relations but upon her children also, who showed increasing pleasure in the thought of the expected visit to their lovely southern home as the time drew near. She felt fully repaid for the sacrifice of feeling that she was making.

CHAPTER EIGHTH

*'Tis easier for the generous to forgive
Than for offence to ask it.*

—THOMPSON

THE ONLY NOTEWORTHY incident of the journey took place in New Orleans, where they halted for a few days of rest to all and sightseeing on the part of the young people.

Mr. Horace Dinsmore, who had some business matters to attend to in connection with Elsie's property in the city, was hurrying back to his hotel one afternoon, when a beggar accosted him, asking for a little help, holding out a very forlorn hat to receive it.

There seemed something familiar in the voice, and Mr. Dinsmore stopped and looked earnestly at its owner.

A seam-scarred face, thin, cadaverous, framed in with unkempt hair and scraggy beard — an attenuated form clothed in rags — these were what met his view, surely for the first time, for there was nothing familiar about either.

No, not for the first time at all; for, with a start of recognition and a low, muttered curse, the mendicant dropped his hat, then stooped, hastily snatching it from the ground and rushing away down an alley.

"Ah, I know you now!" cried Mr. Dinsmore, giving instant pursuit.

He could not be mistaken in the peculiarly maimed hand stretched out to regain the hat.

Its owner fled as if for his life, but, weak from disease and famine, could not outdistance his pursuer.

At last, finding the latter close at his heels, he stopped and faced him—leaning, panting, and trembling against a wall.

"George Boyd, is it you? Have you been reduced to such a condition as this?" exclaimed Mr. Dinsmore, eyeing him searchingly.

"You've mistaken your man, sir," panted the fugitive. "My name's Brown—Sam Brown at your service, sir."

"Then why did you run away from me?" coolly inquired the gentleman. "No, I cannot mistake that hand," pointing to the maimed member.

"And you'd like to hang me, I suppose," returned the other bitterly. "But I don't believe you could do it here. Besides, what's the use? I'll not cumber the ground much longer; can't you see that? Travilla himself," he added, with a fierce oath, "can hardly wish me anything worse than I've come to. I'm literally starving—can hardly get enough food to keep soul and body together from one day to another."

"Then come with me and I will feed you," Mr. Dinsmore said, his whole soul moved with pity for the miserable wretch. "Yonder is a restaurant. Let us go there, and I will pay for all you can eat."

"You don't mean it?" cried Boyd in incredulous surprise at the offer.

"I do—every word of it. Will you come?"

"A strange question to ask a starving man. Of course I will, only too gladly."

They crossed the street, entered the restaurant and Mr. Dinsmore ordered a substantial meal set before Boyd. He devoured it with wolfish voracity, his entertainer watching him for a moment, then turning away in pained disgust.

Time after time plate and cup were filled and emptied, but at last he declared his appetite fully satisfied. Mr. Dinsmore paid the reckoning and they passed out into the street together.

"Well, sir," said Boyd, "I'm a thousand times obliged. Shall be more so if you will accommodate me with a small loan—or gift if you like, for I haven't a cent in the world."

"How much do you think you deserve at my hands?" asked Mr. Dinsmore somewhat severely, for the request seemed to him a bold one under the circumstances before him.

"I leave that to your generosity, sir," was the cool reply.

"Which you expect to be great enough to allow you to escape the justice that should have been meted out to you years ago?"

"I've never harmed a hair of your head nor anyone belonging to you, though I owe a heavy scare to both you and Travilla," was the insolent rejoinder.

"No, your imprisonment was the due reward of your lawless and cruel deeds."

"Whatever I have done," retorted the wretch with savage ferocity, "it was nothing compared to the injury inflicted upon me. I suffered inconceivable torture. Look at me and judge if I do not speak the truth. Look at these fearful scars, these almost blinded eyes." He finished with a torrent of oaths and curses directed at Travilla.

"Stop!" said Mr. Dinsmore authoritatively. "You are speaking against the sainted dead and he entirely innocent of your sufferings."

"What! Is he dead? When? Where? How did Travilla die?"

"At Ion, scarce two months ago, calmly, peacefully, trusting with undoubting faith in the atoning blood of Christ."

Boyd stood leaning against the outer wall of the restaurant. He was evidently very weak from sickness or hunger. He seemed awestruck and did not speak again for a moment—then, "I did not know it," he said in a subdued tone. "So he's gone! And his wife? She was very fond of him."

"She was indeed. She is in the city with her family on her way to Viamede."

"I'm sorry for her, never had any grudge against her," said Boyd. "And my aunt?"

"Is still living and in good health, but beginning to feel the infirmities of age. She had long mourned you as worse than dead. You look ill able to stand. Let me help you to your home."

"Home? I have none." There was a mixture of scorn and despair in the tones.

"But you must have some lodging place?"

"Yes, sometimes it is a door-step, sometimes a pile of rotten straw in a filthy cellar. On second thought, Dinsmore, I rather wish you'd have me arrested and lodged in jail," he added with a bitter laugh. "I'd at least have a bed to lay my weary limbs upon, and something to eat. And before the trial was over I'd be beyond the reach of any heavier penalty."

"Of human law," added Mr. Dinsmore. "But do not forget that after death comes the judgment. No, Boyd, I feel no resentment toward you and since your future career in this world is evidently very short, I do not feel called upon to deliver you up to human justice. Also, for your aunt's sake especially, I am inclined to give you some assistance. I will therefore give you the means to pay for a decent lodging tonight and tomorrow will see what further can be done, if you will let me know where to find you."

Time and place were fixed upon, money enough to pay for bed and breakfast was given to Boyd, and they parted company. Mr. Dinsmore hastened on his way to his hotel—the very best the city afforded—with a light, free step, while Boyd slowly dragged himself to a very humble lodging in a narrow, dirty street near at hand.

Mr. Dinsmore found his whole party gathered in their private parlor and anxiously awaiting his coming. As he entered there was a general exclamation of relief and pleasure on the part of the ladies and his father, and a joyous shout from Rosie and Walter as each hastened to claim a seat upon each knee.

"My dears, grandpa is tired," said their mother.

"Not too tired for this," he said, caressing them with all a father's fondness.

"Are you not late, my dear?" asked his wife. "We were beginning to feel a trifle anxious about you."

"Rather, I believe. I will explain the cause at another time," he said pleasantly.

Tea was brought in, family worship followed the meal, and shortly after that Elsie retired with her little ones to see them to bed. The others drew round the table, each with a book or work, Harold pushing Molly's chair up near the light; and Mr. Dinsmore, seating himself beside his wife, on a distant sofa, gave her in subdued tones an account of his interview with Boyd.

"Poor wretch!" she sighed, "what can we do for him? It is too dreadful to think of his dying as he has lived."

"It is indeed! We will consult with Elsie as to what is to be done."

"The very mention of his name must be a pain to her. Can she not be spared it?"

"I will consider that question. You know I would not willingly pain her," he said with a tenderly affectionate glance at his daughter as she re-entered the room. Then, rising, he paced the floor, as was his habit when engaged in any deep or perplexing thought.

Elsie watched him a little anxiously, but without remark until all the others had retired, leaving her alone with him and Rose.

Then, going to where he sat, in a large easy chair beside the table, looking over the evening paper, "Papa," she said, laying her hand affectionately on his arm, "I fear you are finding my affairs troublesome."

"No, my dear child, not at all," he answered, throwing down the paper and drawing her to a seat upon his knee.

"It seems quite like old, old times," she said with a smile, gazing lovingly into his eyes, then stealing an arm about his neck and laying her cheek to his.

"Yes," he said, "why should I not have you here as I used to twenty odd years ago? You are no larger or heavier nor I a whit less strong and vigorous than we were then."

"How thankful I am for that last," she returned, softly stroking his face, "and it is very pleasant occasionally to imagine myself your own little girl again. But something is giving you anxiety, my dear father. Is it anything in which I can assist you?"

"Yes, but I fear I can hardly explain without calling up painful memories."

He felt her start slightly, and a low-breathed sigh met his ear.

"Still, say on, dear papa," she whispered quietly.

"Can you bear it?" he asked. "Not for me, but for another — an enemy."

"Yes, the Lord will give me strength. Of whom do you speak?"

"George Boyd."

"The would-be murderer of my husband!" she exclaimed, with a start and a shiver, while the tears coursed freely down her cheeks. "I thought him long since dead."

"No, I met him this evening, but so worn and altered by disease and famine, so seamed and scarred by Aunt Dicey's scalding shower, that I recognized him only by the mutilated right hand. Elsie, the man is reduced to the lowest depths of poverty and shame, and evidently very near his end on this earth."

"Papa, what would you have me to do?" she asked in quivering tones.

"Could you bear to have him removed to Viamede? Could you endure his presence there for the few weeks he has yet to live?"

She seemed to have a short struggle with herself; then the answer came in low, agitated tones.

"Yes, if neither my children nor I need look upon him or hold communication with him."

"That would not be at all necessary," her father answered, holding her close to his heart. "And indeed I could not consent to it myself. He is a loathsome creature both morally and physically; yet, for his aunt's sake, and still more for His sake who bids us 'Love your enemies, bless them that curse you, do good to them that hate you,' I shall gladly do all in my power for the wretched prodigal. And who can tell but there may yet be mercy in store for him? God's mercy and power are infinite, and He has 'no pleasure in the death of him that dieth,' but would rather that he turn from his evil way and live."

There was a little pause; then Elsie asked if her father had arranged any plans in regard to Boyd's removal as yet.

"Yes," he replied, "subject of course to your approval. I have thought it would be well to send him on at once and let him settle in his quarters before the arrival of our own party. You must decide what room he is to occupy."

She named one situated in a wing of the mansion quite distant from the apartments that would be used by the family.

"What more, papa?" she asked.

"He must also have an attendant—a nurse. And shall we not write to his aunt, inviting her to come and be with him while he lives? She might remain through the winter with us if she can find it convenient and agreeable to do so?"

"Yes, oh, yes! Poor, dear Mrs. Carrington—it will be but a melancholy pleasure to her. But I think if anyone can do good for him it will be she. I will write at once."

"Not tonight. It is too late. You are looking weary, and I want you to go at once to bed. Tomorrow morning will be time enough for the letter."

"What, sending me to bed, papa!" she said with a slightly amused smile. "I must be indeed your little girl again. Well, I will obey as I used to in the olden time, for I still believe you know what is best for me. So goodnight, my dear, dear father!"

"Good night, my darling," he responded, caressing her with all the old, fatherly tenderness. "May God bless and keep you and your dear children."

CHAPTER NINTH

She led me first to God;
Her words and prayers were
my young spirit's dew.

—*P*IERPONT

ELSIE'S LETTER TO THE elder Mrs. Carrington was dispatched by the first morning mail, and directly after breakfast Mr. Dinsmore went in search of George Boyd.

Hardened as the man was, he showed some sense of gratitude toward the new-made widow of his intended victim when informed of her kind intentions toward himself—some remorse for his attempt to injure him who she had so dearly loved.

"It is really a great deal more than I had the least right to ask even for my aunt's sake, he said. "Why sir, it will be like getting out of hell into heaven."

"It is not for Mrs. Carrington's sake alone, or principally—strong as is the tie of friendship between them," replied Mr. Dinsmore, "but rather for the sake of the Master she loves and serves, and who bids His followers return good for evil."

"Hypocrite!" sneered Boyd to himself, then aloud, "Well, sir, I wish it were in my power to make some suitable return to Mrs. Travilla, but that can never be, and unfortunately I cannot undo the past or its events."

"No, and that is a thought that might well deter us from evil deeds. Now the next thing is to provide you with a bath, decent clothing, and suitable attendant, and get you and him aboard the boat which leaves a few hours hence."

All this was done and Mr. Dinsmore returned to his daughter with a satisfactory report to that effect.

Their party remained a few days longer in the Crescent City, then embarked for Viamede, where they arrived in due season, having met no accident or detention by the way.

As on former occasions, they were joyfully welcomed by the old servants; but many tears mingled with the rejoicings, for Mr. Travilla had been greatly loved by all. They wept for both their own loss and that of their "dear bressed Missus," as they were accustomed to call her who his death had widowed.

She was much overcome at the first memory, vividly recalling former arrivals when he—her dearest earthly friend—was by her side, giving her the support of his loved presence and sharing in her happiness.

Her thoughts dwelt particularly upon the glad days of their honeymoon. And she seemed to see herself again a loved, loving, cherished bride. Now she was wandering with him through the beautiful orange groves or over the velvety, flower-bespangled lawn. Now she was seated by his side on the veranda, the parlor, the library, or on some rustic seat under the grand old trees, his arm encircling her waist, his eyes looking tenderly into hers. Or she was gliding over the waters of the lakelet or galloping or driving through the woods—everywhere and always the greatest delight of each the love and companionship of the other partner.

Ah, how often she now caught herself listening for the sound of his voice, his step—waiting, longing to feel the touch of his hand! Could she ever cease to do so? Could she ever lose that weary homesickness of heart that at all times seemed almost more than mortal strength could endure?

But she had more than mortal strength to sustain her, the everlasting arms were underneath and around her, the love that can never die, never change, was her unfailing support and consolation.

She indulged in no spirit of repining, no nursing her grief. She gave herself with cheerful earnestness to every good work—the careful, prayerful instruction and training of her children as her first duty; then kindly attentions to her old grandfather, to parents and guests; after that the care of house servants, field hands, and the outside poor of the vicinity. She neglected neither their bodies nor their souls. She also helped the cause of Christ in both her own and foreign lands, with untiring efforts, earnest, believing prayer, and liberal gifts. She was striving to be a faithful steward of the ample means God had committed to her trust and rejoiced in the ability to relieve the wants of His people, and to assist in spreading abroad the glad news of salvation through faith in Christ.

There were no parties at Viamede that winter, but the atmosphere of the house was eminently cheerful, its walls often echoing blithe voices and merry laughter of the children—never checked or reproved by mamma. The days went peacefully by in a varied round of useful and pleasant employment and delightful recreation that left no room for ennui—riding, driving, walking, boating for all, and healthful play for the children.

Lester Leland had been heard from, was well, and wrote in so hopeful a strain that the heart of his affianced grew light and joyous. She was almost ashamed to find she could be so happy without the dear father so lately removed.

Her mother reassured her on that point. It was right for her to be happy as she could. It was what her papa would have highly approved and wished. And then, in being so and allowing it to be perceived by those around her, she would add to their enjoyment.

"We are told to 'rejoice in the Lord always,'" concluded the mother, "and a Christian's heart should never be the abode of gloom and sadness."

"Dear mamma, what an unfailing comfort and blessing you are to me and to all your children," cried the young girl. "Oh, I do thank God every day for my mother's dear love, my mother's wise counsel!"

It was very true, and to mamma each one of the six—or seven, for Edward did the same by letter—carried every trouble, great or small, every doubt, fear, and perplexity.

No two of them were exactly alike in disposition—each required a little different management from the others—but attentively studying each character and asking wisdom from above, the mother succeeded wonderfully well in guiding and controlling them.

In this her father assisted her, and she was most careful and decided in upholding his authority, never in any emergency opposing hers to it.

"Mamma," said Harold, coming to her one day in her dressing room, "May I tell you something? Herbie is in trouble with grandpa."

"I am very sorry," she said with a look of concern, "but if so it must be by his own fault. Your grandpa's commands are never unreasonable."

"No, I suppose not, mamma," Harold returned doubtfully, "but Herbie is having a very hard time over his Latin lesson and says he can't learn it; it is too difficult. Mamma," with some hesitation, "if you would speak to grandpa perhaps he would let him off this once."

"Do you think that would be a good plan?" she asked with a slight smile. "Herbert's great fault is lack of perseverance. He is too easily discouraged, too ready to give up and say 'I can't.' Do you think it would be really kind to indulge him in doing so?"

"Perhaps not, mamma; but I feel very sorry to see him in such distress. Grandpa has forbidden him to leave the schoolroom or to have anything to eat but bread and milk till he can recite his lesson quite perfectly. And we had planned to go fishing this afternoon, if you should give permission, mamma."

"My son," she said with an affectionate look into the earnest face of the pleader, "I am glad to see your sympathy and love for your brother, but I think your grandpa loves him quite as well and knows far better what is for his good. I cannot interfere between them. My children must all be obedient and submissive to my father as they are to me."

"Yes, mamma, I know, and indeed we never disobey him. How could we when papa bade us not? And he made him our guardian, too."

Elsie sat thinking for a moment after Harold had gone, then rose and went to the schoolroom.

Herbert sat there alone, idly drumming on his desk, the open book pushed aside. His face was flushed and wore a very disconsolate and slightly sullen expression.

He looked up as his mother came in, but dropped his eyes immediately, blushing and ashamed of his recent behavior.

"Mamma," he stammered, "I—I can't learn this lesson. It's so very hard; and I'm so tired of being cooped up here. Mayn't I go out and have a good run before I try any more?"

"If your grandfather gives permission, and not otherwise, young sir."

"But he won't; and it's a hateful old lesson! And I can't learn it!" he cried with angry impatience.

"My boy, you are grieving your mother very much," she said, sitting down beside him and laying her cool hand on his heated brow.

"Oh, mamma, I didn't mean to do that!" he cried, throwing his arms about her neck. "I do love you dearly, dearly."

"I believe it, my son," she said returning his caress, "but I want you to prove it by being obedient to your kind grandpa as well as to me, by trying to conquer your faults."

"Mamma, I haven't been naughty—only I can't learn such hard lessons as grandpa gives."

"My son, I know you do not mean to be untruthful, but to say that you cannot learn your lesson is really not the truth. The difficulty is not so much in the ability as in the will. And are you not indulging a naughty temper?"

"Mamma," he said, hanging his head, "you don't know how hard Latin is."

"Why, what do you mean, my son?" she asked in surprise. "You certainly know that your mother has studied Latin."

"Yes, mamma, but wasn't it easier for you to learn than it is for me?"

"I think not," she said with a smile, "though I believe I had more real love for study and was less easily conquered by difficulties. And yet—shall I tell you a little secret?"

"Oh yes, mamma, please do!" he answered, turning a bright interested face to hers.

"Well, I disliked Latin at first, and did not want to study it. I should have coaxed very hard to be excused from doing so, but that I dared not, because my papa had strictly forbidden me to coax or tease after he had given his decision. And he said Latin was to be one of my studies. There was one day, though, that I cried over my lesson and insisted that I could not learn it."

"And what did grandpa do to you?" he asked with great interest.

"Treated me just as does you—told me I must learn it, and that I could not dine with him and mamma or leave my room until I knew it. And, my boy, I see now that he was wise and kind, and I have often been thankful since he was so firm and decided with me."

"But did you learn it?"

"Yes, nor did it take me long when once I gave my mind to it with determination. That is exactly what you need to do. The great fault of your disposition is lack of energy and perseverance, a fault grandpa and I must help you to conquer or you will never be of much use in the world."

"But, mamma, it seems to me I shall not need to do much when I'm a man," he remarked a little shamefacedly. "Haven't you a great deal of money to give us all?"

"It may be all gone before you are grown up," she said gravely. "I shall be glad to lose it if possession is to be the ruin of my sons. But I do not intend to let any of you live in idleness, for that would be a sin, because our talents must be improved to the utmost and used in God's service, whether we have much or little money or none at all. Therefore, each of my boys must study a profession or learn some handicraft by which he can earn his own living or make money to use in doing good.

"Now, I am going to leave you," she added, rising, "and if you do not want to give me a sad heart, you will set to work at that lesson with a will, and soon have it ready to recite to your grandpa."

"Mamma, I will, to please you," he returned, drawing the book toward him.

"Do it to please God, your kind heavenly Father, even more than to make me happy," she answered, laying her hand caressingly on his head.

"Mamma, what is the verse that says it will please Him?" he asked, looking up inquiringly, for it had always been a habit with her to enforce her teachings with a passage of Scripture.

"There are a great many that teach it more or less directly," she said. "We are to be diligent in business, to improve our talents and use them in God's service. Children are to obey their parents — and both your grandpa and I have directed you to learn that lesson."

"Mamma, I will do my very best," he said quite cheerfully, and she saw as she left the room that he was really trying to redeem the promise.

An hour later he came to her with a very bright face to say that grandpa had pronounced his recitation quite perfect and released him from the dreaded confinement.

Her pleased look, her smile, and her kiss were a sweet reward and a strong incentive to continue in well doing.

CHAPTER TENTH

To the law and to the testimony: if they speak not according to this word, It is because there is no light in them.

—ISAIAH 8:20

SOME YEARS BEFORE THIS, Elsie had built a little church on the plantation, entirely at her own expense for the use of her dependents and of her own family when sojourning at Viamede. The membership was composed principally of blacks.

A few miles distant was another small church of the same denomination, attended by the local planters and their families.

To these two congregations conjointly Mr. Mason had ministered for a long while, preaching to the one in the morning, to the other in the afternoon of each Sunday.

He had, however, been called to another field of labor, a few weeks previous to the arrival of Elsie and her family, leaving the two congregations pastorless and the pretty cottage built for him at Viamede without a tenant.

Still they were not entirely without the preaching of the Word, now one and now another coming to supply the pulpits for a Sunday or two.

At present they were filled by a young minister who came as a candidate and whose services had been engaged for several weeks.

Elsie and her family were paying no visits now in this time of mourning, but nothing but sickness or a very severe storm ever kept them from church. They attended both services and in the evening the older ones gathered about the table in the library with their Bibles, and with *Cruden's Concordance* and other helps at hand spent an hour or more in the study of the Word.

"Mamma," said little Rosie, one Sunday as they were walking slowly homeward from the nearer church, "why don't we have a minister that believes the Bible?"

"My child, don't you think Mr. Jones believes it?"

"No, mamma," most emphatically, "because he contradicts it. He said there's only one devil, and my Bible says Jesus cast out devils—seven out of Mary Magdalene, and ever so many out of one man, besides other ones out of other folks."

"And last Sunday, when he was preaching about Jonah, he said it was a wicked and foolish practice to cast lots," remarked Harold. "The Bible tells us that the Lord commanded the Israelites to divide their land by lot, and that the apostles cast lots to choose a successor to Judas."

"Yes," said Violet, "and when Achan had sinned, didn't they cast lots to find out who it was that was causing trouble to Israel?"

"And to choose a king in the days of the prophet Samuel," added their older sister. "How strange that anyone should say now that it was a foolish and wicked practice!"

"I don't think his mother can have brought him up on the Bible as ours does," remarked Herbert.

"Mamma, which are we to believe," asked Rosie, "the minister or the Bible?"

"Bring everything to the test of the Scripture," answered the mother's gentle voice. "'To the law and the testimony: if they speak not according to this Word, it is because there is no light in them.' I want you to have great respect for the ministry, yet never to receive any man's teachings when you find them opposed to those of God's Holy Word."

When the Bibles were brought out that evening, Isa proposed that they should take up the question of the correctness of that assertion of Mr. Jones which had led Rosie to doubt his belief in the inspiration of the Scriptures.

"Yes, let us do so," said Molly, "but do you consider it a question of any importance, uncle?"

"I do. No Bible truth can be unimportant. 'All scripture is by inspiration of God, and is profitable for doctrine, for reproof, for correction, for instruction in righteousness, that the man of God may be perfect, thoroughly furnished unto all good works.' And if we have spiritual foes we surely need to know it, that we may be on our guard against them."

"And we have not been left without warning against them," observed old Mr. Dinsmore. "'Put on the whole armor of God, that ye may be able to stand against the wiles of the devil. For we wrestle not against flesh and blood, but against principalities, against powers, against rulers of the darkness of this world, against spiritual wickedness in high places.' How absurd the idea that principalities and powers can mean but one creature!"

"David prays, 'Lead me in a plain path because of mine enemies;' and again, 'Lead me, O Lord, in thy righteousness because of mine enemies, make thy way straight before my face,'" said Mrs. Travilla. "It seems evident to me that it was spiritual foes he meant; that he feared to be left a prey to their temptations, their deceit, the snares and traps they would set for his soul."

"Undoubtedly," returned her father. "On any other supposition some of the psalms would seem to be very bloodthirsty and unchristian."

"I rather took Mr. Jones to task about it as we came out of church," said old Mr. Dinsmore, "and he maintained that he was in the right on the ground that the name devil comes from the Greek *diabolos*, which is applied only to the prince of the devils."

"And what of that?" said his son. "The Hebrew name, Satan, has the very same signification—an adversary, an accuser, calumniator, or slanderer—and Christ called the devils he had just cast out, Satan. 'How can Satan cast out Satan? If Satan rise up against himself, and be divided, he cannot stand.' If they are so like him, so entirely one of him, as to be called himself—and that by Him who has all knowledge and who is the Truth—I cannot see that there is any occasion to deny them the name of devil, or anything to be gained by doing so. On the other hand, there is danger of positive harm as it seems to throw doubt and discredit upon our English translation."

"A very serious responsibility to assume, since the vast majority of the people must depend upon it," remarked Mrs. Travilla. "I think anyone who makes the assertion we are discussing should give a very full explanation and strong warning against the lesser evil spirits we call devils. 'If the foundations be destroyed, what can the righteous do?'"

"Yes," said her father, "and I have very strong faith in the learning, the wisdom, and the piety of the translators."

"Is Satan a real person? Were the devils that Christ and His disciples cast out, real persons?" asked Isadore. "I have heard people talk of Satan as if he were an imaginary creature, a myth, and of the others, with which people were possessed in those days, as probably nothing more than bad tempers."

"'To the law and to the testimony,'" replied her uncle, opening his Bible. "We will consider your questions in the order in which they were asked. 'Is Satan a real person?' There can be no difficulty in proving it to anyone who believes the Bible to be the inspired Word of God. The difficulty is rather in selecting from the multitude of verses that teach it."

Some time was now spent in searching out, with the help of the *Bible Text Book and Concordance,* a very long list of verses bearing on the question — giving the titles, the character and the doings of Satan. These showed that he sinned against God, was cast out of heaven down to hell, that he was the author of the fall, and that he perverts Scripture. He also opposes God's work, hinders the Gospel, works lying wonders, that he tempted Christ, is a liar and the father of lies, is a murderer, and yet appears as an angel of light.

"Here," said Mr. Dinsmore, "is a summing up of what he is, by Cruden, who was without question a thorough Bible scholar. And, remember as I read it that the description applies not to Satan alone but also to those wicked spirits under him. 'He is surprisingly subtle, his strength is superior to ours, his malice is deadly, his activity and diligence are equal to his malice and he has a mighty number of principalities and powers under his command!'"

"Yes," said old Mr. Dinsmore, meditatively, "'the rulers of the darkness of this world.' The word is plural. It seems there must be several orders of them, composing a mighty host."

"I find both my queries already fully answered," said Isa.

"Nevertheless, let us look a little farther into the second question," her uncle answered. "I will give the references as before, while the rest of you turn to and read them."

When this had been done, "Now," said he, "let us sum up the evidence as to their personality, character, works, and right to the name of devil."

"As to the first they sinned, hell is prepared for them. They believe and tremble; they spoke. They knew Christ and testified to His divinity, 'Jesus, thou Son of God.' Wicked tempters could not do any of these things. As to the second, their character, they are called in the Bible 'unclean spirits,' foul spirits. And since Christ called them Satan himself, the description of his character, as I have remarked before, is a faithful description of theirs also. This last proves also their right to the title devil. The Scripture—Christ himself—calls them the devil's angels, his messengers. That is the meaning of angel—they do Satan's bidding, go on his errands and help him in the work of destroying souls and tempting and tormenting those who they cannot destroy. Well, Vi, what is it?" She had given him a perplexed, troubled look.

"There is just one difficulty that I see, grandpa. Here in Jude we are told, 'And the angels which kept not their first estate, but left their own habitation, he hath reserved in everlasting chains under darkness unto the judgment of the great day.' The apostle Peter says the same thing. My difficulty is to reconcile this statement with the other teaching — that they are going about the world on their wicked, cruel errands."

"'To the law and to the testimony,'" repeated Mr. Dinsmore. "Since the infallible Word of God makes both statements, we must believe both, whether we can reconcile them or not. But I doubt not we shall be able to do so if we diligently search the Word with prayer for the teachings of the Holy Spirit."

He then offered a short, fervent petition to that end, after which they resumed their investigation.

"Let us remember," he said, "that the same word often has many meanings, and that hell may be a state or condition rather than a place — I mean that the word may be sometimes used in that sense — so with chains and with darkness."

"We use the expression, 'the chains of habit,'" suggested his daughter. "A spirit could not be bound with a material chain; but in Proverbs we are told, 'His own iniquities shall take the wicked himself, and he shall be holden with the cords of sin.' Think of the awful wickedness and utter despair of those lost spirits — no space for repentance, no hope or possibility of salvation — and I think we have chains on them of fearful weight and strength."

"'The cords of sin are the consequences of crimes and bad habits. Sin never goes unpunished, and the bad habits contracted are, as it were, indissoluble bands from which it is impossible to get free,'" read Mr. Dinsmore from the Concordance, adding, "and to those lost spirits it is utterly impossible. Yes, here in their wicked tempers, malignant desires, and utter despair, we have, I think, the chains that bind them."

"But the darkness, grandpa?" queried Harold.

"We are coming to that. Cruden tells us here that darkness sometimes signifies great distress, perplexity, and calamity, as in Isaiah 8:22 and Joel 2:2. Sometimes it means sin or impurity as in 1 John 1:5. The devils have all these. How great is their sin? How great must be their distress and anguish in the sure prospect of eternal destruction from the presence of God—eternal torment! How dense and fearful must it be beyond the power of words to express! They are darkness, for our Savior calls the exercise of Satan's power 'the power of darkness.' 'This is your hour and the power of darkness.' By the gates of hell, Matthew 16:18, is meant the power and policy of the devil and his instruments. It would seem that they carry their chains, their darkness, and their hell with them wherever they go. And now for the application, the lesson we should learn from all this: What do you think it is, Harold?"

"That we should be constantly on our guard against the wiles of these adversaries, is it not, sir?"

"Yes, and ever looking to the Captain of our salvation for strength and wisdom to do so effectually."

"Putting on the whole armor of God," added old Mr. Dinsmore, "the shield of faith, the helmet of salvation, the sword of the spirit which is the Word of God. What else, Herbert?"

"The breast-plate of righteousness, sir, and the loins are to be girt about with truth, the feet shod with the preparation of the gospel of peace."

"There is yet another lesson," said Mrs. Travilla, her face aglow with holy joy and love. "How it should quicken our zeal for the Master, our gratitude, our joy and love, when we think of His salvation offered to us as His free gift, the purchase of His own blood. He might justly have left us in the same awful state of horror and despair that is the portion of the angels that sinned. And how should we cling to Him who alone is able to keep us from falling into the traps and snares they are constantly spreading for our unwary feet. Ah, my dear children, there is no safety but in keeping close to Christ!"

"But there we are safe," added her father. "'He is able also to save them to the uttermost that come unto God by Him.' He says of His sheep, 'I give unto them eternal life; and they shall never perish, neither shall any man pluck them out of my hand,' He saves His people from sin, from hell and destruction."

"Can't we find some verses about the good angels?" asked little Rosie, who had been permitted to sit up beyond her usual bedtime to share in the Bible lesson.

"Yes," said her grandpa, "we may be thankful for them, because they are kind and good and loving, taking delight in our salvation and ministering to God's people, as they did to the Master when on earth. Which of you can name some instances given in the Bible?"

"One fed Elijah when he fled from wicked Jezebel," answered Rosie promptly.

"They carried Lazarus to heaven," said Herbert.

"And stopped the lions' mouths when they would have eaten Daniel," added Harold.

The others went on, "One comforted Paul when he was in danger of shipwreck."

"One delivered Peter from prison."

"Now who can quote a promise or assurance that we, if the true children of God, shall have help or protection from them?"

"'He shall give His angels charge over thee, to keep thee in all thy ways. They shall bear thee up in their hands, lest thou dash thy foot against a stone,'" repeated the younger Elsie.

Her mother added in low, sweet tones, full of joy and thankfulness, "'The angel of the Lord encampeth round about them that fear Him, and delivereth them.' Is it not a sweet assurance?" she exclaimed. "He is not a transient visitor, but encamps as intending to remain; and not on one side alone, leaving the others exposed to the enemy, but round about. Blessed are they who have the Lord of hosts for their Keeper!"

They united in a song of praise, old Mr. Dinsmore led in prayer, and then with an exchange of the usual affectionate goodnights they separated.

"Mamma," said the younger Elsie, lingering for a little in her mother's boudoir, "tonight's study of the Word has done good for me. I want to live nearer to Jesus, to love Him more, and to serve Him better."

"I, too," said Violet. "I want to give Him the service of my whole heart and life, time, talents, money, everything!"

"It rejoices my heart to hear it, my darlings," the mother answered, folding them in her arms, while glad tears shone in her eyes. "It is what I desire above all things for you, for all my dear ones, and for myself."

CHAPTER ELEVENTH

'Tis not the whole of life to live,
Nor all of death to die.

—*M*ONTGOMERY

MRS. CARRINGTON OBEYED with all speed the call to come to the aid of her unworthy nephew, and her arrival was not delayed by many days after that of their kind entertainers.

She received a cordial welcome; but since that first day the ladies and the children of the family had seen very little of her for Boyd had taken to his bed, and she devoted herself to him.

The gentlemen frequently spent a little time in his room, induced thereto by motives of kindness, but the others never approached it.

Elsie looked upon him as the would-be murderer of her husband, and could scarcely think of him without a shudder.

She was willing, even anxious to give him every comfort that money could buy, and that every effort should be made by her father and others to lead him to repentance and faith in Christ to the saving of his soul. But she shrank from seeing him, though she made kind inquiries, sent messages, and offered many sincere and fervent prayers on his behalf.

Strolling about the grounds one afternoon with her little ones, she saw her father coming hurriedly toward her.

Something in the expression of his countenance as he drew rapidly nearer startled her with a vague and unknown fear.

"What is it, papa?' she asked tremulously.

"Take my arm," he said, offering it. "I have something to say to you. Rosie, you and Walter go to your mammy."

The children obeyed, while he and their mother turned into another path.

Elsie's heart was beating very fast. "Papa, is—is anything wrong with—"

"With any of your loved ones? No, daughter, they are all safe and well so far as I know. But I have a message for you—a request that it will not be easy or pleasant for you to grant, or to refuse. Boyd is drawing very near his end, and with a mind full of horror and despair. He says there is no hope, no mercy for him—nothing but the blackness of darkness forever."

Elsie's eyes overflowed. "Poor, poor fellow! Papa, can nothing be done for him?"

"Could you bear to go to him?" he asked tenderly. "Forgive me, dear child, for paining you with such a suggestion; but the poor wretch thinks he could die easier if he heard you say that you forgive him."

There was a shudder, a moment's struggle with herself; then she said, very low and sadly, "Yes, papa, I will go at once. How selfish I have been in staying away so long. But—oh, Edward! My husband, my husband!"

He soothed her very tenderly for a moment, then asked gently, "Would he not have bidden you go?"

"Oh, yes, yes, he would have forgiven. He did forgive him with all his great, generous heart. And, God helping me, so will I. I am ready to go."

"Lost, lost, lost! No hope, no help, the blackness of darkness forever!" were the words uttered in piercing tones, full of anguish and despair, that greeted Elsie's ears as her father softly opened the door of Boyd's room and led her in.

At those sounds, at the sight that met her view — the wretched man with the seal of death on his haggard, emaciated face, seamed and scarred beyond all recognition, tossing restlessly from side to side, while he rent the air with his cries — she turned so sick and faint that she staggered. And but for the support of her father's arm would have fallen to the floor.

"Call up all your courage, my dear child," he whispered, leaning over her. "Look to the Lord for strength, and who shall say you may not be able to do the poor dying wretch some good?"

She struggled determinedly with her faintness and they drew near the bed.

Boyd started up at sight of her, thrusting the maimed hand under the bedclothes, and holding out the other with a ghastly smile.

"You're an angel, Mrs. Travilla!" he gasped, "an angel of mercy to a miserable wretch who you've a good right to hate."

"No," she said, taking the hand in a kindly grasp, "I have no right to hate you, or anyone—I whose sins against my Lord are far, far greater than yours against me or mine. I forgive you, as I hope to be forgiven. May God forgive you also."

"No, no, it is too late, too late for that!" he groaned. "I have sinned against all light and knowledge. He has called and I refused many, many times. And now the door is shut."

"It is your adversary, the devil, who tells you that," she said, tears streaming from her eyes. "He would destroy your soul. But the words of Jesus are 'Him that cometh to Me I will in no wise cast out.' 'Whosoever will, let him take the water of life freely.'"

"Ah, but He also says, 'Because I have called and ye refused; I have stretched out my hand, and no man regarded; but ye have set at naught all my counsel, and would none of my reproof; I also will laugh at your calamity; I will mock when your fear cometh; when your fear cometh as desolation, and your destruction cometh as a whirlwind; when distress and anguish cometh upon you. Then shall they call upon me, but I will not answer.' Oh, it's all true, every word of it!" he cried with a look of horror and despair that none who saw it could ever forget. "I feel it in my inmost soul. There was a time when mercy's door was open to me, but it's shut now, shut forever."

"Oh, George, George!" sobbed his aunt. "The invitation is without limit—'whosoever will.' If you have a will to come, it cannot be that it is even now too late."

"But those words—those dreadful words," he said, turning eagerly toward her, "'then shall they call upon me, but I will not answer.'"

"Are addressed to those who desire deliverance, not from sin itself, but only from its punishment," said Mr. Dinsmore. "If you have any desire to be saved from your sins, to be cleansed from their pollution, to be made holy, it is not too late—the 'whosoever will' is for you."

He shook his head sadly. "I don't know, I don't know. A deathbed is a poor place to analyze one's feelings. Oh! Warn men everywhere not to put it off, not to put it off! Tell them it is running a fearful risk!"

"We will, we will," said his aunt, "but, oh, George, think of yourself. Cry to Jesus. 'He is able to save to the uttermost.' And He has no pleasure in the death of any soul. He would have you turn now and live. Oh, cry to Him for mercy!"

"Too late, too late!" he muttered faintly, "the door is shut."

They knelt about his bed and poured out fervent prayers for him; they repeated promise after promise, invitations and assurances from the Word of God's willingness to save.

At last, "I'm going, going!" he gasped. "Oh, God be merciful to me, a sinner!" And with the last word the spirit took its flight.

Mrs. Carrington sank, half-fainting, into Elsie's arms and Mr. Dinsmore and the doctor bore her from the room.

It was Elsie's sad task to try to comfort and console where there was little to build hope upon. She could but dwell upon God's great mercy, His willingness to save, and the possibility that that last dying cry came from a truly penitent heart.

"I must try to believe it, else my heart would break," cried the old lady. "Oh, Elsie, my heart has bled for you, but your sorrow is not like unto my sorrow! You can rest in the sure and certain hope of a blissful reunion, you know that your beloved is rejoicing before the throne. While I—alas, alas! I know not whence my poor boy is. And I am tortured with the fear that some of his blood may be found in my skirts—that I did not guide and instruct, warn and entreat him as I might; that my prayers were not frequent enough, my example all that it should have been."

"My dear friend, 'who is sufficient for these things?'" Elsie answered, weeping. "Who has not reason for such self-reproach? I think not you more than the rest of us."

"Ah!" sighed the old lady. "I wish that were so. Had I been but to him and to my own children the mother you are to yours, my conscience would not now trouble me as it does."

⚹ ⚹ ⚹ ⚹ ⚹

Mrs. Travilla had caused a room to be fitted up as a studio for her older daughters, and here they were spending their afternoon—Vi painting, Elsie modeling and thinking, the while, of her absent lover, perchance busy in his studio with hammer and chisel on some sculpture.

"The sun is setting," exclaimed Violet at length, putting down her brush. "What can have become of mamma that she has not been in at all to watch our progress?"

"I hope she has been taking a drive," Elsie answered, ceasing work also. "Come, let us go and dress for tea, Vi. It is high time."

They hastened to do so, and had scarcely finished dressing when Harold rapped and asked if mamma were there.

"No, where can she have gone?" he said. "Herbie and I came in from fishing a little while ago and we have hunted for her almost everywhere."

"Except in the nursery," suggested Herbert. "Let's go and see if she's there."

"The carriage is driving up," said Vi, glancing through the window. "Probably mamma is in it," and all four hurried down to the front veranda eager to meet and welcome her.

Their old grandfather alighted, handed out Grandma Rose, Aunt Enna, Isa, and then, with the help of one of the servant men, Molly.

The carriage door closed. Mamma was not there. Indeed their grandma and Isa were asking for her as they came up the steps.

And childish voices were now heard in their rear making the same inquiry—Rosie and Walter coming from the nursery in search of the mother they never willingly lost sight of for more than an hour.

"Why, what can have become of mamma? Rosie, when did you see her last?" asked Harold.

"Out on the lawn. She was walking with us and grandpa came and took her away."

"Where to?"

"I don't know—where's mamma," cried the child, bursting into tears.

"There, there, don't cry. Dear mamma's sure to be safe along with grandpa," Harold said, putting his arms around his little sister. "And here he comes to tell us about her," he added joyously as Mr. Dinsmore was seen coming down the hall.

They crowded around him, the same question on every tongue.

"She is with Mrs. Carrington," he said, patting the heads of the weeping Rosie and Walter. "Don't cry, my children. She may not be able to join us at tea, but you shall see her before you go to your beds."

Then, to the older ones, speaking in subdued tones, "Boyd is gone, and his aunt is much overcome with her grief."

"Gone, Horace!" exclaimed his wife, looking shocked and awe-struck. "How did he die? Was there any ground for hope?"

"Very little," he sighed. "That is the saddest part of it. The body will be sent away tonight," he added, in answer to a question from his father. "He is to be buried with the rest of his family. Mrs. Carrington will not go with it, will probably remain here through the winter."

All felt it a relief that the burial was not to be near at hand, or the corpse to remain many hours in the house—"a wicked man's corpse," as Harold said with a shudder. But all were saddened and horror struck at the thought that he had gone leaving so little reason for hope of his salvation.

They gathered at the supper table a very quiet, solemn company—few words were spoken. The little ones missed their mother and were glad to get away to the nursery where she presently came to them, looking sad and with traces of recent tears about her eyes.

But she smiled very sweetly upon them, kissed them tenderly, and sitting down, took Walter on her lap and put an arm around Rosie as she stood by her side.

They were both curious to know about Mr. Boyd, asking if he had gone to heaven where dear papa and Lily were.

"I do not know, my darlings," she answered, the tears coming into her eyes again. "He is there if he repented of his sins against God and trusted in Jesus Christ."

Then she talked to them, as often before, of the dear Savior—the great love wherewith He loves all of His people, and the many mansions He is preparing for them.

She spoke to them, too, of God's hatred of sin, and the need of watchfulness and prayer.

"The devil hates us, my darlings," she said. "He goes about like a roaring lion, seeking to kill our souls; but Jesus loves us. He is stronger than Satan, and if we keep close to Him we are safe."

Having seen them safe in bed, she went to her dressing room to find the other four there waiting for her.

They gathered about her with glad, loving looks and words, each eager to anticipate her wishes and to be the first to wait upon her.

"My dear children," she said, smiling through glistening tears, "your love is very sweet to me!"

"And what do you think yours is to us, mamma?" exclaimed Violet, kneeling at her mother's feet and clasping her arms about her waist, while she lifted to hers a face glowing with ardent affection and great admiration.

"Just the same, I hope and believe," and with the words the mother's hand passed caressingly over the golden curls.

"Mamma, you have been crying very much," remarked Harold sorrowfully. "I wish—"

"Well, my son?" as he had paused, leaving his sentence unfinished.

"I wish I could make you so happy that you would never want to shed a tear."

"When I get to heaven, my dear boy, it will be so with me. 'God shall wipe away all tears from their eyes; and there shall be no more death, neither sorrow, nor crying, neither shall there be any more pain.' And that is where your dear papa is now. Oh, how glad we ought to be for him!" she said with mingled smiles and tears. "'Blessed are the dead which die in the Lord;' but, oh, it is not so, my children, with those who have not chosen Him for their portion! 'For to them is reserved the blackness of darkness forever.'"

There was a slight solemn pause, all thinking of the wretched man who had passed away from earth that afternoon.

"Mamma," asked Harold at last, speaking in a quiet, subdued tone, "do you think it is so with Mr. Boyd?"

"My son," she said gently, "that is a question we are not called upon to decide. We can only leave him in the hands of God, in full confidence that the Judge of all earth will do right."

"Mamma, would you like to tell us about it?" asked Herbert.

"It is a painful subject," she sighed, "but—yes, I will tell you, that it may be a warning to you all your lives."

They listened with awe-struck faces and with tears of pity as she went on to give a graphic picture of that death scene so different from the one they had witnessed a few short months ago.

"Oh, my children," she said, "live not for time, but for eternity! Remember that this life is but a preparation for another and endless existence. 'Seek ye first the kingdom of God, and His righteousness.' 'Count all things but loss for the excellency of the knowledge of Christ Jesus our Lord.' Choose His service now while youth and health are yours, and when death comes you will have nothing to fear. 'The wicked is driven away in his wickedness: but the righteous hath hope in his death.' 'Be not deceived, God is not mocked: for whatsoever a man soweth, that shall he also reap. For he that soweth to the flesh, shall of the flesh reap corruption: but he that soweth to the Spirit, shall of the Spirit reap life everlasting.'"

"Yes, mamma," Elsie said in a half whisper, the tears stealing down her cheeks, "surely we have seen it fulfilled in these last few months. Our beloved father sowed to the Spirit, and what a joyous reaping is his! How calmly and sweetly he fell asleep in Jesus."

"Yes," the mother said, mingling her tears with theirs—for all were weeping now—yet with a light shining in her eyes. "I am full of joy and thankfulness tonight in the midst of my grief. Oh how should we love and rejoice in this dear Savior, who through His own death has given eternal life to him and to us, and to as many as God has given Him— to all that will come to Him for it."

CHAPTER TWELFTH

*If any man speak, let him speak
as the oracles of God.*

—1 PETER 4:11

"MAMMA, CAN WE—Elsie and I—have a little private talk with you?" asked Violet as they left the dinner table the next Sunday.

"Certainly, daughter, if it be suited to the sacredness of the day."

"Quite so, mamma," answered Elsie, "it is, at least in part, a question of conscience."

"Then we shall want our Bibles to help us decide it. Let us take them and go out upon the lawn, to the inviting shade of yonder group of magnolias."

"Do you intend to be so selfish as to monopolize your mother's society?" asked her father playfully.

"Just for a little while, grandpa," Vi answered with coaxing look and tone. "Please, all of you, let us two have mamma all to ourselves for a few minutes."

"Mamma," Elsie began, "you saw a young lady talking with us after church? She is Miss Miriam Pettit. She says she and several other young girls belonging to the church used to hold a weekly prayer meeting in Mrs. Mason's parlor. It is the most central place they can find, and she will be very glad, very much obliged, if you will let them use it still. She has understood that nearly all the furniture of the cottage belongs to you and is still there."

"Yes, that is so, and they are very welcome to the use of any of the rooms. But that is not all you and Vi had to say?"

"Oh, no, mamma! She wants us to join them and take part in the meetings—I mean not only to sing and read, but also to lead in prayer."

"Well, my dears, I should be glad to have you do so; and you surely cannot doubt that it would be right?"

"No, mamma," Violet said in her sprightly way, "but we should like to have you tell us—at least I should—that it would not be wrong to refuse."

"My child, do you not believe in prayer as both a duty and a privilege—social and public as well as private prayer?"

"Oh, mamma, yes! But is it not enough for me to pray at home and to unite silently with the prayers offered by ministers and others in public?"

"Are we not told to pray without ceasing?"

"Oh, yes, mamma! And I did not mean to omit silent, even unceasing prayer, but is it my duty to lead the devotions of others?"

"Our Savior gave a precious assurance to those who unite in presenting their petitions at a throne of grace. 'Where two or three are gathered together in my name, there I am in the midst of them.' Someone must lead—there ought always to be several to do so—and why should you be excused more than another?"

"Elsie is willing, mamma, and Miss Pettit, too."

"I am glad to hear it," the mother said with an affectionate look at her eldest daughter. "I know it will be something of a trial to Elsie, and doubtless to Miss Pettit, too—it is to almost everyone. But what a light cross to bear for Jesus compared to that He bore for us—or those borne by the martyrs of old, or even by the missionaries who leave home and dear ones to go far away to reach the heathen! I had hoped my Vi was ready to follow her Master wherever His providence called her—that she would not keep back any part of the price, but give Him all."

"Oh, yes, mamma!" she cried, the tears starting to her eyes, "I want to be altogether His. I have given Him all, and don't want to keep back anything. I will try to do this if you think He calls me to it, though it seems almost impossible."

"My child, He will help you if you ask Him; He will give you the Holy Spirit to teach you how to pray and what to pray for. Try to get your mind and heart full of your own and others' needs, to forget their presence and remember His. Then, words will come and you will find that in trying to do the Master's work and will, you have brought down a rich blessing upon your own soul. And why should we feel it a trial to speak aloud to our Father in the presence of others of His children, or of those who are not?"

"I don't know, mamma; it does seem very strange that it should."

"I should like to attend your meetings, but hardly suppose I should be welcome," Mrs. Travilla said with a smile.

"To us, mamma," both answered, "but perhaps not to the others. Miss Pettit said there were to be none but young girls."

"Isa is invited, I presume?"

"Yes, mamma, and she says she will attend, but can't promise anything more. I think she will, though, if you will talk to her as you have to us," Violet added as they rose to return to the veranda where the rest of the family still lingered.

And she was not mistaken. Isa was too true and earnest a Christian, too full of love for the Master and zeal for the building up of His cause and kingdom, to refuse to do anything that she saw would tend to that, however much it might cost her to attempt it.

"Well, Cricket," Mr. Dinsmore said, giving Violet a nickname he had bestowed upon her when she was a very little girl, "come sit on my knee and tell me if we are all to be kept in the dark in regards to the object of this secret conference with mamma?"

"Oh, grandpa," she said, taking the offered seat and giving him a hug and a kiss, "gentlemen have no curiosity, you know. Still, now it's settled, we don't care if you do hear all about it."

Both he and his wife highly approved and the latter, seeing an interested yet regretful look on poor Molly's face asked, "Why should we not have, in addition, a female prayer meeting of our own? We have more than twice the number necessary to claim the promise."

The suggestion was received with favor by all the ladies present. Time and place were fixed upon, and then, that they might be the better prepared to engage in this new effort to serve the Master, they agreed to take the subject of prayer for that evening's Bible study.

But once entered upon, they found it so interesting, comprehensive, and profitable a theme that they devoted several evenings to it.

The children as well as their elders seemed to be continually finding discrepancies between the teachings of the Bible and those of Mr. Jones, and Elsie was not a little relieved to learn that the time for which his services had been engaged had now nearly expired. She hoped there was no danger that he would be requested to remain.

One day as she was leaving the quarter, where she had been visiting the sick, Uncle Ben, now very old and feeble, accosted her respectfully.

"Missus, I'se be bery thankful to hab a little conversation wid you when it suits yo' convenience to talk to dis chile."

"What is it, Uncle Ben?" she asked.

"May I walk 'longside of de Missus up to de house?" he returned.

"Certainly, Uncle Ben, if you feel strong enough to do so."

"Tank you, Missus. Do dese ole limbs good to stretch 'em 'bout dat much. It's 'bout Massa Jones I'se want to converse wid you, Missus. I hear dey's talkin' 'bout invitin' him to stay, and I want to ascertain if you intends to put him ober dis church."

"I, Uncle Ben!" she exclaimed. "I put a minister over your church? I have no right and certainly no wish to do any such thing. It is for the members to choose who they will have."

"But you pays de money and provides de house for him, Missus."

"That is true, but it does not give me the right to say who he shall be. Only if you should choose one of whose teachings I could not approve—one who was not careful to teach according to God's word— should feel that I could not take the responsibility of supporting him."

"I'se glad of dat, Missus," he said with a gleam of satisfaction in his eyes, "'cause I'se want de Bible truff and nuffin else. And young Massa Jones, he preach bery nice sometimes, but sometimes it 'pears like he disremembers what's in de bressed book, and contradicts it wid some of his own wil' notions."

"Then you don't wish him to stay?"

"No, Missus, dat I don't! I'se hoping you won't be displeased wid me for saying it."

"Not at all, Uncle Ben; I find the very same objection to him that you do."

On reaching the house, she bade the old man a kindly goodbye and directed him to go to the kitchen and tell the cook, from her, to give him a good dinner with plenty of hot, strong coffee.

Rosie and Walter were on the back veranda looking out for mamma.

"Oh, we're so glad you've tum home, mamma!" cried Walter, running to meet her and claim a kiss.

"Yes, mamma, it seemed so long to wait," said Rosie, "and now there is a strange gentleman in the drawing room waiting to see you. He's been here a good while, and both grandpas are out."

"Then I must go to him at once. But I think he is not likely to detain me long away from you, darlings," the mother said.

She found the gentleman—a handsome man of middle age—looking not at all annoyed or impatient, but seemingly well entertained by Isa and Violet, who were there chatting sociably together over some pretty fancy work, when he was shown in by the servant.

They withdrew after Isa had introduced Mrs. Travilla and Mr. Embury.

The former thought it a little singular when she learned that her caller's errand was the same as that of Uncle Ben—to talk about Mr. Jones and the propriety of asking him to take permanent charge of the two churches. Yet with this difference—that he was personally not unfavorable to the idea.

"I like him very well, though he is not by any means Mr. Mason's equal as a preacher," he said. "And I think our little congregation can be induced to give him a call. But we are too few to support him unless by continuing the union with this church, so that the small salary we can give him be supplemented by the very generous one you pay, and the use of the cottage you built for Mr. Mason. I am taking for granted, my dear Madame, that you intend to go on doing for your retainers here as you have hitherto."

"I do," she said, "in case they choose a minister whose teachings accord with those of the inspired Word. I cannot be responsible for any other."

"And do those of Mr. Jones not come up to the standard you have set?"

"I regret to have to say that they do not. His preaching is far from satisfactory to me. He makes nothing of the work of the Spirit, or the danger of grieving Him away forever, nothing of the danger of self-deception, instructing those who are in doubt about the genuineness of their conversion that they must not be discouraged, instead of advising them to go to Christ now and be saved, just as any other sinner must. I fear his teaching may lead some to be content with a false hope. Then he often speaks in a half hesitating way, which shows doubt and uncertainty, on his part, of truths taught most plainly and forcibly in Scripture. In a word, his preaching leaves the impression upon me that he has no very thorough acquaintance with the Bible, and no very strong confidence in the infallibility of its teachings. Indeed so glaring are his contradictions of Scripture, that even my young children have noticed them more than once or twice."

"Really, Mrs. Travilla, you make out a very strong case against him," remarked her interlocutor, after a moment's thoughtful silence, "and upon reflection, I believe a true one. I am surprised at myself that I have listened with so little realization of the important defects in his system of theology. I was not ardently in favor of calling him before; now I am decidedly opposed to it."

He was about to take leave, but the two Mr. Dinsmores came in at that moment, and he resumed his seat and the subject was reopened.

They soon learned that they were all of substantially the same opinion in regard to it.

In the course of the conversation some account was given Mr. Embury of the Sunday evening Bible study at Viamede. He seemed much interested, and at length asked if he might be permitted to join them occasionally.

"My boys are away at school," he said, "my two little girls go early to bed, and my evenings are often lonely — since my dear Mary left me, now two years ago," he added with a sigh. "May I come, Mrs. Travilla?"

"Yes," she said, reading approval in the eyes of her father and grandfather, while her own tender heart sympathized with the bereaved husband, though at the same time her sensitive nature shrank from the invasion of their family circle by a complete stranger.

He read it all in her speaking countenance, but could not deny himself the anticipated pleasure of making the acquaintance of so lovely a family group — to say nothing of the intellectual or spiritual profit to be expected from sharing in their searching of the Scriptures.

Mr. Embury was a man of liberal education and much general information — one who read and thought a good deal and spoke well.

The conversation turned upon literature and Mr. Dinsmore presently took him off to the library to show him some valuable books recently purchased by himself and his daughter.

They were still there when the tea bell rang, and being hospitably urged to remain and partake of the meal with the family, Mr. Embury accepted the invitation with unfeigned pleasure.

All were present even down to little Walter, and not excepting Molly.

Her apartments at Viamede being on the same floor with the dining room, library, and parlors, she joined the family gatherings almost as frequently as anyone else — indeed whenever she preferred the society of her relatives to the seclusion of her own room.

Mr. Embury had occasionally seen her at church. Her bright, intellectual face and crippled condition had excited his interest and curiosity, and in one way and another he had learned her story.

Truth to tell, one thing that had brought him to Viamede was the desire to make her acquaintance — though Molly and the rest were far from suspecting it at the time.

He had no definite motive for seeking to know her. His large, generous heart was drawn out in pity for her physical infirmity and filled with admiration of her cheerfulness under it, and the energy and determination she had shown in carving out a career for herself and steadily pursuing it in spite of difficulties and discouragements that would have daunted many a weaker spirit.

She had less of purely physical beauty than any other lady present, her mother excepted, yet there was something about her face that would have attracted attention anywhere. Her conversation was enviable, as Mr. Embury discovered in the course of the evening. So delightful did he find the society of these new friends, both ladies and gentlemen, that he lingered among them until nearly ten o'clock, quite oblivious of the flight of time until reminded of it by the striking of the clock.

"Really, Mrs. Travilla," he said, rising to take leave, "I owe you an apology for this lengthened visit, which has somehow taken the place of my intended call. But I must beg you to lay the blame where it should fall, on the very great attractiveness of your family circle."

"The apology is quite out of proportion to the offense, sir," she returned, with a kindly smile, "so we grant you pardon and shall not refuse it for a repetition of the misdeed."

"I wish," he said, glancing round from one to another, "that you would all make me a return in kind. I will not say that Magnolia Hall is equal to Viamede, but it is called a fine place; and I can assure you of at least a hearty welcome to its fine hospitalities."

CHAPTER THIRTEENTH

I preached as never sure to preach again,
And as a dying man to dying men.

—RICHARD BAXTER

THERE WAS A STRANGER in the pulpit the next Sunday morning. His countenance, though youthful, by its intellectuality, its earnest thoughtfulness, and a nameless something that told of communion with God and a strong sense of the solemn responsibility of thus standing as an ambassador for Christ to expound His word and will to sinful, dying men, gave promise of a discourse that should send empty away no attentive hearer hungering and thirsting for the bread and the water of life.

Nor was the promise unfulfilled. Taking as his verse the Master's own words, "They hated me without a cause," he dwelt first upon the utter helplessness, hopelessness, and wretchedness of that estate of sin and misery into which all mankind were plunged by Adam's fall. Then, he expounded upon God's offered mercy through a Redeemer, even His only begotten and well-beloved Son. Next, he considered the wondrous love of Christ "in offering himself a sacrifice to satisfy divine justice and reconcile us to God," as shown first in what He resigned—the joy and bliss of heaven, "the glory which he had with the Father before the world was"—secondly in His birth and life on earth, of which he gave a rapid but vivid sketch from the manger to the cross—showing the meekness, patience, gentleness, benevolence, self-denial, humility and resignation of Jesus—how true, guileless, innocent, loving and compassionate He was, describing the miracles He wrought—everyone an act of kindness to some poor sufferer from bereavement, accident, disease, or Satan's power. Then, he gave the closing scenes of that wondrous life—the agony in the garden, the cruel mockery of a trial, the scourging, the crucifixion, the expiring agonies upon the cross.

He paused. The audience almost held their breath for the next words; the silent tears were stealing down many a cheek.

Leaning over the pulpit with outstretched hand, with features working with emotion, "I have set before you, he said in tones thrilling with pathos, "this Jesus in His life and in His death. He lived not for Himself, but for you. He died not for His own sins, but for yours and mine. He offers you salvation as a free gift purchased with His own blood. Yea, risen again and ever at the tight hand of God, He maketh intercession for you. If you hate Him, is it not without a cause?"

The preacher had wholly forgotten himself in his subject, and self did not intrude into the prayer that followed the sermon. Truly he seemed to stand in the immediate presence of Him who died on Calvary and rose again as he poured out his confession of sins, his gratitude for redeeming love, his earnest petitions for perishing souls, blindly, wickedly hating without a cause this matchless, this loving, compassionate Savior. And for Christ's own people, that their faith might be strengthened, their love increased, that they might be very zealous for the Master, abounding in gifts and prayers and labors for the building up of his cause and kingdom.

"The very man we should have here, if he could be induced to come," Mr. Dinsmore said in a quiet aside to his daughter as the congregation began to disperse, going out silently or conversing in subdued tones, for the discourse had made a deep impression.

"Yes, papa. Oh, I should rejoice to hear such preaching every Sunday!" was Elsie's answer.

"And I," Mr. Embury said, overhearing her remark. "But Mr. Keith gave us expressly to understand that he did not come as a candidate. He is here for his health or recreation, being worn out with study and pastoral work, as I understand."

"Keith?" exclaimed Mr. Dinsmore. "I thought there was something familiar in his face. Elsie, I think he must belong to our Keiths."

"We must find out, papa." she said. "Oh, I shall be glad if he does!"

"Shall I bring him up and introduce him?" Mr. Embury asked. "Ah, here he is!" as turning about, he perceived the young minister close at hand.

"Dinsmore! Travilla! Those are family names with us!" the latter said, with an earnest and interested look from one to the other as all of the introductions were made.

"As Keith is with us," Mr. Dinsmore answered, grasping his hand. "I guess that I am speaking to a grandson of my cousin Marcia Keith and her husband, Stuart Keith, of Pleasant Plains, Indiana."

"Yes, sir, I am the son of Cyril, their second son, and bear the same name. And you sir, are the cousin Horace of whom I have so often heard my grandmother and Aunt Mildred speak?"

"The same."

"And Mrs. Travilla is Cousin Elsie?" turning to her with a look of great interest and pleasure mingled with admiration—which quickly changed to one of intense, sorrowful sympathy as he noticed her widow's weeds. He had often heard of the strong attachment between herself and husband, and this was the first intimation he had had of her bereavement.

She read his look and gave him her hand silently, her heart too full for speech.

"You will go home with us, of course," said Mr. Dinsmore, after introducing his wife and the other ladies of the family.

"And stay as long as you possibly can," added Elsie, finding her voice. "Papa and I shall have a great many questions to ask about our cousins."

"I shall be most happy to accept your kind invitation, if Mr. Embury will excuse me from a prior engagement to dine and lodge with him," replied Mr. Keith, turning with a smile to the proprietor of Magnolia Hall, who was still standing near in a waiting attitude.

"I am loath to do so," he said pleasantly, "but relatives have first claim. I will waive mine for the present in your favor, Mrs. Travilla, if you will indemnify me by permission to call frequently at Viamede while Mr. Keith stays, and afterward, if you don't find me a bore. I might as well make large demands while I am about it."

"Being in a gracious mood, I grant them, large as they are," she responded in the same playful tone that he had used. "Come whenever it suits your convenience and pleasure, Mr. Embury."

"Viamede!" said Mr. Keith meditatively, as they drove homeward. "I remember hearing Aunt Mildred talk of a visit she paid there many years ago, when she was quite a young girl, and you, Cousin Elsie, were a mere baby."

"Yes," said old Mr. Dinsmore. "It was I who brought her. Horace was away in Europe at the time, and the death of Cameron, Elsie's guardian, made it necessary for me to come on and attend to matters. Mildred was visiting us at Roselands that winter and I was very glad to secure her as a traveling companion. Do you remember anything about it, Elsie?"

"Not very much, grandpa," she said. "I remember a little of Cousin Mildred's kindness and affection, something of the pain of parting from my dear home and the old servants. But I have a very vivid recollection of a visit paid to Pleasant Plains with papa," and she turned to him with a deeply affectionate look, "shortly before his marriage. I then saw Aunt Marcia, as both she and papa bade me call her, and Cousin Mildred and all the others, not forgetting Uncle Stewart. We had a delightful visit, had we not, papa?"

"Yes, I remember we enjoyed it greatly."

"I was just then very happy in the prospect of a new mamma," Elsie went on, with a smiling glance at her loved stepmother, "and papa was so very good as to allow me to tell of my happiness to the cousins. Your father was quite a tall lad at that time,

Cousin Cyril, and very kind to his little cousin who considered him a very fine young gentleman."

"He is an elderly man now," remarked his son. "You have seen Aunt Mildred and some others of the family since then?"

"Yes, several times. She and a good many of the others were with us at different times during the Centennial. But why did you not let us know of your coming, Cousin Cyril? Why not come to us directly?"

"It was a sudden move on my part," he said, "and indeed I was not aware that I was coming into the neighborhood of Viamede, or that you were there. But I am delighted that it is so—that I have the opportunity to become acquainted with you and to see the place which Aunt Mildred described as a paradise upon earth."

"We think it almost that, but you shall judge for yourself," she said with a pleased smile.

"Beautiful! Enchanting! The half had not been told me!" he exclaimed in delight, as, a few moments later, he stood upon the veranda. From there he gazed out over the emerald velvet of the lawn bespangled with its many hued and lovely flowers and dotted here and there with giant oaks, graceful magnolias, and clusters of orange trees laden with their delicate, sweet-scented blossoms and golden fruit, to the lakelet whose waters glittered in the sunlight and the fields, the groves and hills beyond.

"Ah, if earthly scenes are so lovely, what must heaven be?" he added, turning to Elsie a face full of joyful anticipation.

"Yes," she responded in low, moved tones, "how great is their blessedness who walk the streets of the Celestial City! How their eyes must feast upon its beauties! And yet—ah, methinks it must be long ere they can see them, for gazing upon the lovely face of Him whose blood has purchased their right to enter there."

"Even so," he said, "Oh, for one glimpse of His face! Dear cousin," and he took her hand in his, "let the thought of the 'exceeding and eternal weight of glory' your loved one is now enjoying, and which you will one day share with him, comfort you in your loneliness and sorrow."

"It does, it does!" she said tremulously. "That and the sweet sense of His abiding love and presence who can never die and never change. I am far from unhappy, Cousin Cyril. I have found truth in those beautiful words,

'Then sorrow touched by Thee, grows bright
With more than rapture's ray,
As darkness shows us worlds of light.'"

They had been comparatively alone for the moment, no one near enough to overhear the low-toned talk between them.

The young minister was greatly pleased with Viamede—the more so, the more he saw of it—and with his new-found relatives, the more and better he became acquainted with them. While they found him all his earnest, scriptural preaching had led them to expect.

His religion was not a mask, or a garment to be worn only in the pulpit or on Sunday, but permeated his whole life and conversation, as was the case with most if not all of those with whom he sojourned. And like them, he was a happy Christian, content with the allotments of God's providence, walking joyously in the light of His countenance, making it the one purpose and effort of his life to live to God's glory and bring others to share in the blessed service.

He was strongly urged to spend the winter at Viamede as his cousin's guest and preacher to the two churches.

He took a day or two to consider the matter, then, to the great satisfaction of all concerned, consented to remain, thanking his cousins warmly for their kindness in giving him a sweet home. They made him feel that he was entirely one of themselves, always welcome in their midst, yet at perfect liberty to withdraw into the seclusion of his own apartments whenever duty or inclination called him to do so.

The well-stocked library supplied him with all needed books. There were servants to wait upon him, horses at his disposal. In short, there was nothing wanting for purposes of work or of recreation. Again and again he said to himself, or in his letter to those in the home he had left, that "the lines had fallen to him in pleasant places."

In the meantime, Elsie found the truth as expounded by him Sunday to Sunday, and in the weekday evening service and the family worship most comforting and sustaining, while his intelligence, agreeable conversation, and cheerful companionship were most enjoyable at other times.

"Cousin Cyril" soon became a great favorite with those who claimed the right to call him so, and very much liked and looked up to by Isadore, Molly, and the rest to whom he was simply Mr. Keith.

In common with all others who knew them, he admired his young cousins, Elsie and Violet, extremely, and found their society delightful.

Molly's sad affliction called forth, from the first, his deepest commiseration. Her brave endurance of it, her uniform cheerfulness under it, brought forth his strong admiration and respect.

Yet he presently discovered that Isadore Conly had stronger attractions for him than any other woman he had ever met. It was not her beauty alone, her refinement, her many accomplishments, but principally her noble qualities of mind and heart. These gradually opened themselves to his view as day after day they met in the unrestrained familiar exchanges of the home circle, or walked or rode out together, sometimes in the company of others, sometimes alone.

Mr. Embury made good use of the permission Mrs. Travilla had granted him, and occasionally forestalling Cyril's attentions, led the latter to look upon him as a rival.

Molly watched it all, and though, now one and now the other devoted an hour to her, sitting by her side in the house doing his best to entertain her with conversation, or pushing her wheeled chair about the walks in the beautiful grounds, or taking her out for a drive, thought both were in pursuit of Isa.

It was their pleasure to wait upon Isa, Elsie, and Vi, while pity and benevolence alone led them to bestow some time and effort upon herself—a poor cripple who no one could really enjoy talking about.

She had a modest opinion of her own attractions and would have been surprised to learn how greatly she was really admired by both gentlemen, for her good sense, her talent, energy, and perseverance in her chosen line of work, and her constant cheerfulness. How brilliant and entertaining they often found her talk, pronouncing it "bright, sparkling, witty," and how attractive were her intellectual countenance and her bright, dark, expressive eyes.

CHAPTER
FOURTEENTH

Something the heart must have to cherish,
Must love and joy, and sorrow learn;
Something with passion clasp or perish,
And in itself to ashes burn.

—*L*ONGFELLOW

"MOLLY, HOW YOU DO work, a great deal too hard I'm sure!" said the younger Elsie, coming into her cousin's room. She found her at her writing desk, pen in hand, as usual, an unfinished manuscript before her, and books and papers scattered about.

Molly looked up with a forced smile; she was not in a mirthful mood.

"It is because I am so slow that I must keep at it or I get nothing done."

"Well, there's no need," said Elsie, "and really, Molly dear, I do believe you would gain time by resting more and oftener than you do. Who can work fast and well when brain and body are weary? I have come to ask if you will take a drive with our two dear grandpas, grandma, and Mrs. Carrington."

"Thank you kindly, but I don't believe I can spare the time today."

"But don't you think you ought? Your health is of more importance than that manuscript. I am sure, Molly, you need the rest. I have noticed that you are growing thin and pale of late and look tired almost all the time."

"I was out for an hour this morning."

"An hour! The weather is delightful; everything out of doors is looking so lovely that the rest of us find it next to impossible to content ourselves within doors for an hour. Some of us are going to play croquet. If you will not drive, won't you let one of the servants wheel you out there — near enough to enable you to watch the game?"

"Please, don't think me ungracious," Molly answered, blushing, "but I really should prefer to stay here and work."

"I think Aunt Enna is going with us, and you will be left quite alone — unless you will let me stay or send a servant to sit with you," Elsie suggested.

But Molly insisted that she would rather be alone. "And you know," she added, pointing to a silver hand bell on the table before her, "I can ring if I need anything."

So Elsie went rather sadly away, more than half suspecting that Molly was grieving over her inability to move about as others did and to take part in the active sports they found so enjoyable and healthful.

And indeed she had hardly closed the door between them when the tears began to roll down Molly's cheeks. She wiped them away and tried to go on with her work; but they came faster and faster, till throwing down her pen, she hid her face in her hands and burst into passionate weeping—sobs shaking her whole frame.

A longing so intense had come over her to leave that chair—to walk, to run, to leap and dance—as she had delighted to do in the old days before that terrible fall. She wanted to wander over the velvety lawn beneath her windows to pluck for herself the many-hued, sweet-scented flowers growing here and there in the grass. Kind hands were always ready to gather and bring them to her, but it was not like walking about among them, stooping down and plucking them with her own fingers.

Oh, to feel her feet under her and wander at her own sweet will about the beautiful grounds, over the hills and through the woods! Oh, to feel that she was a fit mate for someone who might some day love and cherish her as Mr. Travilla had loved and cherished her who he so fondly called his "little wife"!

She pitied her cousin for her sad bereavement. Her heart had often, often bled for her because of her loss; but, ah, it was "better to have loved and lost, than never to have loved at all." Never to love, never to be loved, that was the hardest part of it all.

There was Dick, to be sure—the dear fellow! How she did love him! And she believed he loved her almost as well, but the time would come when another would have first place in his heart—perhaps it had already come.

Her mother's affection was something, but it was the love of a stronger nature than her own that she craved—a staff to lean upon; a guiding, protecting love; a support such as is the strong, stately oak to the delicate, clinging vine. There were times when she keenly enjoyed her independence—perfect liberty to control her own actions and choose her own work, her ability to earn a livelihood for herself — but at this moment all that was as nothing.

Usually she was submissive under her affliction; now her heart rebelled fiercely against it. She called it a hard and cruel fate to which she could not, would not be resigned.

She was frightened at herself as she felt that she was so rebellious, that she was envying the happiness of the cousins who had for years treated her with unvarying kindness, and that her lot seemed the harder by contrast with theirs.

And yet how well she knew that theirs was not perfect happiness — that the death of the husband and father had been a sore trial to them all.

Through the open window she saw the handsome, easy-rolling family carriage drive away and disappear among the trees on the farther side of the lawn. Then she saw the croquet party setting out for the scene of their proposed game, which was at some little distance from the mansion, though within the grounds.

She noticed that Isa and Mr. Keith walked first — very close together and looking very like a pair of lovers, she thought. Then came Mr. Embury with Violet's graceful, girlish figure by his side, she walking with a free, springing step that once poor Molly might have emulated as she called to mind with a bitter groan and an almost frantic effort to rise from her chair.

Ah, what was it that so sharpened the sting brought by the thought of her own impotence, as she saw Vi's bright, beautiful face uplifted to that of her companion? A sudden glimpse into her own heart sent a crimson tide all over the poor girl's face.

"Oh, Molly Percival, what a fool you are!" she exclaimed half aloud, then burst into hysterical weeping, but calming herself almost instantly. "No, I will not, will not be so weak!" she said, turning resolutely from the window. "I have been happy in my work, happy and content, and so I will be again. No foolish impossible dreams for you, Molly Percival! No dog in the manger feelings either; you shall not indulge them."

But the thread of thought was broken and lost. She tried in vain to recover it as a distant hum of blithe voices came now and again to her ear with disturbing influence. She could not rise and go away from it.

Again the pen was laid aside and lying back in her chair with her head against its cushions, she closed her eyes with a weary sigh, a tear trickling slowly down her cheek.

"I cannot work," she murmured. "Ah, if I could only stop thinking these miserable and wicked, wicked thoughts!"

Mrs. Travilla, returning from a visit to the quarter, stopped a moment to watch the croquet players. "Where is Molly?" she asked of her eldest daughter. "Did she go with your grandpa and the others?"

"No, mamma, she is in her room hard at work as usual, poor thing!"

"She is altogether too devoted to her work; she ought to be out enjoying this delicious weather. Surely you did not neglect to invite her to join you here, Elsie?"

"No, mamma, I did my best to persuade her. I can hardly bear to think she is shut up there alone while all the rest of us are having so pleasant an afternoon."

"It is too bad," Mr. Embury remarked, "and I was strongly tempted to venture into her sanctum and try my powers of persuasion, but refrained lest I should but disturb the flow of thought and get myself into disgrace without accomplishing my end. Have you the courage to attempt the thing, Mrs. Travilla?"

"I think I must try," she answered with a smile as she turned away in the direction of the house.

She found Molly at work, busied over a translation for which she had laid aside the unfinished story interrupted by the younger Elsie's visit.

She welcomed her cousin with a smile, but not a very bright or mirthful one and traces of tears about her eyes were very evident.

"My dear child," Elsie said, in tones as tender and compassionate as she would have used to one of her own darlings. Laying her hand affectionately on the young girl's shoulder, "I do not like to see you so hard at work while everyone else is out enjoying this delightful weather. How can you resist the call of all the bloom and beauty you can see from your window there?"

"It is attractive, cousin," Molly answered. "I could not resist it if—if I could run about as others do," she added with a tremble in her voice.

"My poor, poor child!" Elsie said with emotion, bending down to press a kiss on the girl's forehead.

Molly threw her arms about her and burst into tears and sobs.

"Oh, it is so hard, so hard! It is so cruel that I must sit here a helpless cripple all my days! How can I bear it—for years and years, it may be!"

"Dear child, 'sufficient unto the day is the evil thereof.' Let us live one day at a time, leaving the future with our heavenly Father, trusting in His promise that as our day our strength shall be. Rutherford says, 'These many days I have had no morrow at all.' If it were so with all of us, how the burdens would be lightened! A very large part of them is apprehension for the future. Is it not?"

"Yes, and I am ashamed of my weakness and my cowardice."

"Dear child, I have often admired your strength and courage under a trial I fear I should not bear half so well."

Molly lifted to her cousin's a face full of wonder, surprise and gratitude; then, it clouded again and tears trembled in her eyes and in her voice as she said, "But, Cousin Elsie, you must let me work. It is my life, my happiness—the only kind I can ever hope for, ever have. Others may busy themselves with household cares, may fill their hearts with the sweet loves of kind husbands and dear little children; but these things are not for me! Oh, cousin, forgive me!" She cried as she saw the pained look in Elsie's face. "I did not mean—I did not intend—"

"To remind me of the past," Elsie whispered, struggling with her tears. "It is full of sweet memories that I would not be without for anything. Oh, true indeed is it that,

*'Tis better to have loved and lost,
Than never to have loved at all.'"*

"Oh, Cousin Elsie, your faith and patience are beautiful!" cried Molly impulsively. "You never murmur at your cross; you are satisfied with all God sends. I wish it were so with me, but—oh, cousin, cousin, my very worst trouble is that I am afraid I am not a Christian—that I have been deceiving myself all these years!" She ended with a burst of bitter weeping.

"Molly, dear," Elsie said, folding her in her arms and striving to soothe her with caresses, "you surprise me very much, for I have long seen the lovely fruit of the Spirit in your life and conversation. Do you not love Jesus and trust Him alone for salvation?"

"I thought I did, and, oh, I cannot bear to think of not belonging to Him! It breaks my heart!"

"Then why should you think so?"

"Because I find so much evil in myself. If you knew the rebellious thoughts and feelings I have had this very day, you would not think me a Christian. I have hated myself because of them."

"You have struggled to cast them out; you have not encouraged or loved them. Is that what they do who have no love for Christ, no desire after conformity to His will? It is the child of God who hates sin and struggles against it. But it is not necessary to decide whether you have or have not been mistaken in your past experience, since you may come to Jesus now just as if you had never come before. Give yourself to Him and accept His offered salvation without stopping to ask whether it is for the first or the ten-thousandth time. Oh, that is always my comfort when assailed by doubts and fears! 'Behold, now is the accepted time; behold, now is the day of salvation.' Jesus says, today and every day, 'Come unto Me, all ye that labor and are heavy laden, and I will give you rest.' 'Him that cometh unto me, I will in no wise cast out.'"

Glad tears glistened in Molly's eyes. "And He will pardon my iniquity though it is so great," she murmured with trembling lip and half-averted face. "He will forgive all my transgressions and my sins, cleanse me from them and love me freely."

"Yes, dear child, He will. And now, put away your work for the rest of this day and come out into the pure, sweet air. If we weary our poor, weak bodies too much, Satan is but ready to take advantage of our physical condition to assault us with temptations, doubts and fears."

"I will do as you think best, cousin," was the submissive reply.

Elsie at once summoned a servant and in a few moments Molly's chair was rolling along the graveled walks, underneath the grand old trees. A gentle breeze from the lakelet, laden with the scent of magnolias and orange blossoms gathered in its passage across the lawn, softly fanned her cheek, her cousin walking by her side and entertaining her with pleasant chat.

Rosie and Walter came running to meet them; they were glad to see Molly out. They filled her lap with flowers and her ears with their sweet innocent prattle, her heart growing lighter as she listened and drank in all the sweet sights and scents and sounds of nature in her most bountiful mood.

They made a partial circuit of the grounds that at last brought them to the croquet players, who, one and all, greeted Molly's arrival with expressions of satisfaction or delight.

Each brought an offering of bud or blossom—the loveliest and sweetest of flowers were scattered so profusely on every hand.

Mr. Embury's was a half-blown rose, and Elsie, furtively watching her charge, noted the quick blush with which it was received, the care with which it was stealthily treasured afterward.

A suspicion stirred in her heart, a fear that made her heart tremble and ache for the poor girl.

Mr. Embury spent the evening at Viamede. Molly was in the parlor with the rest, and the greater part of the time he was close at her side.

Both talked more than usual, often addressing each other, and seemed to outdo themselves in sparkling wit and brilliant repartee.

Molly's cheeks glowed and her eyes shone. She had never been so beautiful or fascinating before, and Mr. Embury hung upon her words.

Elsie's heart sank as she saw it all. "My poor child!" she sighed to herself. "I must warn him that her affections are not to be trifled with. He may think her sad affliction is her shield — raising a barrier that she herself must know to be impassable — but when was heart controlled by reason?

The next morning Enna, putting her head in at the door of the dressing room where her niece was busy with her little ones, said, "Elsie, I wish you'd come and speak a word to Molly. She'll hear reason from you, maybe, though she thinks I haven't sense enough to give her any advice."

"What is it?" Elsie asked, obeying the summons at once, leaving Rosie and Walter in Aunt Chloe's capable charge.

"Just come to her room, won't you?" Enna said, leading the way. "I don't see what possesses the child to act so. He's handsome and rich and everything a reasonable woman could ask. I want you to — but there! He's gone and it's too late!"

Elsie followed her glance through a window and saw Mr. Embury's carriage driving away.

"Did he ask Molly to go with him?" she inquired.

"Yes, and she wouldn't do it, though I did all I could to make her. Come and speak to her though, so she'll know better next time."

Molly sat in an attitude of dejection, her face hidden in her hands, and did not seem conscious of their entrance until Elsie's hand was softly laid on her shoulder, while the pitying voice asked, "What's the matter, Molly dear?"

Then the bowed head was lifted and Elsie saw that her eyes were full of tears, her cheeks wet with them.

"Oh, Cousin Elsie," she sobbed, "don't ask me to go with him. I must not. I must try to keep away from him. Oh, why did we ever meet? Shall I ever be rid of this weary pain in my heart?"

"Yes, dear child, it will pass away in time," her cousin whispered, putting kin arms about her. "He must stay away and you will learn to be happy again in your work, and, better still, in the one love that can never fail you in this world or the next."

"He is a good man; please, don't blame him," murmured the poor girl, hiding her blushing face on her cousin's shoulder.

"I will try not; but such selfish, thoughtlessness is almost unpardonable. He must not be allowed to come here anymore."

"No, no, don't tell him that! Don't let him suspect that I—care whether he does or not. And he enjoys it so much; he is so lonely in his own house."

"Do not fear that I will betray you, unselfish child," Elsie said. "But I must protect you somehow. And, Molly, dear, though I believe married life is the happiest, where there is deep, true love, founded on respect and perfect confidence; I am quite sure that it is possible for a woman to be very happy though she live single all her days. There is my dear, old Aunt Wealthy, for example; she must be nearly ninety. I have known her for more than twenty years, and always as one of the cheeriest and happiest people I ever saw."

"Did she ever meet anyone she cared for?" Molly asked, still hiding her face.

"Yes, she had a sore disappointment in her young days, as she told me herself; but the wound healed in time."

Enna had seated herself in a low rocking chair by the window, and with hands folded in her lap, was keenly eyeing her daughter and niece.

"What are you two saying to each other?" she demanded. "You talk so low I can only catch a word now and then; but I don't believe, Elsie, that you are coaxing Molly to behave as I want her to."

"Poor mother!" sighed Molly. "She simply can't understand it."

CHAPTER FIFTEENTH

Man's love is of man's life a thing apart,
'Tis woman's whole existence.

—*B*YRON

FINDING HER OWN THOUGHTS full of Molly and her troubles to the exclusion of everything else, Elsie presently dismissed her little ones to their play, spent a few moments consulting her best Friend, then went in search of her father.

She would not betray Molly even to him, but it would be safe, helpful, even comforting to confide her own doubts, fears, and anxieties.

She found him in the library and alone. He was standing before a window with his back toward her as she entered, and did not seem to hear her light footsteps till she was close at his side. Then, turning hastily, he caught her in his arms, strained her to himself, and kissed her again and again with fondness.

"What is it, papa?" she asked in surprise, looking up into his face and seeing it full of emotion that seemed a strange blending of pain and pleasure.

"My darling, my darling!" he said in low and tremulous tones, holding her close and repeating his caresses, "how can I ever make up to you for the sorrows of your infancy—the culpable, heartless neglect with which your father treated you then? I see I surprise you by referring to it now, but I have been talking with one of the old servants who retains a vivid remembrance of your babyhood here, and your heart-rending grief when forced away from your home and almost all you had learned to love. Such a picture of it has she given me that I fairly long to go back to that time and take my baby girl to my heart and comfort her."

"Dear papa, I hardly remember it now," she said, laying her head down on his shoulder. "And, oh, I have the sweetest memories of years and years of the tenderest fatherly love and care—love and care that surround me still and form one of my best and dearest earthly blessings. If the Lord will, may we long be spared to each other, my dear, dear father!"

His response was a fervent "Amen," and sitting down upon a sofa, he drew her to a seat by his side.

"I have come to you for help and advice in a new difficulty, papa," she said. "I fear I have made a sad mistake in allowing Mr. Embury's visits here, and yet—I cannot exclude from my house gentlemen visitors of exceptional character."

"No, and he appears to be all that and more—a sincere, earnest Christian. But what is it that you regret or fear? Elsie is engaged, Violet very young, and for Isa—supposing there were any such prospect—it would be a most suitable match."

"But Molly?'

"Molly!" he exclaimed with a start. "Poor child! She could never think of marriage!"

"No, papa, but hearts don't reason and love comes unbidden."

"And you think she cares for him?"

"It would not be strange if she should; he is a very agreeable man. Did you notice them last night? I thought his actions decidedly loverlike, and there was something in her face that made me tremble for the poor child's future peace of mind."

"Poor child!" he echoed. "Poor, poor child! I am glad you called my attention to it. I must give Embury a hint. He cannot, of course, be thinking what he is about; for I am sure he is not the heartless wretch he would be if he could wreck her happiness intentionally."

"Thank you, papa. You will know exactly how to do it without the least compromise of the dear girl's womanly pride and delicacy of feeling or offending or hurting him.

"You spoke just now of Isa," she went on presently. "I should be glad if she and Mr. Embury fancied each other; such a match would be very pleasing to Aunt Louise on account of his wealth and social position, little as she would like his piety, but—"

"Well, daughter?"

"Have you noticed how constantly Cyril seeks her companionship? How naturally the others leave those two to pair off together? They sit and read or chat together by the hour out yonder under the trees. Scarce a day passes without its long, lonely ramble or ride. He talks to her of his work, too, in which his whole heart is engaged; he listens attentively to all she says—turning in the most interested way to her for an opinion, no matter what subject is broached. He listens with delight to her music, too, and sometimes read his sermons to her for the benefit of her criticism, or consults her in regard to his choice of a text."

Mr. Dinsmore's countenance expressed extreme satisfaction. "I am glad of it," he said. "They seem made for each other."

"But Aunt Louise, papa?"

"Will certainly not fancy a poor clergyman for a son-in-law, yet will consider even that better than not seeing her daughter married at all. And if the two most intimately concerned with the arrangement are happy and content, what matter for the rest?"

"Oh, papa!" Elsie returned with a smile that had something of old-time archness in it. "Have not your opinions in regard to the rights of parents and the duties of children changed somewhat since my early girlhood?"

"Circumstances alter cases," he answered with a playful caress. "I should never have objected to so wise a choice as Isa's—always supposing that she has made the one we are talking of."

"And you will not mind if Aunt Louise blames you? Or me?"

"I shall take the blame and not mind it in the least."

Yes, Cyril Keith and Isadore Conly were made for each other and had become conscious of the fact, though no word of love had yet been spoken.

To him, she was the sweetest and loveliest of her sex, in whom he found a stronger union of beauty, grace, accomplishments, sound sense, and earnest piety than in any other young lady of his acquaintance. While to her, he was the impersonation of all that was truly noble, manly, and Christian.

They were dreaming love's young dream, and found intense enjoyment each in the other's society, especially amid all the loveliness of nature that surrounded them at Viamede.

Cyril's was a whole-hearted consecration to his divine Master and that loved Master's work, but this human love interfered not in any way with that, for it was of God's appointment.

"And the Lord God said, 'It is not good that the man should be alone; I will make him an help meet for him.' 'Whoso findeth a wife findeth a good thing, and obtaineth favor of the Lord.'"

"How like you that is, papa dear," Elsie said. "But it would be easier to me to bear blame myself than to have it heaped upon you. I suppose, though, that it would be useless to attempt any interference with the course of true love?"

"Yes, we will simply let them alone."

Mr. Dinsmore rode over to Magnolia Hall that afternoon to seek an interview with its owner but learned that he was not at home, and might not be for a day or two. No one knew just when he would return. So the only course now left seemed to be to wait till he should call again at Viamede.

He had been an almost daily visitor of late and often sent some token of remembrance by a servant—fruit, flowers, game, or fish, or it might be a book from his library that was not in theirs.

But now, one, two, three days passed and nothing was seen or heard of him.

Sad, wearisome days they were to Molly. Mental labor was next to impossible. She could not even read with any enjoyment for her heart was heavy with grief and unsatisfied longing, intensified by her mother's constant reiteration, "You've offended him, and he'll never come again. You've thrown away the best chance a girl ever had; and you'll never see another like it."

Then, too, it was unusually long since she had heard from Dick. And she had waited for news from a manuscript which had cost her months of hard work, and on which great expectations were based, till her heart was sick with hope deferred.

It was on the morning of the fourth day that Molly, having persuaded her mother to go for a walk with her grandfather and Mrs. Carrington, summoned a servant and desired to be taken out into the grounds.

She sat motionless in her chair gazing in mournful silence on all the luxuriant beauty that surrounded her, while the man wheeled her up one walk and down another.

At length she said, "That will do, Joe; you may stop the chair under that magnolia yonder and leave me there for an hour."

"I'se 'fraid you git tired, Miss Molly, and nobody roun' for to wait on you," he remarked when he had placed her in the desired spot.

"No, I have the bell here and it can be heard at the house. I have a book, too, to amuse myself with. And the gardener yonder is within sight. You need not fear to leave me."

He walked away and she opened her book. But she scarcely looked at it. Her thoughts were busying themselves with something else, and her eyes were full of tears.

A quick, manly step on the gravel walk behind her startled her quite severely and sent a vivid color over face and neck.

"Good morning, Miss Percival. I am fortunate indeed in finding you here alone," a voice said, close by her side.

"Good morning, Mr. Embury," she returned, with a vain effort to steady her tones, and without looking up.

He took possession of a rustic seat close to which her chair was standing. "Molly, my dear Miss Molly," he said, in some agitation, "I fear I have unwittingly offended."

"No, no, no!" she answered, bursting into tears in spite of herself. "There, what a baby I am!" dashing them angrily away. "I wish you wouldn't come here and set me to crying."

"Let me tell you something; let me ask you one question. And then, if you bid me, I will go away and never come near you again," he said, taking her hand and holding it fast. "Molly, I love you. I want you to be my wife. Will you?"

"Oh, you don't mean it! You can't mean it! No man in his senses would want to marry me—a poor, helpless cripple!" she cried, trying to pull her hand away. "It's just a cruel, cruel jest! Oh, how can you!" and covering her face with the free hand, she sobbed as if her heart would break.

"Don't, don't, dear Molly," he entreated. "I am not jesting, nor am I rushing into this hastily and thoughtlessly. Your very helplessness draws me to you and makes you doubly dear. I want to take care of you, my poor child. I want to make up your loss to you as far as my love and sympathy can, to make your life bright and happy in spite of your terrible trial."

"You are the noblest, most unselfish man I ever heard of," she said, wiping away here tears to give him a look of amazement and admiration. "But I cannot be so selfish as to take all when I can give nothing in return."

"Do you call yourself—with your sweet face, cheery disposition, brilliant talents, and conversational powers that render you the most entertaining and charming of companions—nothing? I think you a greater prize than half the women who have the free use of all their limbs."

"You are very kind to say it."

"No, I am not, for it is the simple, unvarnished truth. Molly, if you can love me, I should rather have you than any other woman on earth. How your presence would brighten my home! I give all indeed! You will be worth more to me than all I have to give in return. Oh, Molly, have you no love to bestow upon poor me?"

She had ceased the struggle to free her hand from the strong yet tender clasp in which it was held, but her face was averted and tears were falling fast. His words had sent a thrill of exquisite joy to her heart, but instantly it changed to bitter sorrow.

"You cannot have counted the cost," she said. "I am poor; I have nothing at all but the pittance I earn by my pen. And think—I can never walk by your side, I cannot go about your house and see that your comfort is not neglected, or your substance wasted. I cannot nurse you in sickness or wait upon you in health as another woman might. Oh, can you not see that I have nothing to give you in return for all you— in your wonderful generosity—are offering me?"

"Your love, dear child, and the blessed privilege of taking care of you are all I ask, all I want—can you not give me these?"

"Oh, why do you tempt me so?" she cried.

"Tempt you? Would it be sin to love me? To give yourself to me when I want you so much, so very much, Molly?"

"It seems to me it would be taking advantage of the most unheard of generosity. What woman's heart could stand against it?"

"Ah, then you do love me!" he exclaimed, in accents of joy, and lifted her hand to his lips. "You will be mine? My own dear wife? A sweet mother to my darlings? I have brought them with me that their beauty and sweetness, their pretty innocent ways may plead my cause with you, for I know that you love little children." He was gone before she could reply, and the next moment was at her side again, bearing in his arms two lovely little creatures of three and five.

"These are my babies," he said, sitting down with one upon each knee. "Corinna," to the eldest, "don't you want this sweet lady to come and live with us and be your dear mamma?"

The child took a long, searching look into Molly's face before she answered; then, with a bright, glad smile breaking like sunlight over her own, "Yes, papa, I do!" she said emphatically. "Won't you come, pretty lady? Madie and I will be good children and love you ever so much." And she held up her rosebud mouth for a kiss, and Molly gave it heartily.

"Me, too—you mustn't fordet to tiss Madie," the little one said.

Molly motioned the father to set the child in her lap, and, putting an arm about Corinna, hugged and caressed them both for a little, the mother instinct stirring strongly within her all the while.

"There, that will do, my darlings; we must not tire the dear lady," Mr. Embury said presently, lifting his youngest and setting her on her feet beside her sister. "Go back now to your mammy. See, yonder she is waiting for you."

"What darlings they are," Molly said, following them with wistful, longing eyes.

"Yes. Ah, can your heart resist their appeal?"

"How could I, chained to my chair, do a mother's part by them?" she asked mournfully, and with a heavy sigh.

"Their physical needs are well attended to," he said, again taking her hand while his eyes sought hers with wistful, pleading tenderness. "It is motherly counsels, sympathy, love they want. Is it not in your power to give them all these? I would throw no burdens upon you, love; I only aim to show you that the giving need not necessarily be all on my side, the receiving all on your."

"How kind, how noble you are," she said in moved tones. "But your relatives? Your other children? How would they feel to see you joined for life to a —"

"Don't say it," he interrupted in tones of tenderest compassion. "My boys will be drawn to you by your helplessness, while they will be very proud of your talents and your sweetness. I have no other near relatives but two brothers, who have no right to concern themselves in the matter, nor will be likely to care to do so. But, oh, dearest girl, what shall I, what can I say to convince you that you are my heart's desire, that I want you, your love, your dear companionship, more than tongue can tell? Will you refuse them to me?"

She answered only with a look, but it said all he could possibly have wished.

"Bless you, darling!" he whispered, putting his arm about her, while her head dropped upon his shoulder. "You have made me very happy."

Molly was silent; she was weeping, but for very gladness. Her heart sang for joy. Not that a beautiful home, wealth, and all the luxury and ease it could purchase would be hers, but that she was loved by one so noble and generous, so altogether worthy of her highest respect, her warmest affection, the devotion of her whole life—which she inwardly vowed should be his. She would strive to be to him such a wife as Elsie had been to her husband, such a mother to his children as her sweet cousin was to hers.

CHAPTER SIXTEENTH

I saw her, and I loved her —
I sought her, and I won.
Across the threshold led,
And every tear kiss'd off as soon as shed,
His house she enters, there to be a light
Shining within, when all without is night;
A guardian angel, o'er his life presiding,
Doubling his pleasure, and his cares dividing.

—ROGER

"YOU DECLINED A DRIVE with me the last time I asked you," Mr. Embury remarked, breaking a momentary silence that had fallen between them, "but will you not be more gracious today? My carriage is near at hand, and I have a great desire to take you for an airing—you and the babies."

Blushing deeply, Molly said. "Yes, if you wish it and will bring me back before I am missed."

"I shall take good care of you, as who would not his own?" he said, bending down to look into her face with a proud, fond smile. "Yes, you are mine now, dearest, and I shall never resign my claim. Ah," as he lifted his head again, "here comes your uncle, and I fancy he eyes me with distrust. Mr. Dinsmore," and he stepped forward with outstretched hand, "how do you do, sir? What do you say to receiving me into the family? I trust you will not object for this dear girl intends to give me the right to call you uncle."

Mr. Dinsmore grasped the hand, looking in silent astonishment from one to the other. He read the story of their love in both faces—Molly's downcast and blushing, yet happy and Mr. Embury's fairly overflowing with unfeigned delight.

"I assure you, sir" he went on, "I am fully aware that she is a prize any man might be proud to win. Your niece is no ordinary woman—her gifts and graces are many and great."

"She is all that you have said, and even more," her uncle returned, finding his voice. "And yet— you are quite sure that this is not a sudden impulse for which you may some day be sorry?"

He had stepped to Molly's other side and taken her hand in his, in a protecting, fatherly way. "It would wreck her happiness," he added in moved tones, "and that is very dear to me."

"It cannot be dearer to you, sir, than it is to me," the lover answered. "And rest assured your fears are groundless. It is no sudden impulse on my part, but deliberate action taken after weeks of careful and prayerful consideration. You seem to stand in the place of a father to her. Will you give her to me?"

"Mr. Embury, you are the noblest of men, and must forgive me that I had some suspicion that you were thoughtlessly trifling with the child's affections. I see you have won her heart, and may you be very happy together."

Mr. Dinsmore was turning away, but Mr. Embury stopped him.

"Let me thank you, sir," he said, again holding out his hand. "We are going for a little drive," he added, "and please let no one be anxious about Miss Percival. I am responsible for her safe return."

Molly's chair rolled on with rapid, steady movement to the entrance to the grounds where Mr. Embury's carriage stood. Then, she felt herself carefully, tenderly lifted from one to the other and comfortably established on a softly cushioned seat.

How like a dream it all seemed — the swift, pleasant motion through the pure, sweet, fragrant air; beautiful scenery on every hand; the prattle of infant voices and the whispers of love in her ear. Should she not awake presently to its unreality? Awake to find herself still the lonely, unloved woman she was in her own esteem but an hour ago, and who by reason of her sad infirmity could look forward to nothing else through life?

They turned in at an open gateway, and Molly, suddenly rousing herself, said, in surprise, "We are entering someone's private grounds, are we not?"

"Yes," was the quiet reply, "but the owner has no objection. He and I are on the most intimate terms. I admire the place very much, and want you to see it, so we will drive all around the grounds." And he gave the order to the coachman.

Molly looked and admired. "Charming! Almost if not quite the equal of Viamede."

His eyes shone. "Your taste agrees with mine," he said. "Look this way. We have a good view of the house from here. What do you think of it?"

"That it is just suited to its surroundings and must be a delightful residence."

"So it is, and I want to show you the inside, too. There's no objection," as he read hesitation and disapproval in her face. "The master and mistress are not there, and — in fact I have charge of the place just now, and am quite at absolute liberty to show it to strangers."

The next moment they drew up before the front entrance. Mr. Embury hastily alighted and lifted out the little ones, saying in a low tone something that Molly did not hear as he set them down.

They ran in at the open door, and turning to her again he took her in his strong arms and bore her into a lordly entrance hall. Then, it was on through one spacious, elegantly furnished room after another — parlors, library, dining, and drawing rooms — moving slowly that she might have some time to gaze and admire. Now and then he would put her down for a few moments in an easy chair or on a luxurious sofa, usually before a rare painting or some other beautiful work of art which he thought she would particularly enjoy.

The children had disappeared, and they were quite alone.

He had reserved a charming boudoir for the last. Open doors gave tempting glimpses of dressing and bedrooms beyond.

"These," he said, placing her in a delightfully easy, velvet-cushioned chair, and standing by her side, "are the apartments of the mistress of the mansion, as you have doubtless already conjectured. What do you think of them?"

"That they are very beautiful, very luxurious. And oh what a lovely view from yonder window!"

"And from this, is it not?" he said stepping aside and turning her chair a little that she might see through a vista of grand old trees, the lagoon beyond sparkling in the sunlight.

"Oh, that is finer still!" she cried. "I should think one might almost be content to live a close prisoner here."

"Then I hope my dear wife will not be unhappy here? Will not regret leaving the beauties of Viamede and the charming society there for this place and the companionship of its owner? Molly, dearest, this is Magnolia Hall. You are its mistress and these are your own rooms." He said, kneeling by her side to fold her to his heart with tender caresses.

"It is too much! Oh, you are too good to me!" she sobbed, as her head dropped upon his shoulder.

❧ ❧ ❧ ❧ ❧

On leaving Mr. Embury and Molly, Mr. Dinsmore hastened to join his wife and daughter, who were sitting together on the lawn. The interview between the lovers having taken place in a part of the grounds not visible from where they sat, they had seen nothing of it.

"You look the bearer of glad tidings, my dear," Rose remarked, glancing inquiringly at her husband as he seated himself at her side.

"And so I am, dear wife," he answered joyously. "Elsie, you may spare yourself any further regrets because of your kindness to Mr. Embury. Indeed, he is a noble, generous-hearted fellow, and very much in love with our poor, dear Molly. They are engaged."

"Engaged?" echoed both ladies simultaneously, as much surprised and pleased as he had hoped to see them.

"Yes," he said, and went on to repeat what had passed between himself and the newly-affianced pair.

"Dear Molly," Elsie said with tears trembling in her eyes, "I trust there are many very happy days in store for her. And how pleased Aunt Enna will be. She was so desirous to bring about the match."

"Molly herself should have the pleasure of telling her all about it then."

"Yes, indeed, papa."

"There is something else," Mr. Dinsmore said. "At Mr. Embury's suggestion I wrote to Dick two or three weeks ago, telling him that there was a good opening for a physician here, and asking if he would not like to come and settle if pleased with the country. His answer came this morning, and he will be with us in a few days."

"How glad I am!" was Elsie's exclamation. "Molly's cup of happiness will be full to overflowing."

Rose, too, was rejoicing, but she had heard before of the invitation to Dick and was less surprised at this news than Elsie was.

The ladies had their work, Mr. Dinsmore the morning paper, and the three were still sitting there when Mr. Embury's carriage returned.

Molly' face was radiant with happiness; Mr. Embury's also. And the faces of the friends who gathered about them in the library, whither he carried her, seemed to reflect the glad light in theirs.

Everybody was rejoicing at Molly's good fortune and pleased to receive Mr. Embury into the family, for they all respected and liked him.

Enna's delight on hearing the news was unbounded. She smothered her daughter with kisses and exclaimed over and over again, "I knew he wanted you! And didn't I tell you there'd be somebody better worth having than Elsie's lover coming after you some day? And I'm glad as can be that my girl's going to be married the first of all—before Louise's girls, or Elsie's either!"

"I can't see that that makes the least difference, mother," Molly said, laughing for very gladness. "But, oh, what a good and kind man he is! And what a lovely home we are to have! Mother, he says you are to live with us always if you like."

"Now that is nice!" Enna said, much gratified. "And is it as pretty as Viamede?"

"It is almost if not quite as beautiful as Viamede, though not quite so large. Both house and grounds are, I believe, a little smaller."

"How soon are you going to be married?"

"I don't know just when, mother; the day has not been set."

"I hope it will be soon, just as soon as we can get you ready."

This was a little private chat in Molly's room after Mr. Embury had gone away. She had asked to have her chair wheeled in there, and to be left alone with her mother while she told her the news of her engagement.

"I must consult with uncle and aunt and Cousin Elsie about that," she said in answer to her mother's last remark. "Will you please open the door now and ask them to come in? I don't care if the rest come too."

"Well, Molly, when, where, and by whom is the knot to be tied?" asked Mr. Dinsmore playfully, as he stood by her side looking down with a kindly smile at her blushing, happy face.

"Oh, uncle, so many questions at once!"

"Well, one at a time then. When?"

"That foolishly impatient man wanted me to say tonight," she answered, laughing; and when I told him how absurd an idea that was, he insisted that a week was quite long enough for him to go on living alone."

"A week!" exclaimed her aunt. "You surely did not consent to that?"

"No, Aunt Rose, but I believe I half consented to try to make my preparations in two weeks. I doubt if we can quite settle that question now."

"There must be time allowed for furnishing you with a handsome trousseau, my dear child," Elsie said, "but possibly it can be accomplished in a fortnight. As to the next question—where?—you surely will let it be here, in my house?"

"Gladly, cousin, if pleasing to you," Molly answered with a grateful, loving look. "And Mr. Keith shall officiate, if he will. Of course, it must be a very quiet affair; I should prefer that under any circumstances."

"You will invite Dick, will you not?" her uncle asked with a twinkle in his eye.

"Dick! Oh, dear fellow! I ought to have him. I wonder if I could persuade him to leave his practice long enough to come. Two weeks would give him time to get here if I write at once."

"No need," her uncle replied quickly. "Providence permitting, he'll be here in less than half that time."

Then the whole story came out in answer to Molly's look of astonished inquiry, and her cup of happiness was indeed full to overflowing.

"Where did you drive, Molly?" asked Isa. "But I suppose you hardly know; you could see nothing but—your companion?"

"Ah, Isa, do you judge of me by yourself, dear?" queried Molly gleefully. "By the way, though, I had three companions. But don't I know where I went?"

Then smiling, laughing, blushing, rosy, and happy as they had never seen her before, she described the darling baby girls and the beautiful home.

But the sweet words of love that had been as music to her ear were too sacred for any other.

She had quite a large and certainly very attentive and interested audience, the whole family having gathered in the room. Enna and the young girls were especially delighted with the tale she had to tell.

"It's just like a story—the very nicest kind of a story!" cried Vi, clapping her hands in an ecstasy of delight when Molly came to that part of the narrative where she learned that she herself was to be the mistress of the lordly mansion she had entered as a stranger visitor, with all its wealth of luxury and beauty.

The next two or three weeks were full of pleasant bustle and excitement, preparations for the wedding were being pushed forward with all possible dispatch—Mr. Embury pleading his loneliness and that he wanted Molly's relatives and friends to see her fairly settled in her new home before they left Viamede for the north.

Mr. and Mrs. Dinsmore, with Enna, Isa, the younger Elsie and Violet took a trip to New Orleans and spent several days in shopping there, laying in great stores of rich, costly, and beautiful things for Molly's adornment.

Mr. Embury, too, paid a flying visit to the city that resulted in an elegant set of jewels for his bride and some new articles of furniture for her apartments.

Dick arrived at about the expected time and was joyfully welcomed. His surprise and delight in view of Molly's prospects were quite sufficient to satisfy her, and so greatly was he pleased with the country that in a few days he announced his purpose to remain.

Cyril received a unanimous call from the two churches and after mature deliberation accepted it, upon which Elsie doubled the salary she had formerly paid. She told him playfully and in private that if he would get a wife who she could approve she would repair, enlarge, and refurbish the cottage.

"You are extremely kind and generous, cousin," he stammered, coloring deeply, "and I—I would be only too glad to follow out your suggestion."

"Well," she returned in the same playful tone, "what is there to hinder?"

"The only woman I fancy, could love, is so beautiful, fascinating, accomplished, so altogether attractive in every way, that—I fear she could hardly be expected to content herself with a poor minister."

"I cannot say how that is," Elsie answered with a smile, "but judging by myself, I should think she would give her hand wherever her heart had gone; and if I were a man, I should not despair until I had asked and been refused. And Cyril, though not rich in this world's goods, I consider you a fit match for the highest—you who are a son of the King."

"That sonship is more to me than all the world has to give," he said, looking at her with glistening eyes, "but to others it may seem of little worth."

"Not to anyone who is of the right spirit to be truly a helpmeet to you. I think I know where your affections are set, my dear cousin, and that by her the true riches are esteemed as by you and me."

He thanked her warmly by word and look for her kind sympathy and encouragement, and there the interview ended.

But that night, when Elsie was retiring, Isa came to her, all smiles and tears and blushed to tell the story of love given and returned. She and Cyril had spent the evening wandering about the grounds alone together in the moonlight, and he had wooed and won his heart's choice.

"Dear Isa, I am very, very glad for you and Cyril," Elsie whispered, clasping her cousin close and kissing again and again the blushing cheek. "I cannot wish anything better for you than that you may be as happy in your wedded life as my dear husband and I were."

"Nor could I ask a better wish," Isa returned. "But, ah, I fear I can never be the wife you were. And I can hardly hope for mamma's approval of my choice."

"Do not trouble about that now; I think we shall find means to win her consent."

"I think grandpa and uncle are sure to approve."

"Yes, and they will be powerful advocates with Aunt Louise; so I think you need not hesitate to be as happy as you can." Elsie answered with a smile. "Do you wish the matter kept secret?"

"Mr. Keith is with grandpa and uncle now," Isa said, blushing, "and I don't care how soon Aunt Rose and the girls and Dick know it; but, if you please, the rest may wait until mamma is heard from."

Molly was delighted, though not greatly astonished when Isa told her the next morning.

"How nice that we shall be near neighbors," she exclaimed. "I wish you would just decide to make it a double wedding."

"Thank you," laughed Isa, "but do you forget that it is now just one week from your appointed day? Or do you think my trousseau could be gotten up in a week, though it takes three for yours?"

"I really didn't stop to think," Molly acknowledged with a happy laugh. "But, Isa, you are so beautiful that you need no finery to add to your attractions, while my plainness requires a good deal."

"Molly," Isa said standing before her and gazing fixedly and admiringly into the glad, blooming face, "I think you have neglected your mirror of late or you wouldn't talk so."

A great surprise came to Molly on the morning of her wedding day. Her cousin Elsie gave her ten thousand dollars, and Mr. Embury settled fifty thousand upon her, besides presenting her with the jewels he had purchased—a lovely set of diamonds and pearls.

Also, she received many handsome presents from uncle, aunt, brother, and cousins, and from Mr. Embury's children.

He had sent for his two boys, fine manly fellows of ten and twelve, to be present at the marriage which was to take place in the evening, and had brought them that morning for a short call upon his chosen bride.

She and they seemed mutually pleased, and Molly, who had been somewhat apprehensive lest they should dislike the match, felt as if the last stone were removed from her path.

She gratified Mr. Embury greatly by a request that the baby girls and all the servants from Magnolia Hall might be present, and that he would let Louis, his elder son, stand up with them as third groomsman—Dick and Harold Travilla being first and second.

Isa, younger Elsie, and Violet were the bridesmaids, all wearing white for the occasion.

It was a very quiet wedding, indeed; no one at all present but the members of the two families, servants included — grouping themselves about the open door into the hall.

Molly sat in her chair looking very sweet and pretty in white silk, point lace, and an abundance of orange blossoms freshly gathered from the trees on the lawn.

The bridesmaids looked very lovely also; groom and groomsmen, handsome and happy.

Mr. Keith made the ceremony short but solemn and impressive. The usual greetings and congratulations followed. Elsie's to the bride was a whispered hope, accompanied with tears and smiles, that every year might find her and her husband nearer and dearer to each other.

An elegant banquet succeeded, and shortly after the happy bridegroom bore his new-made wife away to her future home.

CHAPTER
SEVENTEENTH

But happy they! The happiest of their kind!
Whom gentler stars unite, and in one fate
Their hearts, their fortunes,
and their beings blend . . ; for naught but love
Can answer love, and render bliss secure.

—*T*HOMSON'S *S*EASONS

𝒜S NO INVITATIONS TO THE wedding were to be sent to relatives at a distance, it was thought quite as well not to inform them of Molly's engagement until after the marriage had taken place. Besides, as the preparations were so hurried, no one had much time for correspondence.

Isadore Conly did not once during the three weeks write to Roselands, excusing herself on the double plea that her last letter remained unanswered and that she was particularly busy about the trousseau.

She found little time to spare from that which was not taken in walking or riding with Cyril.

He proposed writing to her mother immediately after declaring his love, but she begged him to delay a little till her grandfather and uncle should have time to consider how to bring their influence to bear upon Mrs. Conly in the way most likely to win her approval of his suit.

The day after the wedding saw a number of letters directed to Roselands, dropped into the Viamede mailbag, and a few days later they reached their destination.

The family—consisting of Mrs. Conly, Calhoun, Arthur, Virginia, Walter (who was at home for a few days on a furlough, being now a lieutenant in the U. S. Army), and several younger ones—were at breakfast when Pomp came in with the mailbag.

Calhoun opened it and distributed the contents.

"Letters from Viamede at last," he remarked. "Three are for you, mother, from grandpa, uncle and—somebody else. One is for Walter (Dick's handwriting! I didn't know he was there) and one for Virginia."

"From Isa," Virginia said as she glanced at the address. Then, tearing open the envelope and glancing down the first page, "Molly is married! To a rich planter, too! Will wonders never cease?"

A simultaneous exclamation of surprise came from all present.

"Nonsense, Isa's hoaxing you," said Walter, stirring his coffee. "Here let me see the letter."

"No. Open your own."

"That's not in Isa's line," remarked Arthur, "but really it is very astonishing news. What does Dick say, Wal? He went down there to attend the wedding, I presume?"

"No, didn't know a word about it till he got there," Walter said, giving a hasty perusal to the not very lengthy epistle. "He went to settle, good opening for a doctor, splendid country, everything lovely, likes brother-in-law immensely, is overjoyed at Molly's good luck, says she's as happy as a queen."

"Which may mean much or little," remarked Calhoun pensively.

His mother cleared her throat emphatically and all eyes turned to her. She held an open letter in her hand, and her face looked flushed and angry.

"Isa, too, it seems, has lost her heart," she said in a bitter, sarcastic tone, "and with her usual good sense has bestowed it upon a poor clergyman. Doubtless he has heard of her Aunt Delaford's intentions—Elsie perhaps has given him the hint, he being a relative of hers—and thinks he is securing a fortune. But if Isa throws herself away in such fashion, Sister Delaford may change her mind."

Calhoun and Arthur both repelled with warmth the insinuation against Elsie. The latter added that he thought Isa's personal charms were quite sufficient of themselves to captivate a man who was not in pursuit of wealth.

"And Isa," remarked Calhoun, "is so unworldly that wealth would be a matter of small consideration to her where her heart was concerned."

"A fact that should make her friends the more careful how they encourage her in taking a poor man," said her mother. "But, my father and brother are both strongly in favor of this adventurer's suit."

"Adventurer, mother! I thought you said he was a clergyman!"

"Well, Calhoun, I don't see any contradiction there. But his name is Keith, and that explains it all—for my father was always very partial to those relatives of his first wife. Horace, too, of course."

"But as Isa is a good deal more nearly related to them, they are very fond of her, and, men not easily deceived or taken in, I think we may safely trust their judgment. You won't oppose what they so highly approve, mother?"

"I don't know; must take time to think it over. Do you and Arthur come with me to the library," she said, rising with the letter in her hand. "I see you have both finished your breakfast."

They rose instantly and followed her from the room, Walter looking after them and muttering discontentedly, "I think mother might take me into her counsel, too."

"You are too young and foolish," said Virginia.

"The first objection doesn't lie against you, though the second may," he retorted. "You'd better look to your laurels. Isa and Molly are both well ahead of you."

"What of that?" she said, reddening with vexation. "Isa's two years older than I, and taking a poor minister whom I wouldn't look at."

"Sour grapes," suggested her brother, teasingly. "And Molly's not a year older than you, and has married rich."

"A second-hand husband!" sneered Virginia, at which Walter laughed uproariously.

"Oh, Virgie, Virgie, those grapes are terribly sour! But do let us hear what Isa has to say about it."

"I haven't finished the letter; but, there, take it. What do I care about her fine dresses and presents, and the splendor of Magnolia Hall?"

"Well," he cried presently, "Cousin Elsie did the thing handsomely! And he's a splendid fellow even if he is second-hand. No wonder Dick's pleased. I only wish my sisters might all do as well."

In the library, Calhoun was saying, as he laid down his uncle's letter that he had just read aloud, "Cousin Elsie is certainly the most generous of women! Mother, you could not have read this when you uttered that insinuation against her a few moments since?"

Mrs. Conly colored violently under her son's searching gaze.

"Twenty-five thousand is a mere trifle to her," she said, bridling, "and you perceive she promises Isa that dowry in the event of her marrying that poor relation of her own."

"Mother, it is extremely generous, nevertheless!" exclaimed both her sons in a breath.

"And I do not think it by any means a bad match for Isa," Arthur went on—"a good man, of fine talent, receiving a very comfortable salary, a lovely home rent free, very little expense except for clothing, seeing they are—as uncle says—to have all the fruit, vegetables, nearly their whole living, in fact, from the Viamede fields and orchards, even the use of carriages and horses, whenever they like."

"No, it isn't bad," their mother acknowledged, "and if she gets her Aunt Delaford's money, she will really be very far from poor. But I dislike the thought of having her, with her beauty and talents, buried, as one may say, in that out-of-the-way corner of the world."

"But she chooses for herself and ought to be the best judge of what is for her own happiness," Calhoun said. "So you will consent, mother?"

"Oh, yes, yes, of course! But I'll take no blame from your Aunt Delaford, nor from Isa either, if she sees cause to repent."

So at long last a letter was sent that made glad the hearts of the lovers, in spite of some slight ungraciousness of tone.

Isa's letter, giving as it did, a minute description of the trousseau, the wedding, Magnolia Hall, Mr. Embury and his children, and telling of the generous settlements upon the bride made by him and her cousin Elsie, was read and re-read by Mrs. Conly and Virginia with great interest, which was yet not altogether pleasurable.

They were glad that Molly had a new home of her own, and particularly that her mother was to share it. This home was so far away from Roselands that Enna was not likely to trouble them any more, for her feebleness of intellect made her something of a mortification to them of late years. Yet the good fortune of the poor crippled niece and cousin was too great, too strongly in contrast with their own distressed circumstances not to arouse some feelings of envy and jealousy in persons of their haughty and overbearing disposition.

"Dear me, I wonder why some people have all the good fortune and others none!" exclaimed Virginia angrily. "I should say five thousand was quite enough for Molly—especially in addition to the rich husband and loads of handsome presents—and that ten thousand would have been better bestowed upon you or me, mamma."

"You've only to get married, sis, and probably she'll do the same handsome thing by you," remarked Walter, who happened to be within hearing.

"Not she! I never had the good fortune to be one of her favorites."

"Well, Isa can't say that, for she's certainly doing the handsome thing by her."

"What?"

"So mother hasn't told you? She's promised that the day Isa marries her cousin, Cyril Keith, she'll hand over twenty-five thousand dollars to them."

"That was to get mamma's consent. Mamma, I wouldn't be bought if I were you," Virginia said quite scornfully.

"You wouldn't?" laughed Walter. "I tell you you'd sell yourself today to any man worth half a million, or even something less."

"Walter, you are perfectly insulting," cried Virginia, her eyes flashing and her cheeks flushing hotly. "I wish your furlough ended today!"

"Thank you, my very affectionate sister," he said, bowing low as he stood before her. "Why don't you wish I'd get shot in the next fight with the Indians? Well, I'll tell you what it is," he went on presently. "If I were one of Elsie's children—Ed, for instance—I'd enter a pretty strong protest against these wholesale acts of benevolence toward poor relations."

"She can afford it," said his mother loftily, "and I must say I should have a much higher appreciation of her generosity if she had given Isa the money without any conditions attached."

"But Isa wouldn't, or I'm greatly mistaken."

"Do you mean to say you think there has been a conspiracy between them?" demanded his mother, growing very red and angry.

"No, no, mother, nothing of the kind! But Cousin Elsie is a woman of keen observation, delicate tact, and great discernment; and she had Isa's happiness much at heart."

"Really," she sneered, "I have but just discovered that I have a Solomon among my sons!"

"I think it is mean not to invite us to the wedding," said Virginia.

"No, that was right enough," corrected her mother. "Being in deep mourning for her husband, she could not, of course, give Molly anything but the quietest sort of wedding."

"Well, will Isa come home to be married?"

"Of course, and I shall insist upon time to have everything done properly and without anyone being hurried to death."

Immediately upon the reception of Mrs. Conly's letter giving consent to the match between her daughter and Cyril Keith, the work of adding to, repairing, and improving the cottage destined to be the future home of the young couple was begun.

It was a matter of great interest, not to Cyril and Isa alone, but to the whole family of Dinsmores and Travillas. Their departure from Viamede was delayed some weeks that Elsie and her father might oversee and direct the workmen.

It was going to be a really commodious and beautiful residence when completed. Elsie determined that it should be prettily furnished, too, and found great pleasure in planning for the comfort and enjoyment of these cousins.

And Molly's happiness was a constant delight to her. There were daily exchanges between Viamede and Magnolia Hall, Mr. Embury driving Molly over almost every day to see her relatives, and Dick bringing his mother, usually on horseback.

Dick was making his home with his sister for the present, at Mr. Embury's urgent request, and was showing himself a good and affectionate son to Enna.

The visits were returned, too, even Elsie going over frequently for a short call, because she saw that Molly very keenly enjoyed being in a position to extend hospitality to all her friends, and especially herself, as one to whom she had long been indebted for a happy home.

"Oh, cousin," Molly said to her one day when they were alone together in her beautiful boudoir, "I am so happy! My husband is so kind, so affectionate! I cannot understand how it is that he is so fond and even proud of me — helpless cripple that I am. But I have learned to be thankful even for that," she added, tears springing to her eyes, "because he says it was that that first drew his attention to me. And, strangely enough, his pity soon turned to admiration and love. Oh, he has such a big, generous heart!"

"He has indeed!" Elsie said. "But, Molly, dear, you underrate yourself. I do not wonder that he admires you and is proud of your brave, cheerful courage under your hard trial, and of your talents and the name you are making for yourself as both a translator and original writer. I hope you will not give up your work entirely now that there is no pecuniary necessity for it, for I think it is bringing a blessing to yourself and to others."

"No, oh, no, I shall not give up while I can believe it is doing something for the Master's cause. Louis does not wish me to while I enjoy it. And I find he is just the critic I need to help me to improve. I had a letter from Virgie yesterday," she went on with a happy laugh, "congratulating me on being no longer compelled to work, yet pitying me because I am a stepmother."

"That does not trouble you, Molly?" Elsie gently inquired of her.

"Oh, no! The boys, Louis and Fred, are so much like their father—seeming to love me all the better for my helplessness. By the way, Louis, my husband, says it is a positive delight to him to take me in his arms and lift me about. And the baby girls are as lovely and dear as they can be. I wouldn't for anything part with one of the whole four."

"Dear child!" Elsie said, embracing her with full heart and eyes, "I am so glad, so happy for you that it is so! And how your mother and brother seem to enjoy your good fortunes!"

"Yes, Dick is such a dear fellow and mother— really it is just a pleasure to see how she delights in it all. And I think she couldn't be fonder of the children if she were their own grandmother."

"How glad, how thankful I am that we came to Viamede this winter," Elsie said, after a moment's silent musing. "Grandpa has so entirely recovered his health, a favorable opening has been found for Dick, and four other people are made happy in mutual love who might, perhaps, never have met otherwise. Besides, dear Mrs. Carrington had the melancholy pleasure of nursing her poor nephew through his last illness. How true is the promise, 'In all thy ways acknowledge Him, and He shall direct thy paths.'"

"You take a very unselfish delight in other people's happiness, my cousin," Molly remarked. "And Isa is very happy."

"Yes, and Cyril, too," Elsie answered with a smile. "I sometimes think my Elsie half envies them—thinking of Lester so far away. But her turn will come, too, I trust, poor, dear child!"

May was well advanced, the weather already very warm in the Teche country when at last the family set out upon their return to their more northern homes.

Everything there was looking very lovely on their arrival. Friends, kindred, and servants rejoiced over their return, all in good health.

Elsie and her children took up again the old, quiet life at Ion, missing Molly not a little, and feeling afresh, for a time upon their arrival at home, the absence of one far nearer and dearer.

Mr. and Mrs. Dinsmore spent some weeks with their other children, then again made their home at Ion, at Elsie's earnest supplication. In the loneliness of her widowhood she knew not how to do without her father.

In order to secure her cousin Elsie's presence at her wedding, Isa insisted upon a very quiet one, only relatives and very intimate friends to be invited to witness the ceremony; but to please her mother and Virginia, there was afterward a brilliant reception. The marriage took place the last of June, and the next two months were spent principally among Cyril's relatives up north.

CHAPTER
EIGHTEENTH

The sea! The sea! The open sea!
The blue, the fresh, the ever free!

—*P*ROCTOR

THE USUAL SUMMER VACATION brought Edward Travilla home just in time for his cousin Isa's wedding. He had grown so manly and so like his father in appearance that at sight of him his mother was much overcome.

His first, his warmest, tenderest greeting was for her. He held her to his heart, his own too full for speech, while she wept upon his shoulder.

But only for a moment—lifting her head, she gazed long and searchingly into his face, then, with a sigh of relief, "Thank God," she whispered, "that I can believe my boy has come back to me as pure and innocent as he went!"

"I hope so, mother. Your love, your teachings, and my father's have been my safeguard in many an hour of temptation," he answered with emotion.

"Did you not seek help from above, my son?' she asked gently.

"Yes, mother, you had taught me to do so and I knew that you, too, were daily seeking it for me."

"Yes, my dear boy; I think there was scarce a waking hour in which I did not ask a blessing on my absent son."

The mother dried her tears; grandparents, brothers and sisters drew near and embraced the lad, servants shook him by the hand, and Ion was filled with rejoicing as never before since the removal of its master and head.

Tongues ran nimbly as they sat about the tea table and on the veranda afterward. So much had happened to the young collegian, so many changes had taken place in the family connection since he went away, that there was a great deal to tell and to hear on both sides.

The voices were blithe and there was many a silvery peal of laughter mingled with the pleasant, cheery talk.

Isa and Molly's matches were discussed in a most kindly way, for Edward was quite curious to hear all about them and the preparations for the approaching wedding.

Cyril had arrived earlier in the day, was taking tea at Roselands, but would pass the night at Ion, which Edward was glad to hear, as he wished to make his acquaintance.

A summer at the seashore had been decided upon some weeks ago, and Edward, to his great gratification, had been empowered to select a cottage for the family to occupy during the season, his Aunt Adelaide and her husband assisting him with their excellent advice.

He announced with much satisfaction that he had secured one that he thought would accommodate them well—several guests in addition, if mamma cared to invite any of her close and intimate friends — and please everyone.

"It is large, convenient, well — even handsomely furnished — and but a few yards from the shore," he said. "The country is pretty about there, too — pleasant walks and drives through green lanes, fields, and woods."

"But where is it, Edward?" asked Violet.

"Not far from Long Branch, and there are easily some half-dozen other seaside places within an easy driving distance."

There were exclamations of both delight and impatience to be there from the younger ones. The mother covered up with a smile and a few words of commendation to Edward the pain in her heart at the thought that her best beloved would not be with his wife and children beside the sea this summer, as in former years.

Her father and Rose were thinking of that, too, with deep sympathy for her.

In a moment the same thought presented itself to Edward and Violet, and they drew closer to their mother with loving, caressing looks and words. But memories of Lester and their walks and talks together when last she was at the seashore were filling the mind of the younger Elsie with emotions, half of pleasure, half of pain. When should they meet again? Then the sudden silence that had fallen upon the group about her mother, and a glance at that loved mother's face, reminded her also of the father who would return no more, and whose companionship had been so dear a delight to her and to them all.

It was Rosie who broke the silence at length. "Mamma, can we not go pretty soon?"

"Yes, daughter, in about a week."

The journey was made without incident, and the cottage and its vicinity found to be all that Edward had represented to them.

They had brought some of their own servants with them, and had nothing to do with hotel or boarding house life. Elsie had always loved the quiet and seclusion of home, and clung to it now, more than ever. Yet, for her children's sake she would not shut out society entirely. Both Edward and his sisters were free to invite their young friends to partake of the hospitalities of their mother's house, but without noise or revelry, for which indeed, they themselves had no heart.

For a while the society of his mother and sisters was quite sufficient for Edward and his for them — they were all so strongly attached to each other and he had been so long away from home that it was very delightful to be together once more.

Mr. and Mrs. Dinsmore were at that time visiting relatives in Philadelphia and its vicinity. His grandfather's absence gave Edward the long coveted opportunity to try how nearly he could fill his father's place as his mother's earthly prop. It was dear delight to have her lean upon his arm, rely upon his strength, and consult him about business or family matters.

He was very proud and fond of his lovely sisters, prouder and fonder still of his sweet and beautiful mother. He quite longed to show her off to all his college friends, yet would not for the world have her grief intruded upon by them with their thoughtless merriment.

During these weeks that they were entirely alone, she gave herself wholly to her children, seeking to secure for them the greatest possible amount of innocent enjoyment. No tasks were set, there was no attempt at regular employment, and almost the whole day was spent in the open air. Together they sported in the surf, strolled on the beach, or sat in the sand reveling in the delicious sea breeze and the sight of the ever restless, ever changing, beautiful ocean, with its rolling, tumbling, dashing waves. They were there early in the morning, sometimes in season to watch the sun rise out of the water, and often again when the silvery moonlight lent its witchery to the scene.

But there came a day when the rain poured down so continuously and heavily that they were glad to take refuge from it in the house.

They gathered in a room overlooking the sea. The ladies had their fancywork. Rosie played with her doll, while Harold and Herbert helped little Walter build blockhouses; Edward read aloud a story selected by the mother as entertaining and at the same time pure and wholesome.

She was careful in choosing their mental food; she would no sooner have suffered her children's mind to be poisoned than their bodies.

As Edward closed the book upon the completion of the story, the younger Elsie said, "Mamma, do you quite approve of all of the teachings the author has given? Or perhaps I should rather say the sentiments she has expressed?"

"Not quite, but what is it you do not approve?" the mother answered with an affectionate and pleased look at the earnest face of the questioner. "I am glad to see that you are not ready to be carried off by every wind of doctrine."

"It is her comment about her heroine's effort to escape from her trouble by asking help from God.

She speaks as if, had the girl been older and wiser, she would have known that God had the welfare and happiness of other people to consult as well as hers, and couldn't be expected to sacrifice them for her sake."

"Well, daughter?"

"It seems to me to show a very low estimate of God's power and wisdom. Since He is infinite in both, can He not so order events as to secure the best good to all His creatures?"

"Yes, my child, I am sure He can and we need never fear that He is not able and willing to help His people in every time of trouble. 'The name of the Lord is a strong tower: the righteous runneth into it, and is safe.' 'The righteous cry, and the Lord heareth, and delivereth them out of all their troubles.' He does not always answer just as we desire, it is true, but often in a better way, for we, in our folly and short-sightedness, sometimes ask what would prove in the end a curse instead of a blessing."

"Mamma, how happy we should be if we had perfect faith and trust," said Violet.

"Yes, if we fully believed the inspired assurance, 'We know that all things work together for good to them that love God,' we should not fret or grieve over losses, crosses or disappointments. Strive after such faith, my children, and pray constantly for it, for it is the gift of God."

There was a little pause broken only by Walter's prattle, the splash of the rain, and the not so distant murmur of the sea.

Edward seemed in deep thought. Taking a low seat at his mother's knee, he said, "Mamma, I want to have a talk with you and perhaps this is as good a time as any."

"Well, my dear boy, what is it?"

"Do you think, mamma, that I ought to go into the ministry?"

"My son," she said, looking at him in some surprise, "that is not a question to be decided in a moment, or without asking God's guidance."

"You would be willing, mother?"

"More than willing—glad and thankful—if I saw reason to believe that you were called of God to that work. To be truly an ambassador of Christ is, in my esteem, to stand higher than any of earth's potentates, yet if your talents do not lie in that direction, I would not have you there. It is every man's duty to serve God to the utmost of his ability, but all are not called to the ministry. Some can do far better service in other walks of life, and I should prefer to have a son of mine a good carpenter, mason, or shoemaker, rather than a poor preacher."

"You do not mean poor in purse, do you, mamma?" queried Harold, joining in the little group.

"No, a poor sermonizer—one lacking the requisite talents, diligence, or piety to proclaim God's truth with faithfulness and power."

"How can one tell to what work he is called, mamma?" Edward quietly asked, with an anxious, perplexed look.

"By watching the leadings of God's providence and by earnest prayer for His direction. Also, I think if a lad already has a decided bias for any one profession or employment it is a pretty sure indication that that is what he is called to, for we can almost always do best what we most enjoy doing."

"Then I think I should study medicine," said Harold, "for I should very greatly prefer that to anything else. And don't you think, mamma, that a doctor may do really as much good as a minister?"

"Quite as much if he is a devoted, earnest Christian, ready to do good as he has opportunity; therefore, I entirely approve your choice."

"Thank you, mamma. So I consider it quite settled," Harold returned with a look of great satisfaction. "Now, Ed and Herbie, what will you be?"

"As Herbert never likes to be separated from you, I presume he too will choose medicine," the mother remarked, with a smiling glance at her third son, as he too came and stood at her side.

"I don't know, mamma; it seems to me doctors have a dreadfully hard life."

"Ah, I fancy a life of elegant leisure would suit you best, my laddie," laughed his eldest brother.

But the mother's look was very grave and also a little anxious.

Herbert saw it. "Don't be troubled about me, mamma dear," he said, putting his arms round her neck and gazing lovingly into her eyes. "I do mean to fight against my natural laziness. But do you think I ought to choose so very hard a life as Harold means to?"

"Not if you have talent for something useful which would better suit your inclinations. Can you think of any such thing?"

"Couldn't I be a lawyer?"

"You could never rise to eminence in that profession without a great deal of hard work."

"An author then?"

"The same answer will fit again," his mother returned with a slight smile. "Has not your Cousin Molly worked very hard for a number of years?"

Herbert drew a long, deep sigh, then brightening, "I might be a publisher," he said. "I don't suppose they work very hard, and they can have all the new books to read."

"Oh, Herbie," said Violet, "think of the great number of letters they must have to write, and manuscripts to read, beside many other things."

"No, my boy, you cannot do or be anything worth while without work, and a good deal of it," said his mother. "So I hope you will make it your earnest, constant prayer that you may have grace to overcome your besetting sin of indolence and to 'be not slothful in business; fervent in spirit; serving the Lord. The Bible bids us, 'Whatsoever ye do, do it heartily, as to the Lord, and not unto men.'"

"Edward, you have not told us yet what you wish to be," said his sister Elsie.

"My inclination," he answered in grave, earnest tones, "is to take my father's place in every way possible, first in the care of my darling, precious mother." Taking her hand and lifting it to his lips he continued, "After that, in cultivating the Ion plantation and making myself a good, upright, useful church member and citizen."

"A worthy ambition, my boy," the mother said with emotion. "My strong desire is that you may follow as closely as possible in the footsteps of your honored father. I never knew a better man, in the pulpit or out of it. His was a truly Christian manhood, and, like his Master, he went about doing good."

"Then, mother, with your approval my choice is made; and, with your permission, I shall spend some time in an agricultural college after finishing the course where I am."

"You should do as you wish. You shall have every advantage I can give you. My other boys, also, if they will improve them."

"Your girls, too, mamma?" asked Rosie.

"Yes, indeed," mamma answered, bestowing a smile and a kiss upon the questioner.

At that moment the tea bell summoned them to their evening meal. Edward took his father's seat at the table, his father's place in asking a blessing upon the food.

As they left the table they perceived that the rain had ceased. The clouds had broken away from the setting sun and its red light streamed over the dark waters like a pathway of fire.

They were all gathered on the porch, watching, as usual, the changing beauty of the sea and clouds, when a young man, in the undress uniform of a lieutenant in the army, opened their gate and came with a brisk, manly step up the walk leading to the house.

As he drew near, he lifted his military cap, bowed low to the ladies, then, stepping upon the porch, handed a card to Mrs. Travilla.

"Donald Keith," she read aloud. And holding out her hand with a sweet, welcoming smile, she said, "How do you do, cousin? I am very glad to see you. But, to which branch do you belong?"

"I am the younger brother of the Reverend Cyril Keith, lately married to a Miss Conly," the young officer answered as he took the offered hand. "He wrote me of your great kindness to him and when I learned, a few hours since, who were the occupants of this cottage, I felt that I must come and thank you. I hope I do not intrude, cousin."

"No, indeed; we are always ready to welcome near or far relatives. Now let me introduce these other cousins — my boys and girls."

The young man spent the whole evening in the company of these newfound relatives and went away highly delighted with them all.

He had several weeks' furlough, was staying at a hotel near by, and promised himself great enjoyment in the society of the dwellers in the cottage.

And they were pleased with him.

"He seems a very nice, clever fellow, mother," Edward remarked.

"Yes," she said, "he has very agreeable manners and talks well. And, knowing that he comes of a godly race, I hope we shall find him in all respects a suitable companion for you and your sisters. I am glad of his coming for your sakes, for I fear you may have felt the want of young society."

"Oh, no, mamma," they all protested, "we could not have enjoyed ourselves better. It has been so nice to have you quite to ourselves."

CHAPTER
NINETEENTH

A mother is a mother still,
The holiest thing alive.

—COLERIDGE

THE NEXT MORNING'S MAIL brought a letter from Mr. Dinsmore announcing his speedy coming with his wife, father, Mr. and Mrs. Allison, and several of their children.

"There shall be the end to our quiet, good times!" sighed Violet.

"Shall you be so very sorry to see your grandpa?" her mother asked with a slight smile, knowing that her father was dearly loved by all her children, and by none more than by Violet herself.

"Oh, no, mamma, nor grandma, nor any of them," was the quick reply. "Only, it was so nice to have you entirely to ourselves."

"Haven't you enjoyed it, too, mamma?" asked several voices, while every face turned eagerly and inquiringly to hers.

"Yes, indeed, my darlings," she said, "and yet so dearly do I love my father that my heart bounds at the very thought that he will be with me again in a few hours."

"Then, mamma, we are glad for you," Elsie said. Violet added, "and for ourselves, too; for it is nice to have grandpa and grandma with us, and Aunt Adelaide also. She is always so kind."

"Very different from Aunt Louise," remarked Edward. "Who would ever think they were sisters? Isa and Virginia are quite as unlike, too, though they are sisters. I hope Aunt Louise and her old-maid daughter won't visit us this summer!"

"Edward!" his mother said in a tone of reproof.

"Excuse me, mother," he said, "but if I dislike them, it is because they have always treated me so badly."

"They have never done me any injury, my son," she answered, with gentle gravity, "and I would not have you feel unkindly toward them. Much less am I willing to hear you speak of them as you did just now. Virginia is not an old maid, and if she were I should be sorry to have you apply that epithet to her."

"She is several years older than I am, mother," he said, blushing.

"About three, and you are only a boy."

Edward felt this as the most cutting rebuke his gentle mother had ever administered to him. He had begun to think of himself as a man, old enough and strong enough to be his mother's stay and support, and a guide to his younger brothers and sisters.

But, sensible that he justly deserved the reproof, he bore it in silence. Yet he could not rest until, seizing an opportunity to speak to her without being overheard by others, he whispered, looking beseechingly into her eyes, "Dear mamma, will you not forgive my thoughtless, uncharitable speech of this morning?"

"Certainly, my dear boy," she answered with one of her sweetest smiles. "And I trust you will try to cultivate more kindly feelings toward your grandpa's sister and niece for his sake, and because it is your Christian duty.

Mr. Dinsmore and his party arrived that afternoon. The next day they were followed by Mrs. Conly and her daughter, Virginia.

"We thought we would give you a surprise," was the greeting of the former. "The heat and threats of yellow fever drove us north. I scattered the younger children about among other relatives, leaving several at your house, Adelaide, then came on here with Virgie, knowing that Elsie would, of course, have room enough for us two."

"We will find room for you, Aunt Louise," Elsie said with pleasant cordiality and trying hard to feel rejoiced at their coming.

A very difficult task as they never were at the slightest pains to make themselves agreeable and the house was already comfortably filled.

Edward waited only to shake hands hastily with his aunt and cousin, then slipped away for a solitary stroll on the beach, while he should fight down his feelings of disgust and irritation at this unwelcome and unwarranted invasion.

He had asked that morning if he might invite his college chum, Charlie Perrine, to spend a week or two with him and had received a prompt and kind permission to do so. It seemed hard enough to have to entertain, instead, these relatives, between whom and himself there had always been a cordial dislike. For from early childhood, he had perceived and strongly resented the envy, jealousy, and ill will indulged in by them toward his mother.

He paced hurriedly to and fro for some minutes, striving, with but indifferent success, to recover his equanimity, then stood still, gazing out to sea, half-inclined to wish himself on board an outward-bound vessel in the offing.

Presently a hand took quiet possession of his arm, and turning his head he found his mother standing by his side.

"I am grieved to see my boy's face so clouded," she said in her sweet and gentle tones.

"Then, mother, it shall not be so any longer," he answered, resolutely forcing a smile. "I have been really trying to feel good-natured, but it is not easy under the circumstances. Not to me, I mean. I wish I had inherited your sweet disposition."

"Ah, you can judge only from outside appearances," she said with a sigh and a smile. "No one knows what a battle his neighbor may be fighting in his own heart, while outwardly calm and serene. "I know you are disappointed because you fear you must give up inviting your friend for the present, but that will not be necessary, my dear boy. We can still manage to make room for him by a little crowding which will hurt no one. My room is so large that I can easily take Walter and all your sisters in with me, and if necessary, we will pitch a tent for the servants."

"Or for Charlie and me, mother," he exclaimed in delight. "We should not mind it in the least. Indeed, it would be good fun to live so for a while."

At this moment they were joined by Elsie and Violet, both full of sympathy for Edward, and anxious to consult mamma as to still making room for the comfortable accommodation of his friend.

They listened with delight to her proposed arrangement. It would be a great pleasure to them to share her room, if it would not inconvenience her, and she assured them it would not.

"I was afraid," said Elsie, "that Aunt Adelaide might hurry away to make room for the others; but now I hope she will not, for we all enjoy having her with us."

"No," Mrs. Travilla said, "we will keep her as long as we can. Ah, here come my father and grand-father. I think we shall astonish them with the news of the arrival."

"Cousin Donald is with them, too," remarked Elsie. "Mamma, I think Virginia will be rather pleased to see so fine looking a gentleman haunting the house."

"Her sister's brother-in-law," said Vi. "Perhaps she will claim him as more nearly related to her than to us."

The young man had found favor with both Mr. Dinsmores, and the three were just returning from a pretty long tramp together which had caused them to miss seeing the arrival of Mrs. and Miss Conly.

The news seemed to give more surprise than pleasure.

"It was very thoughtless of Louise," the old gentleman said with some vexation, "but it is just like her. I think we must find rooms for them at one of the hotels, Elsie. I don't see how your house is to accommodate us all."

"I do, grandpa," was her smiling rejoinder, "so make yourself perfectly easy on that score."

"I hope our excursion is not to be interfered with, cousin?" Donald said inquiringly, for arrangements had been made for a long drive that afternoon, taking in several of the neighboring seaside resorts. As his three lady cousins had promised to be of the party, he was loath to give it up.

"No," she said, "Aunt Adelaide and Aunt Louise will doubtless be well pleased to be left alone together for a few hours, after a separation of several years."

"Besides, both my aunt and cousin will need a long nap to refresh them after the fatigue of their journey," remarked Edward.

The young people exchanged congratulatory glances. They were all eager for the drive. It was just the day for it, they had all decided — the roads in excellent condition after the late rain, a delicious sea-breeze blowing, and light fleecy clouds tempering the heat of the July sun.

They set off directly after an early dinner — all the Dinsmores and Travillas, Mr. Allison and his children, and Mr. Keith — in two covered carriages, and well provided with waterproofs for protection against a possible shower.

They were a pleasant, congenial party — cheerful and companionable, full of life and spirit.

They had visited Seagirt, Spring Lake, and Asbury Park, and were passing through Ocean Beach, when Edward, catching sight of a young couple sauntering leisurely along on the sidewalk, uttered an exclamation. "Why there's Charlie Perrine!" Then, calling to the driver to stop, he sprang out and hurried toward them.

"His college chum — and how glad they are to meet," Violet said as the two were seen shaking hands in the most cordial manner.

Then Perrine introduced Edward to his companion, and the lad's sisters noticed that his face lighted up with pleased surprise as he grasped her hand.

"Why, I know her!" cried Donald. "Excuse me one moment, ladies," and he too sprang out and hastened to join the little group on the sidewalk.

He and the lady met like very intimate friends, greeting each other as "Donald" and "Mary." Then he led her to the side of the carriage and introduced her. "My cousin Mary Keith, Uncle Donald's daughter, our cousins, Miss Elsie and Miss Violet Travilla."

The girls shook hands and exchanged glances of mutual interest and admiration. Mary had a very bright, pleasant face, dark eyes and hair, plenty of color, ladylike manners, and a stylish figure well set off by inexpensive but tasteful attire.

The other carriage, containing the older people had now come up and halted beside the first.

There were more introductions, then Mary was persuaded to take Edward's place in the carriage with her young cousins, and drive with them to the Colorado House, where she was staying, while he and his friend followed on foot.

Here the whole party alighted, seated themselves on the porch and chatted together for a half-hour.

"How long do you stay here, Cousin Mary?" Mrs. Travilla asked.

"Another week, Cousin Elsie. I have engaged my room for that length of time. I wish you would let one of your girls stay with me, or both if they will, though I'm afraid that would crowd them. I should be so glad if you would. I want to become acquainted with them, and besides, I have just lost my roommate, and I don't like to be left alone."

After a little consultation between the elders of the party, it was decided that Violet should accept the invitation. Her mother promised to send her trunk in the morning and Mary agreed to return the visit later in the season, when her cousin's cottage would have parted with some of its present occupants.

Edward, too, would remain and room with Charlie Perrine, on the same floor with the girls, so that Violet would feel that she had a protector.

"I hope it will be a pleasant change for you, dear child," the mother whispered in parting from Violet. "And, if you grow tired of it, you know you can come home at any time. And Edward," she added, turning to him, "I trust your sister to your care, particularly in swimming. Don't let her go in without you, and don't either of you venture too far out or into any dangerous spot."

"We will be very careful, mamma," they both replied, "so do not feel in the least uneasy."

"I shall owe you a grudge for this," Donald was saying in a rueful aside to Mary.

"Why, you needn't," she returned. "You can come, too, if you wish, unless you object to my society." "That wouldn't mend matters," he answered, with a glance at the younger Elsie.

"Nonsense! I've found out already that she's engaged. Didn't you know it?"

"Not I. Well, it takes a woman to find out the secrets of her sex!"

"Then you own that a woman can keep a secret?" was her laughing rejoinder. "But do tell me," in a still lower tone, "has cousin lost her husband lately?"

"Within a year, and they were devotedly attached."

"Oh, poor thing! But isn't she sweet?"

"Yes! It didn't take even me long to find that out."

The carriages rolled away amid much waving of handkerchiefs by the travelers and the little party left behind. Then Mary carried Violet off to her room for a long talk before it should be time to dress for tea. All this while the lads strolled away together along the beach, their tongues quite as busy as the other two, for there were various college matters to discuss, beside plans for fishing, boating, riding, and driving.

And Edward must sound his mother's praises and learn whether Charlie did not think her the loveliest woman he ever saw.

"Yes," Charlie said with a sigh, "you are a lucky fellow, Ned. I hardly remember my mother — was only five years old when she died."

"Then I pity you with all my heart!" Edward exclaimed. "For there's nothing like a mother to love you and stand by you through thick and thin."

He turned his head away to hide the tears that sprang unbidden to his eyes, for along with pity for his friend came a sudden recollection of that dreadful event in his childhood when by an act of disobedience he had come very near killing his dearly loved father. Ah, he should never forget his agony of terror and remorse, his fear that his mother could never love him again, or the tenderness with which she had embraced him, assuring him of her forgiveness and continued affection.

Meantime, Donald was speaking in glowing terms of Cousin Mary. "One of the best girls in the world," he pronounced her — "so kindhearted, so helpful and industrious. Uncle's circumstances are moderate," he said. "Aunt's health has been delicate for years, and Mary, as the eldest of eight or nine children, has had her hands full. I am very glad she is taking a rest now, for she needs it. A maiden sister of her mother's is filling her place for a few weeks, she told me, else she could not have been spared from home."

"You make me glad that I left Violet with her," Mrs. Travilla said with a look of pleased content.

Edward and his chum returned from their walk, made themselves neat, and were waiting on the piazza before the open door, as Mary and Violet came down at the call to tea.

The dining room was furnished with small tables each accommodating eight persons. The four young friends found seats together. The other four places at their table were occupied by two couples — a tall, gaunt, sour-visaged elderly man in green spectacles and his meek little wife, and a small, thin, invalid gentleman who wore a look of patient resignation and his wife, taller than himself by half a head.

A fine head of beautiful gray hair was the only attractive thing about her. Her features were coarse and her countenance was fretful. She occupied herself in filling and emptying her plate with astonishing rapidity, and paid little or no attention to her husband, who was so crippled by rheumatism as to be almost helpless. He had entirely lost the use of one hand and so nearly that of his lower limbs that he could not walk without assistance.

He had a nurse, a young German, who was with him constantly day and night. He helped him about and waited upon him, but in a very awkward fashion. The man's clumsiness was, however, borne with patience by the sufferer and did not seem to trouble the wife.

She eyed Violet curiously between her immense mouthfuls and whispered to her husband loud enough for the child to hear, "Isn't that a pretty girl, William? Such a handsome complexion! I reckon she wears make-up."

The sudden crimsoning of Vi's cheeks contradicted that suspicion instantly, and the woman corrected herself. "No, she don't, I see. I wonder who she is."

"Hush, hush, Maria!" whispered her husband. "Don't you see she hears you?" and he gave the young girl such a fatherly look, gentle and tender, that quick tears sprang to her eyes. It was a very strong reminder of one whose look of parental love she should never meet again on earth.

People at other tables were noticing her, too, remarking upon her beauty and grace, and asking each other who she was.

"We'll soon find out, mamma; don't you see she is with Miss Keith? And she will be sure to introduce her to us," said a nice looking girl about Vi's age, addressing a sweet-faced lady by whose side she sat.

They all met in the parlor shortly afterward, and Vi, Mrs. Perkins, her daughter Susie, and her son Fred, a lad of nineteen or twenty, were formally presented to each other.

"I don't want to get into a crowd; I don't care to make acquaintances," Vi said, half tearfully.

Mary understood and respected the feeling, but answered, "Yes, dear cousin, I know, but do let me introduce Mrs. Perkins and her children. She is so sweet and lovely, a real Christian lady—and her son and daughter are very nice. We have been together a great deal and I feel as if they were old friends."

Vi did not wonder at it after talking a little with Mrs. Perkins, who had made room for her on the sofa by her side. Her thought was, "She is a little like mamma, not quite so sweet nor half as beautiful, though she is very pretty."

Several other ladies had come in by this time, the invalid gentleman's wife among the rest. "Mrs. Moses," Vi heard someone call her.

"How do you do, Miss?" she said, drawing forward an armchair and seating herself directly in front of Violet. "You're a newcomer, ain't you?"

"I came this afternoon," Vi answered, and turned to Mrs. Perkins with a remark about the changing beauty of the sea and clouds, for they were near an open window that gave them a view of the ocean.

"Where are you from?" asked Mrs. Moses.

"The south, Madame."

"Ah! I should hardly have suspected it. You've such a lovely complexion and how beautiful your hair is! Like spun gold."

The German manservant appeared in the doorway.

"Mrs. Moses, Herr wants to see you."

"Yes, I hear." Turning to Vi again, "Well, you must have had a long, tiresome journey; and I suppose you didn't come all alone?"

Vi let the inquiry pass unnoticed, but the woman went on, "I've never been south, but I'd like to go. Perhaps I shall next winter. It might help my William's rheumatism."

"I believe your husband wants you, Mrs. Moses," remarked Mary Keith.

"Oh, yes, he's always wanting me. I'll go presently."

"Cousin," said Mary, "shall we stroll on the beach?"

Violet caught at the suggestion with alacrity, and they went at once, the rest of their party and Mrs. Perkins and hers accompanying them.

"That poor man!" sighed Mary. "I thought if we all left her, perhaps she would go to him."

"Isn't it strange?" said Susie. "He seems to love her dearly, and she to care nothing about him. And he is so nice, good, and patient, and she so disagreeable."

"A very poor sort of wife, I think," pursued Mary. "She will not even sleep on the same floor with him, for fear of being disturbed when pain keeps him awake. Day and night he is left to the care of that awkward, blundering German. But there! I ought to be ashamed of myself for talking about an absent neighbor."

"I don't think you are doing any harm, Cousin Mary," said Charlie, "for we can all see how utterly selfish the woman is."

"What! Are you two cousins?" asked Edward in surprise.

"First cousins, sir," returned Charlie, laughing, "sisters' children. Can't you and I claim kin, seeing she's cousin to both of us?"

A sudden dash of rain prevented Edward's reply and sent them all scurrying into the house.

CHAPTER TWENTIETH

*A little more than kin
and a little less than kind.*

—*S*HAKESPEARE

THEIR LITTLE PARTY HAD scarcely seated themselves in the parlor where a number of the guest of the house were already gathered, when the invalid gentleman was assisted in by his servant and took possession of an easy chair which Mrs. Perkins hastened to offer him.

He thanked her courteously as he sank back in it with a slight sigh as of one in pain.

Violet, close at his side, regarded him with pitying eyes. "I fear you suffer a great deal, sir," she said, low and feelingly, when Mary, her next neighbor, had introduced them.

"Yes, a good deal, but less than when I came."

"Then the sea air is doing you good, I hope."

"I'm thankful to say I think it is. There's an increase of pain tonight, but that is always to be expected in rainy weather."

"You are very patient, Mr. Moses," Mary remarked.

"And why shouldn't I be patient?" he returned. "Didn't Christ suffer far more than I do?"

"And He comforts you in the midst of it all, does He not?" asked Mrs. Perkins.

"He does, indeed, ma'am."

"I've always found Him faithful," she said.

"Humph! It's plain to be seen that you two don't know what trouble is," put in Mrs. Moses, glancing fretfully at her crippled spouse.

Vi's tender heart ached for him, and her countenance expressed sincere pity and sympathy.

A child began drumming on the piano, and Mr. Moses sent a helpless, half-despairing glance in that direction that spoke of tortured nerves.

Vi saw it, and as he turned to her with, "Don't you play and sing, my dear? You look like it, and I should be much gratified to hear you," she rose and went at once to the instrument, thinking of nothing but trying to bring help and comfort to the poor sufferer.

"Will you let me play a little?" she said to the child, with look and tone of winning sweetness, and the piano stool was promptly vacated.

Seating herself, she touched a few chords and instantly a hush fell upon the room.

She played a short prelude; then, in a voice full, rich, and sweet, she sang—

"O Jesus! Friend unfailing,
How dear art thou to me!
And cares or fear assailing,
I find my rest in thee!
Why should my feet grow weary
Of this my pilgrim way;
Rough though the path and dreary
It ends in perfect day.

"Naught, naught I count as treasure,
Compared, O Christ, with thee;
Thy sorrow without measure
Earned peace and joy for me.

I love to own, Lord Jesus,
Thy claims o'er me and mine,
Bought with thy blood most precious,
Whose can I be but thine!

"'For every tribulation,
For every sore distress,
In Christ I've full salvation,
Sure help and quiet rest.
No fear of foes prevailing,
I triumph, Lord, in thee.
O Jesus, Friend unfailing!
How dear art thou to me!'"

Edward had made his way to her side as soon as he perceived her purpose.

"You have left out half," he whispered, leaning over her, "and the words are all so sweet."

"Yes, I know, but I feared it was too long."

There were murmurs of admiration as he led her back to her seat. "How well she plays!" "Such an exquisite touch!" "What a sweet voice!" "Highly cultivated." "Yes, and what a beauty she is!"

Some of the remarks reached Violet's ears and deepened the color on her cheek, but she forgot them all in the delight of having given pleasure to the invalid. He thanked her with tears in his eyes.

"The words are very sweet and comforting," he said. "Are they your own?"

"Oh, no, sir!" she answered. "I do not know whose they are, but I have found comfort in them, and hoped that you might also."

Edward and Mary were conversing in low, earnest tones.

"I am delighted!" Mary said.

"With what?"

"Words, music, voice, everything."

"The music is her own, composed expressly for the words which she found in a religious newspaper."

"Indeed! She is a genius then! The tune is lovely."

"Yes, she is thought to have a decided genius for both music and painting. I must show you some of her pictures when you pay us that promised visit."

Mr. Moses presently found himself in too much pain to remain where he was, and summoned his servant, retiring to his own room.

His wife, paying no regard to a wistful, longing look he gave her as he moved painfully away, remained where she was and entertained the other ladies with an account of the family pedigree.

"We are lineal descendants of Moses, the Hebrew lawgiver," she announced. "But don't suppose we are Jews, for we are not at all."

"Belong to the lost ten tribes, then, I suppose," remarked Charlie Perrine dryly.

The morning's sun shone brightly in a clear sky. And on leaving the breakfast table the little party went down to the beach and sat in the sand, watching the incoming tide, before which they were now and then obliged to retreat, sometimes in scrambling haste that gave occasion for much mirth and laughter.

Mrs. Moses came down and joined them, a not invited and not over-welcomed companion. But, of course, the beach was as free to her as to them.

"How is your husband?" inquired Mrs. Perkins.

"Oh, about as usual."

"I do believe it would do him good to sit here awhile with us, sunning himself."

"Too damp."

"No, the dampness here is from the salt water and will harm nobody."

"Where is he?" asked Fred, getting on his feet.

"On the porch yonder," the wife answered in a tone of indifference.

"Come boys, let's go and bring him!" said Fred, and at the word the other two rose with alacrity and all three hurried to the house.

They found the poor old gentleman sitting alone, save for the presence of the uncouth servant standing in silence at the back of his chair. The old gentleman was watching with wistful, longing eyes the merry groups moving hither and thither, to and fro, between the houses and the ocean, some going down to swim, others coming dripping from the water, some sporting among the waves, and others still, sunning themselves on the beach.

"We have come to ask you to join us, sir," Fred said in hearty tones. "Won't you let us help you down to the beach? The ladies are anxious to have you."

The poor man's face lighted up with pleased surprise, then clouded slightly. "I should like to go, indeed," he said, "if I could do so without troubling others; but that is impossible."

"We should not feel it any trouble, sir," the lads returned, "but a pleasure, rather, if you will let us help you there."

"I ought not to ask it. Jacob can give me an arm."

"No," said Edward, "let Jacob take this opportunity for a swim, and we will take his place."

He yielded, and found himself moved with far more ease and comfort than he had believed possible.

The ladies—his wife, perhaps, excepted, greeted him with smiles and pleasant words of welcome. They had arranged a couch with their waterproofs and shawls far enough from the water's edge to be safe from the waves and here the lads laid him down with gentle carefulness.

Mrs. Perkins had seated herself at his head and shaded his face from the sun with her umbrella, while the others grouped themselves about, near enough to carry on a somewhat disjointed conversation in spite of the noise of the water.

"I think a sun bath will be really good for you, Mr. Moses," said Miss Keith.

"It's worth trying anyhow," he answered with a patient smile. "And it's a real treat to do so in such pleasant company. But don't any of you lose your swim for me. I've seen a number go in and I suppose this is about the best time.

"Just as is said," was the rejoinder of the young men.

"I do not care to swim today," Violet said with decision. "The rest of you may go, and I will stay and take care of Mr. Moses."

"Well, I'll go then. He'll not be wanting anything," said his wife. "Ain't the rest of you coming?"

After some discussion, all went but Mrs. Perkins and Violet. They were left alone with the invalid.

Vi had conceived a great pity for him, great disgust for that selfish, unsympathetic wife.

"How different from mamma!" she said to herself. "She never would have wearied of waiting upon papa if he had been afflicted. She would have wanted to be beside him, comforting him every moment. And how sweetly it would have been done."

"Little lady," the old man said with a longing look into the sweet, girlish face, "will you sing me that song again? I must say, it was the most delightful, consoling thing I've heard for many a day."

"Yes, indeed, sir. I would do anything in my power to help you to forget your pain," she said, coloring with pleasure.

She sang the whole of the one he had asked for, then perceiving how greatly he enjoyed it, several others of like character.

He listened intently, sometimes with tears in his eyes, and thanking her warmly again and again.

Finding that the old gentleman felt brighter and freer from pain during the rest of the day and thinking he had received benefit from his visit to the beach, the lads helped him there again the next day.

They set him down, then wandered away, leaving him in the care of the same group of ladies who had gathered round him the day before.

Each one was anxious to do something for his relief or entertainment, and he seemed both pleased with their society and grateful for their attentions.

Mrs. Perkins suggested that the lame hand might be benefited by burying it in the sand while he sat there.

"No harm in trying it, anyhow," he said. "Just turn me round a little, Maria, if you please."

His wife complied promptly with the request, but in a way that the other ladies thought rough and unfeeling, seizing him by the collar of his coat and jerking him round to the desired position.

But he made no complaint.

"I think it does ease the pain," he said after a little. "I'm only sorry I can't try it every day for a while."

"What is there to hinder?" asked Mrs. Perkins.

"We're going tomorrow," replied Mrs. Moses.

"Oh, why not stay longer? You have been here but a week and Mr. Moses has improved quite a good deal in that time."

"Well, he can stay as long as he chooses, but I'm going to New York tomorrow to visit my sister."

The ladies urged her to stay for her poor husband's sake, but she was not to be persuaded.

"Take some sand with you, then, to bury his hand in, won't you?" said Mrs. Perkins.

"I haven't anything to carry it in," was the reply.

"Those newspapers."

"I want to read them."

"Well, if we find something to put it in, and get it ready for you, will you take it in your trunk?"

"Yes, I'll do that."

"I have a good-sized paper box which will answer the purpose, I think," said Mary Keith. "I'll get it."

She hastened to the house, returned again in a few moments with the box, and they proceeded to fill it, sifting the sand carefully through their fingers to remove every pebble.

"You are taking a great deal of trouble for me, ladies," the old gentleman remarked.

"No trouble at all, sir," said Mary. "It's a real pleasure to do anything we can for you, especially remembering the Master's words, 'Inasmuch as you have done it unto one of the least of these my brethren, you have done it unto me.'"

CHAPTER
TWENTY-FIRST

How happy they
Who, from the toil and tumult of their lives,
Steal to look down where naught but ocean strives.

—BYRON

XViolet was alone, lying on the bed, resting after her swim, not asleep, but thinking dreamily of home and mother.

"Only one more day and my week here will be up," she was saying to herself. "I've had a delightful time, but oh, I want to see mamma and the rest!"

Just then the door opened and Mary came in with a face all smiles. "Oh, Vi, I'm so glad!" she exclaimed, seating herself on the side of the bed.

"What about, cousin?" Violet asked, rousing herself and with a keen look of interest.

"I have just had the offer of a furnished cottage for two or three weeks—to keep house in, you understand—and I can invite several friends to stay with me. And it won't cost half so much as boarding here, beside being great fun," Mary answered, talking very fast in her excitement and delight. "Charlie will stay with me, I think, and I hope you and Edward will, and I have two girl friends at home who I shall invite. One is an invalid and needs the change, oh, so badly. Though they are not exactly poor people, not the kind one would dare offer charity to. Her father can't afford to give her even a week at any of these hotels or boarding houses and she did look so wistful and sad when I bade her goodbye. 'I can hardly help envying you, Mary,' she said, 'though I'm ever so glad you are going. But I have such a longing to get away from home for a while—to go somewhere, anywhere for a change. I'm so weak and miserable and it seems to me that if I could only go away I should get well. I haven't been outside of this town for years.'"

Violet's eyes filled with tears. "Poor thing!" she said. "I have always traveled about so much and enjoyed it greatly. I wonder why it is I have so many more pleasures and blessings than other people."

"I hope they may never be fewer," Mary said, hugging her. "But isn't it nice that now I can give poor Amy Fletcher—for that is her name—two or three weeks here at the seashore?"

"Yes! But you haven't told me how it happened."

In reply to this, Mary went on to say that a married friend who had rented the cottage for the year, now found that he must take his family away for a short time. Mountain air was being recommended for his wife, who was in poor health. And as it would cost no more to have the cottage occupied in their absence than to leave it empty, he had offered her the use of it rent free.

"He saw mother and father last week," she added, "and talked it over with them. They have written me to accept his offer by all means, and stay as long at the shore as I can."

"But you are to visit us, you know."

"Yes, afterward, if that will do. I don't intend to miss that pleasure if I can help it," Mary answered gleefully. "Now about my other friend, Ella Neff—she is not an invalid, but she teaches for her support. She wanted to come with me, but couldn't afford it; yet, I'm sure she can in this way. For besides the difference of board, there will not be the same necessity for fine dress."

"I should never have thought of that," said Vi.

"No, of course not, you fortunate little lassie. You have never known anything about the pinchings of poverty—or the pleasures of economy," she added merrily, "for I do assure you there is often real enjoyment in finding how nicely you can contrive to make one dollar do the work of two—or 'auld claes amaist as weel's the new.' But, oh, don't you think it will be fun to keep house, do our own cooking and all?"

"Yes," Violet said. "Yes, indeed."

"And you'll stay, won't you? Don't you think you'd enjoy it?"

"Oh, ever so much! But I don't believe I can wait any longer than till tomorrow to see mamma. Besides, I don't know whether she would approve."

"Well, if you should spend a day at home and get her consent to come back, how would that do?"

Vi thought that plan might answer, if Edward were willing to be one of the party at the cottage.

"We must consult the lads at once," said Mary. "Let me help you dress, and we'll go in search of them."

Vi sprang up, and with her cousin's assistance got dressed quickly.

They found Edward and Charlie in the summer house, just across the road, waiting for the call to dinner. Fortunately no one was within hearing, and Mary quickly unfolded her plan.

It was heard with delight. "Splendid! Capital! Of course, we'll be glad to accept your invitation," they said. Edward, however, put in the provision, "If mamma sees no objection."

"Or grandpa," added Violet.

"All the same," said Edward. "Mamma never approves of anything that he does not."

"Where is the cottage? Can we see it?" asked Charles.

"Yes, the family left this morning, and I have the key," Mary answered. "We could take possession tonight, if we chose; but I must plan and lay in some provisions first."

"Let's walk up (or down, whichever it is) after dinner and take a look at it."

"Yes, Charlie, if Edward and Vi are agreed. It is up, on this street, about two blocks from here."

"Directly in front of the ocean? That's all right."

"Or the ocean directly in front of it," Mary returned laughingly.

"All the same, don't be too critical, Miss Keith," said Charlie.

They did not linger long over dinner or dessert, but made haste to the cottage, eager to see what accommodations it afforded.

It was small, the rooms few in number, and mere boxes compared to those Edward and Violet had been accustomed to at Ion and Viamede. Very much more contracted than those of the cottage their mother was occupying, yet all four were quite satisfied to take up their residence in it for a season.

"Four bedrooms," remarked Mary reflectively. "Two will do for the lads and two for the lasses. Parlor and dining room are not very spacious, but will hold us all when necessary. I don't suppose we'll spend much of the daytime within doors. By the way, I think we must add Don Keith to our party—if he'll come."

The boys said, "By all means," and Vi raised no objection at all.

"When do you expect Ella and Amy?" asked Charles, who was well acquainted with both.

"I telegraphed to mother at once to invite them, and shall expect to see them about day after tomorrow."

"What sort of provisions do you propose to lay in, Miss Keith?" inquired Charlie. "I am personally interested in that."

"I do not doubt that in the least, Mr. Perrine," she answered demurely. "I intend to buy some of the best flour and groceries that I can find."

"Can't you buy bread here?'

"Yes, but perhaps I may choose to exhibit my skill in its manufacture; also, in that of cake and pastry."

"Ah! Well, no objection to that except that we don't want you shut up in the kitchen when the rest of us are off pleasuring. What about other supplies?"

"I see you have some idea of what is necessary in housekeeping, Charlie. I'll give you a good recommendation to—the first nice girl who asks if you'll make a good husband," Mary returned, looking at her cousin with laughing eyes.

"Am I to have an answer to my question, Miss Keith?" he inquired with dignity.

"Yes, when I see fit to give it. The Marstons were, of course, served with butter, eggs, milk, and cream, fish, flesh, and fowl, and Mr. Marston told me he had spoken to the persons thus serving him and his to do likewise by me and mine. Does this explanation relieve your mind, Mr. Perrine?

"I think we are very fortunate," Mary remarked, resuming her ordinary tone. "They have left us bedding, table and kitchen furniture, and we have nothing whatever to provide except food, drink, and clothing."

"I shall order a carriage for an early hour tomorrow morning," said Edward, "and drive over to see my mother. Vi will, of course, go along, and I wish, Cousin Mary, that you and Charlie would go, too."

"Thank you very much," Mary said. "I should enjoy it extremely, but there are some few arrangements to be made here. The girls may come tomorrow evening, and I must be here and ready to receive them."

Then Charlie decided that he must stay and take care of Mary. So, it was finally arranged that Edward and Violet should go alone, and the former attend to the ordering of groceries and anything else he could think of that was desirable and did not require to be fresh.

When the carriage containing Edward and Violet drove up to their mother's door, nearly all the family and their guests were out upon the beach. There was instantly a glad shout from Harold, Herbert, and Walter, "There they are!" and they, their sisters, and grandfather started at once for the house, while Mrs. Dinsmore and Mrs. Travilla, who were within, hastened to the door.

Mrs. Conly and Virginia, slowly sauntering along within sight of the cottage, looked after those who were hurrying toward it, with smiles of contempt.

"Such hugging and kissing as there will be now!" sneered Virginia. "They will make as much fuss as if they hadn't seen each other for five years."

"Yes," returned her mother, "and I don't wish to be a spectator of the sickening scene. Thank fortune I'm not of the overly affectionate kind."

"Mamma, mamma!" cried Violet, springing into the dear arms so joyfully opened to receive her. "Oh, I am so glad, so glad to see you again!"

"Not more glad than mamma is, darling," Elsie said, clasping her close with tender caresses.

"And you've come home a day sooner than you were expected! How good of you!" the younger Elsie exclaimed, taking her turn.

"Yes, but not to stay; that is, I mean if mamma consents to—"

But the sentence remained unfinished for awhile, for there were so many claiming a hug and kiss from both herself and Edward. Indeed Virginia was correct in her prediction that there was as much embracing and rejoicing, perhaps even more, than there would have been in the Conly family in receiving a brother and sister who had been absent for years.

But when all that had been attended to, and the pleasant little excitement began to subside, it did not take many minutes for mamma and grandpa and grandma to learn all about the proposed effort in housekeeping on the part of the young people.

"What, does my Vi want to leave her mother again so soon?" Mrs. Travilla said with half reproachful tenderness, putting her arm about the slender, girlish waist, and pressing another kiss on the softly rounded, blooming cheek.

"No, mamma dearest," Vi said, blushing and laying her head down on her mother's shoulder, "but the house here is as full as ever, isn't it?"

"Yes, but that makes no difference; there is plenty of room."

"Well, mamma, I don't like to be away from you, or any of the dear ones, but I do think it would be

227

great fun for a little while. Don't you? Wouldn't you have liked it when you were my age?"

"Yes, I daresay I should, and I see no great objection, if you and Edward wish to try it. What do you say, papa?"

"That I think their mother is the right person to decide the question, and that I do not suppose they can come to any harm," Mr. Dinsmore answered with a kindly look and smile directed to Edward and Violet. "I doubt if I should have allowed you to do such a thing at Vi's age, Elsie," he added, "but I believe I grow more indulgent with advancing years — perhaps more foolish."

"No, papa, I cannot think that," she said, lifting her soft eyes to his with a world of filial tenderness and reverence in their depths. "I lean very much upon the wisdom of your decisions. Well, dears, since grandpa does not disapprove, you have my full consent to do as you please in this matter."

They thanked her warmly.

"Cousin Mary would be delighted if Elsie would come, too," said Violet, looking wistfully at her sister, "and so would I. I don't suppose, mamma, you could spare us both at once, but if Elsie would like to go, I will stay, and not feel it the least bit of a hardship either," she added, turning to her mother with a bright, affectionate smile.

"I should be lonely with both my older daughters away," the mother said, "but I will not be selfish in my love. Elsie may go, too, if she wishes."

"Mamma, selfishness is no part of your nature," her namesake daughter responded promptly, "but I haven't the slightest desire to go. Yet I thank my sweet sister all the same for her kind and unselfish offer," she added, giving Violet a look of affection.

"But what is grandpa to do without his merry little Cricket?" asked Mr. Dinsmore, drawing Vi down upon his knee. "For how long is it? Three weeks?"

"I don't know, grandpa; perhaps I shall grow tired and homesick and want to come back directly."

"Well, no one would be sorry to see you."

"You will always be joyously welcomed," added mamma, "nor Edward less so. Now let us consider what you will need, and how best to provide it. I claim the privilege of furnishing all the groceries and everything else for the larder that need not be procured upon the spot."

"Oh, thank you, mamma!" said Edward. "But I knew you would."

Violet asked and obtained permission to sleep with her mother that night and all day long was scarcely absent from her side. Evidently the child had a divided heart, and was at times more than half-inclined to stay at home.

But Edward urged that he would not half enjoy himself without her, that she had promised to go if mamma did not withhold consent, and that Mary would be sadly disappointed if she failed to return with him. Donald Keith, too, who was still there and had accepted Mary's invitation, added his persuasions. He was sure they would have a pleasant time and if she grew homesick, she could drive home any day in a couple of hours. He would be glad to bring her over himself if she would let him, or she could come in less time by the cars.

Then mother came to her help. "I think it will be best for you to go, dear, even if you should stay but a day or two," she said. "And if your grandpa likes, he and I will drive over with you and see your snug little cottage, and whether there is anything we can do to add to the comfort and enjoyment of those who are to occupy it for a season."

"A very good idea, daughter," Mr. Dinsmore said, and Vi's rather troubled face grew bright.

"Oh, how nice, mamma!" she exclaimed. "I will go without any more foolish hesitation, although I do not think Edward is quite correct in saying I promised."

"Foolish enough!" sneered Virginia, who prided herself on her audacity in making disagreeable remarks. "I should be very much ashamed of myself if I were half the mamma's baby you are."

"And I," remarked Mr. Dinsmore severely, irritated out of all patience by the pained look on Vi's face, "should be more ashamed of my sweet little granddaughter if she were as heartless and ready to wound the feelings of others as a certain niece of mine seems to be."

ᘏ ᘏ ᘏ ᘏ ᘏ

"Will you come to my house-warming, Mrs. Perkins, you and Fred and Suzie?" asked Mary Keith as they left the breakfast table the next morning. "I expect my cousins, the Travillas, about dinner time, and the morning train may bring the other guests. The dinner is to be prepared with my own hands, and though it will be on a small scale compared with those served here, you have a hearty welcome.

"Thank you, we would be delighted, but are already engaged for the picnic," Mrs. Perkins said.

So they parted with mutual good wishes, each hoping the other would have an enjoyable day.

Charles and Mary made themselves busy in seeing to the removal to the cottage of their own and cousin's luggage, making some purchases at the provision stores, and rearrangements of furniture. Then, about the dinner—Mary pressed Charlie into her service as sheller of peas, husker of corn, and beater of eggs.

They had a merry time over the work, though Charlie protested vigorously against being set at such menial tasks, and declared that Ned should be made to do a fair share of them in the future.

Mary sent him to the train to meet the girls, while she stayed behind to watch over the dinner.

He had scarcely gone when a carriage drew up at the door and Mr. and Mrs. Dinsmore, Mrs. Travilla, Edward and Violet, and Donald Keith alighted therefrom and came trooping in—most of them laden with parcels. The driver brought up the rear, carrying a large hamper that seemed to be well filled and heavy.

Mary's first emotion on seeing the arrival was delight, the second—a sudden fear that her dinner would not suffice for so many.

But that fear was relieved at the sight of the hamper and a whisper from Vi, who headed the procession, that it contained such store of provision as would obviate the necessity of much cooking for several days to come.

"Oh, how good and kind of your mother!" Mary exclaimed in a like low tone, then hastened to welcome her guests with unmixed pleasure.

"Oh, Cousin Elsie, how nice of you to come and to bring Edward and Violet! You are going to let them stay, then? I am so glad. So glad to see you, too, Cousin Rose and Cousin Horace. It seems as if I ought to call you aunt and uncle, though."

"Then suppose you do," Mr. Dinsmore said, shaking hands with her and kissing her rosy cheek. "You have my permission."

"I shall, then, and thank you," she returned in her bright, merry tones. "Oh, Don," turning to Mr. Keith with outstretched hands, "so here you are! That's a good boy."

"Yes, and a good boy must not be put off with less than others," he said, following Mr. Dinsmore's example.

"Well, as you are only a cousin it doesn't matter," she remarked indifferently. "Please, all make yourselves at home. Oh, there's the stage stopping at the gate! The girls have come!" and she flew out to welcome them.

The little parlor was quite inconveniently crowded, but that afforded subject for mirth, as Mary introduced her friends and bustled about trying to find seats for them all.

"We shall have to take dinner in relays or else set a table in here in addition to the one in the dining room," she said, laughing.

"Let Amy and I go to our room and dress while your first set eat, and give us our dinner afterward," suggested Ella Neff.

"Yes, I should much prefer it," Miss Fletcher said. "We are really too dusty and dirty to sit down to your table now."

"And I shall act as waiter to the first table and eat with these ladies at the second," said Charlie.

"Very well, I can manage to seat the rest," Mary said; and so it was arranged.

The dinner proved very nice and very abundant with the help of the contents of the hamper. Mary's cooking received many praises, in which Charlie claimed a share, because, as he said, he had assisted quite largely.

CHAPTER
TWENTY-SECOND

O spirits gay, and kindly heart!
Precious the blessings ye impart!

—JOANNA BAILLIE

"WELL CRICKET, ARE WE to carry you back with us?" Mr. Dinsmore asked, with a smiling look at Violet. "If so, 'tis time to be tying on your hat, for the carriage is at the door."

"No, grandpa, I am going to stay," she answered, holding up her face for a parting kiss.

"I am well satisfied with your decision, dear child," her mother said when bidding her goodbye, as they and Edward stood alone together for a moment on the little porch. "I think these young people are all safe associates for you and your brother," turning to him and taking a hand of each, "and that you will enjoy yourselves very much with them. But, my darlings never forget in the midst of your mirth and merriment—or in trouble, if that should come—that God's eye is upon you, and that you have a Christian character to maintain before men. Let me give you a parting verse, 'Whether therefore ye eat, or drink, or whatsoever ye do, do all to the glory of God.' And yet another for your joy and comfort, 'The Lord God is a sun and shield: The Lord will give grace and glory: no good thing will He withhold from them that walk uprightly.'"

"Was there ever such another dear, good mother as ours?" Violet said to her brother as together they watched the carriage out of sight.

"I wish there were thousands like her," he answered. "Ever since I can remember, it has been plain to me that what she most desired for all her children was that they might be real, true, earnest Christians. Vi, if we are not all that, we can never lay the blame at our mother's door."

"Nor papa's either," Violet said with a sigh and a tear to his memory, "for he was just as careful as she is to train us up for God and heaven."

"Yes," Edward assented with emotion. "Oh Vi, if I could but be the man he was!"

They went into the house. In the little parlor Amy Fletcher reclined on a sofa gazing out through the open door upon the sea.

"I have had my first sight of the ocean today," she said glancing up at them as they came in, "and, oh, how beautiful it is! How delicious is this breeze coming from it! It surely must bring health and strength to anyone who is not very ill indeed!"

"I hope it will bring it to you," Violet said sitting down by her side.

"I hope so," she returned with a cheerful look and smile, "for the doctors tell me I have no organic disease, and that nothing is more likely to build me up than sea air and sea bathing."

Amy was small and fragile in appearance, but not painfully thin. She had large, dark gray eyes, brown hair, a sweet patient expression, a clear complexion, and though usually rather too pale and quiet, when excited or greatly interested the color would come and go on her cheek, her eyes shine, and her whole face light up in a way that made her decidedly pretty.

She was weary now with her journey and a visit to the beach.

Merry sounds of jest and laughter were coming from the kitchen.

"The girls are washing the dishes," Amy said with a smile, "and the lads helping or hindering, I don't know which."

"The dinner dishes?" asked Violet.

"Yes, Mary set them aside for a time, to enjoy the company of your family while they stayed."

"Do you think I could be of any assistance out there?" queried Edward with gravity.

"I've an idea that the place is quite full now," Amy said with a merry glance up into his face. "I wish there was room for us all, for they seem to be having a great deal of fun. Just listen how they are laughing! Don't you think we are going to have a jolly time here?"

The door opened and the two young men came in.

"You don't know what you've missed, Ed," said Charlie helping himself to a chair near Amy's couch. "Housework's jolly good fun."

"When you haven't too much of it," remarked Amy.

"And do it in pleasant company," added Donald.

"And under a capable and kind instructor," supplemented Mary, speaking from the kitchen.

"What are your terms for tuition, Miss Keith?" inquired Edward, as she and Ella Neff joined the circle in the parlor.

"Beginners get their board, which is sometimes more than they earn."

"Is that all?" said Donald. "Then I think I shall retire from the service."

"I advise you to do no such thing," said Ella. "The knowledge that you gain may prove to be invaluable in some future emergency—some time when you find yourself out on the plains or buried in the forests of the far west with no gentle, loving woman at hand to prepare your meals."

"In that case, there would doubtless be an ungentle and obedient orderly to do so," rejoined Donald with feigned gravity.

"Well, women are often lectured by newspaper writers and others on the paramount duty of making themselves acquainted with the culinary arts, as well as everything else pertaining to housewifery, in order that they may be fully capable of directing the labors of their servants. I see no reason why the rule shouldn't hold good for men," remarked Ella.

"There, sir, you're cornered, Don!" laughed Charlie.

"Now that we are all here together, suppose we make such arrangements as are necessary to constitute ourselves a tolerably orderly household," said Mary.

"I understood that you were commanding officer, and the rest of us had nothing to do but obey orders," said Donald.

"Quite a mistake. This is not an army, but a democracy, in which the majority rules. All important questions, therefore—"

"Such as the bill of fare for dinner," suggested Charlie. "Excuse the hint, ma'am."

"Are to be put to a vote," Mary went on not deigning to notice the interruption. "Mr. Keith, I propose that you, as the eldest of the party, take the chair."

"Which?" he asked with serious air.

"That large easy one, which each of us is politely leaving for somebody else."

Donald promptly took possession. "Is the meeting ready for business?" he asked.

"Ready!" responded Charles and Edward.

"Somebody make a motion, then."

"I move that Mary Keith be elected housekeeper and cook extraordinary," said Ella.

"I second the motion," said Edward.

"You have all heard the motion and to save useless repetition, I put it to the vote. All in favor—"

A simultaneous "Aye!" from all present.

"Who are to be my assistants?" she asked.

"All of us, I suppose," said Charles. "No, not Amy—she's the invalid and must be taken care of by the heartiest and strongest, which is probably your humble servant, ladies and gentlemen."

"Doubtful that!" said Edward, with a downward glance at his own stout limbs.

"I think we should all help in that and with the housework," remarked Vi modestly. "Cousin Mary, I can make beds, sweep, and dust very nicely, mamma says. It was her wish that I should learn, and I did."

"So can I," said Ella, "and we'll undertake that part of the work together, if you like, Miss—"

"Please, call me Violet or Vi."

"Yes," said Charlie. "I move that everybody be called by their Christian name—or some abbreviation thereof—as a saving of trouble and showing a friendly disposition toward each other."

"Agreed," said Donald, "but let it be understood that there's no objection to the prefix of cousin."

"At what hours shall we take our meals?" asked Mary.

"Make a motion," said Donald.

"Breakfast at eight, dinner at one, tea at six—will these hours suit all? If not, let us have objections."

"Speak now, or forever hold your peace," said Charlie. "They suit me well enough if the rule be not too rigidly enforced, so as to interfere with pleasuring."

"I didn't mean they should do that," said Mary. "They are only to be a general guide."

"And if anybody happens to indulge in an extra morning nap, what's to be the penalty?"

"A cold and lonely breakfast, I suppose. Perhaps to wash his own dishes besides."

"All in favor of the hours named for meals please signify it by saying 'aye,'" said Donald.

"Aye!" from every tongue.

"Anything else, Miss Keith?" he asked.

"Just one thing more," she answered, speaking with a sudden seriousness, and in a low, almost tremulous tone that sobered them all instantly.

She went on with an effort. "We all profess to be Christians. Shall we live together, even for the short space of two or three weeks, like heathen?"

A moment's silence, then Donald said with quiet gravity, "Surely not, Mary."

"We will not partake of the food God provides for our nourishment and enjoyment without asking His blessing upon it, or begin or end the day without prayer and praise, will we?" she asked.

"Oh, no!" came softly from the lips of Amy and Violet, and was echoed by the other voices.

"Then which of you, my three cousins—Don, Edward and Charlie—will take the lead in these acts of worship?"

A longer silence than before, then Vi turned a wistful, pleading look upon her brother.

There was no mistaking its meaning. And his mother's words were ringing in his ears.

"If no one else is willing," he said, "I will do it."

"Thank you, Edward," said Charlie, rising and grasping his hand. "But it would be too selfish to leave you to do it alone, so I will take my turn."

"I, too," said Donald. "It should never be said of a soldier that he refused to stand by his colors."

"Or of a follower of Christ that he was ashamed of his Master's service," added Edward.

So it was arranged that they should take turns, a day at a time, according to their age.

"Five o'clock—just an hour to tea time," Charlie said, consulting his watch. What shall we do with it? Amy, do you feel equal to a stroll on the beach, with the support of my arm?"

"Thank you, it would be very nice, but I am tired enough to think it still nicer just to lie here and look at the sea," she said. "I shall not mind being left alone, though; so, please, all the rest of you go. And tomorrow I shall be able to join you, I hope."

"Ah, no," said Mary, "for I am going to stay with her. I am weary enough just now to prefer resting in this easy chair to a ramble on the beach or anywhere else. And, besides, I want a chat with Amy."

"Secrets to tell, eh?" said Charlie, picking up his hat. "Goodbye, then. Speak well of the absent."

"Oh, I am so glad to be alone with you for a little while, Mary," Amy said when the others had all gone. "I want to thank you for your kindness in asking me to come here. Such a blessed relief as it was! For it seemed to me the very monotony of my life was killing me."

"The thanks hardly belong to me," Mary said between a smile and a tear, as she leaned over Amy, gently smoothing back the hair from her forehead. "I think they should be given first to our heavenly Father, and second to Mr. Marston."

"Yes, and third to you, Mary. I used to wonder over that verse in Isaiah—'He that believeth shall not make haste.' I didn't know what it meant, but I believe I do now."

"Well, dear, what is your explanation?"

"I think it means he that is strong in faith will patiently and calmly wait God's time for the fulfillment of His promises, and for relief from trouble and trial. Oh, if I could but do it always!"

"And I," sighed Mary, "but, oh, how often I am guilty of making haste for myself or for others—my dear ones especially. There is poor mother so often sick. It is so hard to see her suffer when she is so good, too, so patient and cheerful and resigned."

"I think that must be harder than suffering yourself."

"Amy," Mary said after a pause, "you must not forget that it is a very great pleasure to me to have you here, and that if you and the others had refused to come and stay with me I could not have accepted Mr. Marston's offer."

"It is very generous of you to set it in that light," Amy answered with a grateful look and smile.

They found so much to talk about that time flew fast and they were greatly surprised to see Ella and Violet coming up the path to the house.

"Surely it is not six yet!" Mary exclaimed.

"No, only half-past five," Vi said, taking out her watch. "But you are tired and Ella and I want you to let us get tea."

"Good girls!" returned Mary happily. "I feel quite rested now, but you may help if you like. I'm not going to cook much, though—only to make tea and stew a few oysters."

Tea and the clearing up after it well over, they all gathered on the porch. There they had the full benefit of the breeze and could get a glimpse of the sea by the light of the stars, and listen to its ceaseless murmur, while amusing themselves with cheerful chat and in making arrangements for various pleasure excursions about the vicinity.

It was unanimously decided to reserve the long walks until Amy should grow stronger in order that she might share the enjoyment.

In the meantime, they would fill up the time with bathing, lounging, short strolls, driving, and boating.

They finished the evening with the singing of hymns, a chapter of the Bible read aloud by Donald, and a short, earnest prayer well suited to their needs, offered by him.

The next day their plans were interfered with by a constant, steady rainfall, but no one fretted or looked dull. Most of them took their swim in spite of it, and there were books and games with which to while away the time within doors.

The second day was bright and clear. Amy felt herself already so greatly improved that she was eager for a proposed boating excursion on Shark River. Breakfast was prepared, eaten, and cleared away in good season. Mary was an excellent manager, working rapidly and well herself and skillfully directing the labors of others.

They took the stage down to the river, hired a boat large enough to carry the whole party, spent a couple of hours in rowing back and forth and up and down, then returned home as they came. They reached home in time for their swim and the preparation of a good though not very elaborate dinner, Mary pressing Ella and the lads into her service, while Amy and Violet were ordered to lie down and rest after their swim.

"What's the program for this afternoon?" asked Charlie, finishing his dessert and pushing his plate aside.

"Dish washing, a long lounge on beds and couches, the tea and a second chapter of cleansing of utensils, followed by an evening stroll on the beach," answered Mary decidedly.

"And what for tomorrow?" queried Donald.

"Ah, that reminds me," said Edward, "that Mrs. Perkins told me she expects her husband by the evening train and wants us to join them tomorrow in getting up a fishing party. The plan is to drive over to Manasquan, hire a boat there, and go out on the ocean. What do you say about it?"

The young men were highly in favor of the trip. Amy would see how she felt in the morning. Violet demurred, lest there might be danger in going upon the ocean and because she could not see any pleasure in catching fish. It seemed so cruel.

"But you eat them," reasoned her brother.

"Yes, I know, and I suppose it is very inconsistent to object to catching them, but I do. I could not enjoy seeing them suffer."

"You can go with us without feeling obliged to share in that, can you not?" asked Donald.

"Needn't even go out in the boat unless you choose," put in Charlie. "We'll find a shady spot under the trees near the shore where you can sit and watch us."

Violet thought that plan would do very well. She could take a book along and the time would not seem tedious.

"Mary has not spoken," said Donald, turning to her.

"I see no objection for any or all of you," she answered brightly, "but I must be excused."

"But why?" they all asked in various tones of disappointment and inquiry.

"Because tomorrow is Saturday, and the cook and housekeeper must make ready for Sunday's rest by doing two days' work in one."

"Can't we manage it somehow?" asked Donald.

Mary shook her head. "No, but I shan't mind it at all. Go and enjoy yourselves, my children, and leave me to attend to my duties at home."

"The rest can go if they choose, but if you stay at home, cousin, I shall stay with you," announced Violet with decision.

They rose from the table.

"Mary," said Charlie, "let the dishes stand a bit. I'm going to the post office," and seizing his hat he disappeared, followed by the laughter of the others."

"Quick, now, lads and lasses, let's have them all out of the way before he gets back," said Ella, beginning to clear the table in hot haste.

The heat of the sun was too great and Charlie was gone a full half-hour. When he returned, he found them all sitting at their ease in the parlor.

"I think I'll leave those dishes till the cool of the evening, Mary," he said, wiping the perspiration from his forehead.

"No, I can't consent to that—not on ordinary occasions," she answered demurely.

"Then back to the post office goes this letter!" he cried threateningly, holding aloft one with her address upon it.

"Silly boy, the dishes are done without your help. Give it to me!" she cried, springing up and catching it out of his hand.

"A fortunate day" he said, pulling several more from his pocket and distributing them.

The tongues were silent for a moment; then, Vi uttered a joyous exclamation. "Oh, Mary, you needn't stay at home tomorrow! Mamma says she will send a hamper by the evening train tomorrow with provision to last us over Sunday, so that you need not be troubled with Saturday cooking."

Everybody was glad, everybody thankful.

"But tomorrow's dinner," said Mary presently. "Shall we be back in time for me to cook it?"

"I don't know," said Edward, "but there are hotels where we can dine, and I invite you all to be my guests at whichever one the party may select. Now, Cousin Mary," as he read hesitation on her face, "I shall be hurt if anybody refuses my invitation."

So no one ventured an objection.

The day proved auspicious. Amy was unusually well, everybody else in good health and spirits, no excuse for staying at home. So all went and spent the entire day, taking an early start and not returning till late in the afternoon.

CHAPTER
TWENTY-THIRD

Macbeth: If we should fail—
Lady M: We fail!
But screw your courage to the sticking place,
And we'll not fail.

—SHAKESPEARE

SUNDAY MORNING CAME and our young friends met at the breakfast table, not in their usual jesting, mirthful mood, but with cheerful gravity of demeanor, suited to the sacredness of the day.

"There is no preaching, no sort of religious service within our reach today," Edward remarked.

"Then shall we not have one of our own?" asked Mary. "I have a book of sermons—one might be read aloud. Then, we can have three prayers and as many hymns as we please. We all sing."

"We might have a Bible reading, also," suggested Ella. "And suppose we take up the *International Sunday School Lesson* and study it."

All these propositions were received with favor and eventually carried out.

They did not think it wrong to stroll quietly along the shore, or to sit there watching the play of the billows. And thus they ended their afternoon.

The evening was pleasantly spent in serious talk and the singing of hymns on the front porch, where they could feel the breeze and see the foam-crested waves by the light of a young moon.

They retired early, feeling that they had had an enjoyable, restful day, and rose betimes, full of life and vigor—except Amy. And even she felt equal to a longer stroll than she had yet taken.

The days flew by on swift wings, each bringing its duties and enjoyments with it. And so pleasant was the merry, free life they led that at times they half regretted that it must come to an end.

Yet there were other times when some, if not all, anticipated with real satisfaction, the return to the more serious business of life.

There was a very frequent exchange of visits between their party and the one to which Edward and Violet more properly belonged. This was sometimes by way of the cars, at others by riding or driving—so that Violet was never many days without sight and speech of her mother and some of the other dear ones at home. That reconciled her to a longer absence from it.

At length the younger Elsie was persuaded to come and spend a few days with Mary and her party, the mother consenting to spare both daughters for that length of time. The sweet girl's presence added much to the enjoyment of all, especially her sister, for their mutual attraction had always been very strong.

One day there was a large fishing party, composed principally of guests from the other houses, which both Elsie and Violet declined to attend. But Vi, fired with the laudable ambition to emulate her cousin Mary's skill in the culinary art, volunteered to get dinner, and have it ready by the time the others returned from their outing.

Each one of them offered to stay and assist, but she would not hear of it. She laughingly asserted that she wanted all the honor and glory, and wouldn't have anybody with her but Elsie, who knew nothing about cooking, but would keep her from being 'lone and lorn.' Perhaps Elsie would help a little in those things that were so easy that even the lads could do them.

Edward was not there — some errand having taken him home by the morning train.

"Can you stand that insinuation, Donald?" asked Charlie. "I vote that you and I stay at home tomorrow and get dinner, just to prove our skill in that line."

"Agreed," said Donald. "But what's to be done with the lasses in the meantime. We can't let them go off pleasuring alone."

"Oh, Edward can take care of them all for once. He's to be back by dinner time today, you know, so will be on hand here tomorrow."

"Thank you," said Ella, laughing, and with a mock curtsy, but we are entirely capable of taking care of ourselves, as perhaps we may prove to you one of these days. But here's the carriage at the gate. Come, Amy, I'll help you in. Let us show these lords of creation that they are of not quite so great importance as they are pleased to imagine."

She ran happily out, Amy following a little more slowly, with a regretful good-bye to the two who were to remain at home.

The lads hurried after in season to forestall Ella in assisting Amy into the vehicle, which the former had hastily entered unaided, before they could reach it.

Mary lingered behind a moment to say to Elsie and Violet that she did not in the least care to go, indeed, would prefer to stay with them.

"No, no, Cousin Mary," they both said, "we would not have you miss the sport, or deprive the rest of the pleasure of your society."

"Besides," added Violet with a merry look and smile, "if you were here I know very well I should miss the opportunity to distinguish myself as a capable and accomplished cook. So, away with you, fair lady! See, the lads are waiting to hand you into the carriage."

"Good-bye then, but don't attempt an elaborate dinner," Mary returned, as she hastened away.

The sisters stood on the little porch watching the departure till the carriage was out of sight.

Just then a boy carrying a large basket opened the gate and came in.

"That's right, you are just in good time," was Vi's greeting. "Please carry them into the kitchen. Have you brought all I ordered?"

"Yes'm. Potatoes, corn, beans, tomatoes, cabbage, lettuce, and young beets. All right fresh and nice.

Violet paid him and he left.

"There, I shall have a variety of vegetables," she remarked, viewing her purchase with satisfaction.

"Oh, Vi," sighed Elsie with a look of apprehension, "do you in the least know what you are about?"

"Why, of course, you dear old goosie! Haven't I watched Mary's cooking operations for over two weeks? Oh, I assure you I'm going to have a fine dinner! There's a chicken all ready for the oven—cousin showed me how to make the stuffing and all that. I've engaged fresh fish and oysters—they'll be coming in directly. I shall make an oyster pie and broil the fish. I mean to make a boiled pudding and sauce for dessert, and have bought nuts, raisins, and almonds, oranges, bananas, and candies besides, and engaged ice cream and cake."

"Your bill of fare sounds very good, but what if you should fail in the cooking?"

"Oh, no such word as fail for me!" laughed Vi. "I've screwed my courage to the sticking place, and don't intend to fail. Now we must don our big aprons and to work; you'll help me with the vegetables, I know."

"Willingly, if you'll show me how."

Violet felt very wise and important as she gave her older sister the requested instruction, then went bustling about making her pudding and pastry— for she decided to add tarts to her bill of fare, and the oyster pie must have a very nice crust.

But as she proceeded with her preparations, she discovered that her knowledge was deficient in regard to many of the details of the business at hand. She did not know exactly how much time to allow for the cooking of each dish—how long it would take for the chicken to roast, pie and tarts to bake, pudding and vegetables to boil.

She grew anxious and nervous in her perplexity. There was no one to give her the needed information, and in sheer desperation she filled her oven, her pots and kettles as fast as possible, saying to Elsie it would surely be better to have food a little overdone than not sufficiently cooked.

It proved an unfortunate decision, especially as the fishing party was an hour later in returning than had been expected.

Poor Violet was too much mortified to eat when she discovered that there was no sweetness left in the corn, that her potatoes were water-soaked, her oysters tough as leather, the chicken scorched and very overdone, the fish burned almost to a cinder, and—oh, worst of all, cooked with the scales on. She had forgotten they had any.

Her friends all comforted her, however, taking the blame on themselves. "If we had not been so late, things would not have been so overdone. It was our fault. And the lettuce, the cole slaw, and bread and butter were all very nice. The tarts, too."

But as soon as she tasted them, Violet knew she had forgotten the salt in her crust and that it was tough compared to her Cousin Mary's.

And then the pudding! Why did it turn out so heavy? Ah, she had made it with sour milk and put in no soda.

"Oh, what shall I do?" she said despairingly to Mary, who was helping her to dish it up. "There's hardly anything fit to eat and I know you are all very hungry."

"Indeed, dear little cuz, there is a great deal that's fit to eat," Mary said, glancing toward the table on which the last course was set out—except the ice cream, which had not yet been taken from it's freezer.

"Yes, those are nice, but the substantials of the meal—just what are most needed—are all spoiled. Oh, what's that?" with a sudden change of tone as a man bearing a large hamper appeared at the open door. "Something from mamma, I do believe."

"Yes," said Edward, stepping in after the man as the latter set the hamper down, "and I suppose it's very well I didn't come empty handed."

"Oh, Ned, Ned, you dear, good fellow!" cried Violet, springing to his side and throwing her arms around his neck.

"Yes, you may well say that!" he returned, laughing as he gave her a kiss, then put her aside and stooped to open the basket. "I told mother what you were attempting today and she said, 'The poor, dear child! She will surely struggle, so I'll send some provisions with you when you go.' And here they are, all of the best, of course, for mamma never does anything by halves," he added, beginning to hand out the viands—a pair of cold roast fowls, a boiled tongue, pickles, jellies, pies, and cakes in variety. Mary and Vi received them with exclamations of satisfaction, delight and thankfulness which quickly brought the others on the scene, just as the bearer of the hamper, who had gone out on setting it down, re-entered with a basket of beautiful, luscious peaches and grapes.

"Hello!" exclaimed Charlie in high glee, "what's all this? A second dinner?"

"Yes," returned Violet, "my dear, good mother's atonement for her conceited daughter's failure."

"No, no, we don't call it a failure, nor the cook conceited," cried a chorus of voices. "Some things are very nice, and others were spoiled by our fault in coming home so late."

"Well, please come back to the table and we'll begin again," said Violet, carrying the fowls into the dining room. Mary followed with the tongue, Elsie and Ella with other edibles.

"Please, help me carry away dinner number one to make room for dinner number two," said Vi, replacing the dish containing her unfortunate chicken with the one on which she had put the new arrivals.

Upon that, everybody seized one or more of the dishes and hurried back to the kitchen. And so, with a great rushing to and fro and amid much laughter and merry jests, they respread the board.

Violet's spirits and appetite had returned, and she joined the others in making a hearty meal.

The next morning was cloudy and cool for the season. All agreed it was just the day for a long stroll inland, and shortly after breakfast they set out in a body—Mary, Ella, and Edward leading the group, Donald and Edward's two sisters coming next, Charlie and Amy bringing up the rear.

There seemed to be a tacit understanding that those two were always to be together and no remark was ever made about it. But Charlie always took possession of the fragile little lady, just as if he had entered into bonds to be her caretaker and entertainer. He accommodated his pace to hers, which was so much slower than that most natural to the others that they often unintentionally left her far behind.

They presently met Mrs. Perkins, Fred, and Susie, who were also starting out for a walk, and the two parties joined their forces.

They passed through the village and sat down for a little while on some rustic benches under the trees on the riverbank to rest.

The village lay behind them. Before them, green slopes dotted here and there with trees standing singly or in groups. Then the sparkling river, to the left, beyond the bridge, widened into a lake like expanse, to the right pouring its waters into the great ocean, on which many ships, steamers and smaller craft could be seen—some near, others far away in the distance.

The surface of the river too was enlivened by a number of small sailboats slowly moving before the wind and skiffs that darted hither and thither. On the further bank the scene was diversified by woods and fields with here and there a farm house, then the sandy beach bordering the wide, blue sea.

"Are you quite tired out, Amy?" Charlie asked after a little.

"Oh, no, I'm quite rested," she answered merrily, "and feel able to walk a good deal farther. I am really surprised to find how strong and well I am."

"The seashore's the place for you, evidently," he said. Then as she sprang up nimbly to join the others as they rose and moved on again, "But I don't know that it would be best to keep you here too long. You might grow so strong as to feel capable of dispensing with any help from other folks."

"Which would be very delightful indeed," she returned with an arch look and smile as she accepted his offered arm.

They hastened on after the rest of their party, over a bridge and along the roadside for some distance. Then they all struck into a narrow footpath on the farther side of the fence. The young men let down the bars to give the ladies easier entrance, and followed that through a bit of woods, crossing a little stream by a broken bridge, where again the lads had the pleasure of giving assistance to their companions of the weaker sex. Then, they crossed some cornfields, making a circle that brought them back to the river.

The path now ran along its bank, and still pursuing it they came at length to a little inlet where was neither bridge nor boat. There they stopped and held a consultation. No one wanted to go back by the way they had come, it was too long and roundabout. If they could but cross this inlet, they could soon reach one of the life-saving stations on the other side, and there probably find someone who would carry them across the river in a boat. Then a short walk along the beach would take them to their temporary home.

"The water is not deep, I think," said Donald. "I propose that we lads strip off boots and stockings, wade through and carry the ladies over. I will wade across first and try its depth."

He did so in spite of some protests from the more timid of the ladies, and found it hardly knee deep. All then agreed to his proposition.

"Edward and I will make a chair by clasping hands," he said merrily, "and Fred and Charlie can do likewise if they will, and we will divide the honor of carrying the ladies over dryshod."

Donald had a purpose in selecting Edward as his companion and helper in the undertaking, fairly certain that Elsie and Violet would choose to be carried by their brother — which they did.

"I see through you, young man," Charlie said to Donald in a laughing aside while making ready for the trip, but I don't care much, if you leave Miss Fletcher for me."

"All right," returned Donald, "I intended to, for I see which way the wind blows. She's light, too, my lad, and will be the better suited to your strength."

"Strength, man! I'm as able to lift and carry as Lieutenant Keith, if I'm not greatly mistaken," Charlie said with pretended wrath. "And to prove it, I speak for the carrying of Mrs. Perkins and Miss Neff, who must be a trifle heavier than any of the other ladies."

"All right, but fortunately there isn't one in the party heavy enough to be any great burden to either of us."

So amid a good deal of mirth and laughing and some timidity and shrinking on the part of the younger girls, the short journey was made, and that without mishap or loss.

Then, a short, though toilsome walk through the soft yielding sand brought them to the life-saving station, a small two-story frame building standing high on the sandy beach, the restless billows of the ocean tossing and tumbling not many yards away.

They were courteously treated by the brave fellows who make this their abode during eight months of the year. They were shown the room on the lower floor where they sleep and eat, the two above where they sleep, and also all the apparatus for saving the shipwrecked and any others who may be in danger of drowning within reach of their aid.

These friends were all greatly interested in looking at these things — the colored lamps and flags for signaling, the lifeboat, the breeches buoy, and the life-car — this last especially. It was of metal, shaped like a rowboat, but covered in over the top, except a square opening large enough to admit one passenger at a time, and having a sliding door, the closing of which after the passengers are in, makes the car completely water tight.

How many will it hold?" asked Edward.

"Six or seven grown folks, if they are not very large sized."

"I should think they would smother!" cried Violet.

"It is only about three to four minutes they'd have to stay in it," said the exhibitor.

Then he showed them the thick, strong rope or hawser on which it runs, and the mortar by means of which they send a line to the distressed vessel with a tally-board attached on which are printed directions — English on one side, French on the other — for the proper securing of the hawser to the wreck.

"The other end is made fast on shore, I suppose?" said Amy inquiringly.

"Yes, Miss."

"And when they have made their end fast and got into the car—"

"Then we pull 'em ashore."

"Not a particularly pleasant ride to take, I imagine," remarked Donald.

"Not so very, sir. She's apt to be tossed about pretty roughly by the big waves, turn over several times, more likely than not."

"Yes, I suppose so."

"Oh," cried Amy with a shudder, "I think I'd almost rather drown."

"No, Miss," said the man, "I guess you'd find even that better'n drowning."

Having fully satisfied their curiosity, they inquired if there were anybody about there who would take them across the river.

"Yes, sir, I'll row you across, half of you at a time," answered the man, addressing Donald, who had acted as spokesman for the party. "All of you at once would be too big a load for the boat."

It was but a short walk to the river, a few minutes' row across it, and soon they were all on the farther side and walking along the beach toward home.

"Dinner time!" exclaimed Ella, looking at her watch. "What's to be done about it?"

Her question seemed to be addressed to Mary.

"Don't ask me," was the demure reply. "It's none of my concern today. Didn't you hear the agreement between Charlie and Don yesterday?"

"There! Mr. Charles Perrine, see the scrape you have got yourself and me into?" exclaimed Donald with a perplexed and rueful look.

"What in the world are we to do!" cried Charlie, stopping short with his hands upon the gate and turning so as to face the others.

"Get in out of the sun for the first thing," replied his cousin.

"Yes, yes, of course!" and he stepped back and held the gate open for the ladies to pass in.

"We are all hungry as bears, I suppose," he said when they were all in the house. "Come, Mary, be good and tell us what to do. Shall we go to one of the hotels?"

"No, make the fire, set the table, and grind some coffee," she answered, laughing, "I foresaw that I'd have to come to the rescue and am prepared. We'll have coffee, stewed oysters, cold fowl left from yesterday, plenty of good bread, rolls and butter, fruits and cake, and it won't take many minutes to get it ready."

"Mary, you're simply a jewel!" Charlie returned, catching her about the waist and kissing her on both cheeks.

"Be gone, you impertinent fellow!" she said laughingly as she released herself and pushed him away. "Even cousins shouldn't take such liberties."

CHAPTER
TWENTY-FOURTH

O pilot! 'tis a fearful night,
There's danger on the deep.

—BAYLY

ELSIE HAD GONE HOME, and in a few days the little party would break up entirely—Ella and Amy would return to their homes; Mary, Donald, and Charlie would go with Edward and Violet to their mother's cottage to spend some time as Mrs. Travilla's guests.

The Allisons had all gone and there was now abundance of room, though the Conlys—mother and daughter—still lingered, loath to leave the delightful sea breezes.

The quiet life led under her Cousin Elsie's roof was not much to Virginia's taste, but nothing better had been offered as yet.

Breakfast was over, the morning tasks the girls had set themselves were all done, and all four came trooping out upon the porch where the three lads were standing—apparently very intent upon some object out at sea.

Edward was looking through a spyglass that he handed to Donald, "See if you can make out the name."

"Not quite, but she is certainly a yacht," was Donald's reply, after a moment's steady gaze at one of the many vessels within sight. They had counted more than forty of various sorts and sizes—some outward bound, others coming in. The one that so excited their interest was drawing nearer.

"Let me look," said Mary. "I have the reputation of being very far-sighted."

Donald handed her the glass and pointed out the vessel they were looking at.

She sighted it and in another moment said, "Yes, I can read the name—the '*Curlew*.'"

"Ah, ha!" cried Edward in a very pleased tone, "I was correct. It is Will Tallis's yacht."

"And really it looks as if he meant to call at Ocean Beach," added Charlie. "Must have heard, Ned, that you and I are here."

"Doubtless," laughed Edward.

"Will Tallis?" repeated Violet, inquiringly. "Is he a friend of yours, Edward?"

"Why, yes. Have you not heard me speak of him? He's a splendid fellow, one whom I should very willingly introduce to my mother and sisters."

"And has a yacht of his own?"

"Yes, he's very rich and delights in being on the sea. Inherits the taste, I suppose—his father was a sea captain. He told us—Charlie and me—that he meant to go yachting this season and wished he could persuade us to go with him."

"And I, for one, should like nothing better," said Charlie. "Why, Ned, he's coming ashore! See, they have dropped anchor and are putting off from the yacht in a boat! Yes, here they come, pulling straight for this beach. Grab your hat; let's run down, boys, and meet them as they land!" cried the lad, excitedly.

Amy had found his hat and silently handed it to him. Edward and Donald seized theirs and all three rushed to the beach.

"Come, girls," said Ella, "let us go, too. Why should we miss the fun, if there is to be any?"

They put on their hats, took their sun umbrellas, and started. They, however, went only as far as the sidewalk in front of the Colorado House—so many people were thronging the beach to witness the landing, which was now evidently taking place just below there—and the modest, refined, young ladies did not like to be in a crowd.

Mrs. Perkins and Susie joined them. Fred was away—had gone over to New York, expecting to return by the evening train.

"Not much to be seen by us but the waves and the crowd," remarked Ella, a little impatiently. "Nor much to be heard but the murmur of their voices."

"They must have landed, I think," Mrs. Perkins said. "Yes, here they come—our lads, I mean, and a stranger with them. A very nice looking fellow he is, too."

The four young men drew near and Edward introduced "My friend, Mr. Tallis," to the ladies.

He was very gentlemanly in appearance and had a pleasant, open countenance; a cordial, hearty manner as he shook hands with the matronly married lady and lifted his hat to the younger ones.

"I am happy to make your acquaintance, ladies," he said with a genial smile and an admiring glance at Violet, "and have come to ask the pleasure of your company on board my yacht. I am bound for Boston and the coasts of New Hampshire and Maine—a short sea voyage that I trust you will find enjoyable if I can but persuade you to try it."

Mrs. Perkins declined, with thanks, for herself and Susie. Violet did likewise. The other three hesitated, but finally yielded to the persuasions of the lads.

"Oh, Edward, you will not go, surely?" whispered Violet, drawing her brother aside.

"And why not?" he returned impatiently.

"Because you haven't mamma's consent, or grandpa's either."

"No, but that's only because they are not here to give it. I'm sure there's nothing objectionable. Will's the very sort of fellow they would approve, the vessel is new and strong, and the captain and crew understand their business."

"But a storm might come up."

"Why, Vi, how silly! There's no appearance of a storm and we are not intending to go far out to sea. Besides, you might just as well bring the objection to any trip by sea."

"Yes, but if you had mamma's consent it would be different."

"I don't see that. I'd ask it, of course, if I could—and be sure to get it, too, I think—but there isn't time. They don't want to lose this favorable wind and fine weather, and will take off again within an hour. Come; make up your mind to go with us. I want you along, for I think it will be a delightful little voyage."

"Thank you, brother, but I don't wish to go, and couldn't enjoy it if I went without mamma's knowledge and consent. And I do wish you would not go."

"Vi, I never knew you so unreasonable! But if you will not go along, perhaps I ought to stay to take care of you. I had not thought of that before. Mother left you in my charge, but I am sure she would not want me to lose this pleasure, and it strikes me as a trifle selfish of you to make it necessary for me to do so."

"I don't want you to stay on my account," she said, tears springing to her eyes. "And I don't think you need to stay. I can go home this afternoon by the cars. Probably mamma would not mind my taking so short a ride alone."

"I don't know, but I should enjoy the voyage far more with you along."

"What is the matter?" asked Mrs. Perkins, over-hearing a part of the talk. "I will take charge of your sister, Mr. Travilla, if she prefers to stay behind."

"Thank you," Edward responded with brightening countenance. "But—Vi, you will not care to swim while we are gone?"

"No, Ned, I shall not go in without you, as mamma desired me not."

"And are you willing for me to go?"

"Not quite. I wish you wouldn't, only don't stay to take care of me."

Edward looked a good deal vexed and annoyed.

"Mrs. Perkins," he said, turning to her, "if Fred were here, would you object to his going?"

"No, not at all. I should leave him to follow his own inclination. But," as Edward turned triumphantly to Violet, "I am not meaning to encourage you to go, if your sister thinks your mother might object. All mothers do not see alike, you know."

"Well," he said, "I imagine I am as competent a judge of that as Violet is. I feel well nigh certain that she would bid me go and enjoy myself. She's not one of the fussy kind of mothers who are afraid to let their children stir out of their sight."

"Then you will go?" said Mr. Tallis.

"Yes," Edward answered, resolutely avoiding Violet's pleading looks.

"I wish we could persuade your sister," Mr. Tallis said, turning to her. "Are you timid about venturing on the sea, Miss Travilla?"

"Not particularly," she said, coloring slightly.

"Then do come with us! The more the merrier, you know, and I should be so happy. I do not feel quite comfortable carrying off all the rest of your party and leaving you alone."

The girls joined their entreaties to his, but Violet was firm in her resolution to remain on shore.

Then Mary offered to stay with her, but as Violet was convinced that it would involve a sacrifice on her cousin's part, she would not consent.

They now all hastened back to the cottage to make such preparations as might be needed. It was not much to any of them, as they expected to return the next day or the one following.

"Edward, can I be of any assistance to you?" Violet asked, going to the door of his room.

"Yes, if you'd like to pack this valise. Maybe you would do it better than I. I'm alone, so come in."

Violet accepted the invitation and did the little service quite to his satisfaction.

"You are a nice, handy girl, if I do say it," he remarked laughingly. "But what's the matter?" as he saw that her eyes were full of tears.

"Oh, Edward, don't go away vexed with me!" she exclaimed, putting her arm around his neck. "Suppose a storm should come up, and—and we should never see each other again."

These words came with an irrepressible burst of tears. The loving, young heart was sore from recent bereavement and ready to fear for all its dear ones.

"Come, don't fret about possibilities," he said kindly. "I'm not vexed now, and you must forgive me for calling you selfish."

"You don't think I am?"

"No, indeed! But just the most darling little sister ever a fellow had. I shouldn't like—if anything should happen—to have you remember that as one of the last things I said to you. No, I was the selfish one. Now, goodbye and don't worry about me." He said, holding her close and kissing her several times. "You know, Vi, dear, that we are under the same protecting care on sea and on land."

"Yes," she whispered, but with some hesitation and drawing a deep sigh.

"Ah!" he said, "you doubt whether I shall be taken care of because I'm going without permission. Are you not forgetting that we have always been trained to think and decide for ourselves in all cases where it is right and proper to do so? And why should I need permission to go on the sea in a yacht any more than in a fishing boat? Can you answer me that?" he concluded, half laughingly.

"No," she said with a slight smile, "and I daresay you are in the right about it."

"Then you won't change your mind—'tis a woman's privilege, you know—and go along? It's not yet too late.

"No, thank you. I do not care to claim all the woman's privileges yet," she answered with playful look and tone.

"Hello, Ned! 'Most ready?" shouted Charlie from below. "Time's about up."

They went down at once.

The other girls were on the porch quite ready to start, Donald standing with them. Mrs. Perkins and

Susie could be seen down on the beach waiting to see them off—Mr. Tallis, too, chatting with some of the other ladies.

The young men gathered up the ladies satchels and their own. Charlie offered his arm to Amy, but she declined it with a laughing assurance that she was now strong enough to walk without support.

"Miss Neff," he sighed, turning to Ella, "I've lost my situation—will you?"

"And you will, maybe, lose something else if we don't hurry," she answered lightly.

"'Time and tide wait for no man,' so let us make haste before they fail us."

These three were very merry, the other three sober almost to absolute quietness as they made their way to the waiting boat.

Edward kissed his sister again as he was about to step into it and she clung to his neck for a moment whispering, "Ah, I shall pray that you may come back safely!"

"Don't borrow trouble, you dear, little goose," he said as he let her go.

At the last moment it appeared that Donald was not going.

There were various explanations of surprise and disappointment from the voyagers when his purpose to remain behind became apparent. They had understood he was going. "Why did you change your mind?" was the query.

"Well," he said with a quiet smile, "a man is not bound to give all his reasons, but the fact is Mrs. Perkins has held out strong inducements to me to stay where I am."

"And he couldn't be in better company, could he?" was her laughing addition.

Violet was as much taken by surprise as the others, but in her secret heart not at all sorry — "It would be so much less lonely with Cousin Donald there."

They stood on the beach, waving their handkerchiefs to their departing friends until the latter had reached the deck of the yacht. Nor did they cease to watch the vessel so long as the smallest portion of it was visible, as it faded quite out of sight.

Violet felt a strong inclination to indulge in a hearty cry, but putting a determined restraint upon herself, chatted cheerfully instead. Yet, her friends perceived her depression and exerted themselves for her entertainment.

"It seems to me," Donald said with a glance at Violet, but addressing Mrs. Perkins, as they went into a summer house near by and sat down, "that this little lady has less of inquisitiveness than most people — I will not say most of her sex, for I think my own is by no means deficient in the characteristic — or she would have made some inquiry in regard to the strong inducements I spoke of."

"What were they?" asked Violet. "You have roused my sleeping curiosity."

"Mrs. Perkins has kindly offered to come to the cottage and help us with our housekeeping while the rest of the lads and lassies are away, and to bring Miss Susie and her brother with her."

Vi's face lighted up with pleasure. "It is very kind," she said. "Now I shall not mind the absence of the others half so much as I had expected. I like my little room at the cottage, and do not fancy living in a crowd as I must anywhere else."

"Then, you will not go home to see your mamma?" Donald said inquiringly.

"No, upon second thought I have decided against that plan, because if I did go I must tell mamma how it happened, and then if a storm should come up she would be tortured with useless anxiety about my brother."

"You are very thoughtful of your mother."

"As anyone would be who had such a mother as ours, Cousin Donald."

"She is certainly very lovely and lovable," he said. "Now, about our meals, cousin. Do you object to taking them in a crowd? At one of the public houses here?

"No, I think it the least of the two evils," she answered with a smile, "for I own to being somewhat tired of the fun of housework and cooking."

"Then we will settle upon that plan," Mrs. Perkins said. "We will sleep and live at the cottage; breakfast, dine, and sup elsewhere."

Mrs. Perkins was a good talker, full of general information, anecdotes and entertaining reminiscences—a delightful companion even to one as young as Violet.

Time passed swiftly to them all. Life at the cottage, because it took them out of the crowd, was more enjoyable than at the hotels, which were all very full at this season and as a consequence, very noisy.

The cottage seemed very peaceful and quiet by contrast. Indeed it was far quieter now than it had been at any time in the past two or three weeks, and Violet, who was beginning to weary of so much sport and mirthfulness, really found the change quite agreeable.

By the middle of the afternoon of the next day they began to watch for the reappearance of the *Curlew*, but night closed in again without the sight.

There was a fresh and stormy breeze from the northeast when they went to bed. In the morning it blew almost a gale, and as Violet's eyes turned seaward her face wore a very anxious expression.

"No sign of the *Curlew* yet," she sighed, as she stood at the parlor window gazing out upon the wind-tossed billows, plunging, leaping, roaring, foaming as if in furious passion.

"No, and we may well thank God that we do not," said Donald's voice close at her side, "for the wind is just in the quarter to drive them ashore. I hope they are giving the land a wide berth."

She looked up into his face with frightened eyes.

"Do not be alarmed," he said. "Let us not anticipate evil. They may be safe in port somewhere, and at all events we know Who rules the winds and the waves."

"Yes," she murmured, in low, tremulous tones, "the stormy wind fulfills His word. And no real evil shall befall any of His children."

There was a moment of silence; then, "It is about breakfast time now," he said, "but you will not venture out in this gale, surely? Shall I not have your meal sent in to you?"

"Thank you, but I prefer to make the effort to go," she said. "I want to get a nearer view of the sea."

The others felt the same desire and presently they all started out together.

The ladies found it as much as they could do to keep their feet even with the assistance of their stronger companions, and the great, wind-driven waves sometimes swept across the sidewalk.

It was clearly dangerous, if not impossible, to approach nearer to the surging waters. The gale was increasing every moment, the sky had grown black with clouds and distant mutterings of thunder. And an occasional lightening flash gave warning that the worst was yet to come. Evidently it would be no day for outdoor exercise or amusement.

Regaining the cottage with difficulty, after eating their breakfast they brought out books, games, and fancywork, resolved to make the best of circumstances. Yet, anxious as they were for the fate of their friends, the voyagers in the yacht, they did little but gaze out upon the sea, looking for the *Curlew*, but glad that neither she nor any other vessel was in sight.

✂ ✂ ✂ ✂ ✂

The *Curlew's* cabin was comfortably, actually, luxuriously furnished, her larder well supplied with all the delicacies of the summer season. Favored with beautiful weather and propitious winds, the friends found their first day out from Ocean Beach most enjoyable.

They passed the greater part of their time on deck, now promenading, now reclining in extension chairs, chatting, laughing, singing to the accompaniment of flute and violin — the one played by Edward, the other by Charlie.

The yacht was a swift sailor, her motion easy, and until the afternoon of the second day they were scarcely troubled with any seasickness. Most of the time they kept within sight of land touching in at Boston, Portsmouth, and several other New England seaports. They continued on their course until the wind changed, when they turned, with the purpose of going directly back to Ocean Beach.

For some hours all went well, a stiff breeze carrying them rapidly in the desired direction. But it grew stronger and shifted to a dangerous quarter, while the rough and unsteady motion of the vessel made all the passengers so seasick that they began to heartily wish themselves safe on land.

The ladies grew frightened, but the captain assured them there was as yet little cause for alarm. He had shortened sail and put out to sea, fearing the dangers of the coast.

But the wind increased constantly until by night it was blowing a gale, and though every stitch of canvas had been taken in and furled, they were being driven landward.

All night long the seamen fought against the storm, striving to keep out the sea, but conscious that their efforts were nearly futile. There was little sleep that night for passengers or crew.

Morning broke amid a heavy storm of rain accompanied by thunder and lightening, while the wind seemed to have redoubled its fury, blowing directly toward the shore.

The girls, conscious that they were in peril of shipwreck, had gone to their berths without undressing. Amy had been very sick all night, and the other two, who stood it better, had done their best to wait upon her, though it was little that could be done for her relief. The pitching and rolling of the vessel frequently threw them with violence against each other or the furniture.

"It is morning," said Ella at length. "See, it grows light in spite of the storm, and I hear voices in the salon. Shall I open the door?"

"Yes," said Mary, "let us learn the worst, and try to be prepared for it."

The three young men were in the salon and the girls joined them, Amy looking like a ghost of herself.

Charlie, who had stationed himself near her door, instantly gave her the support of his arm, while he held fast to the furniture with the other hand, and her head dropped on his shoulder.

With death staring them in the face, they did not care for the eyes of their companions in peril, who, indeed, were too full the danger and solemnity of their own position to pay any attention to the matter.

"Oh, darling," Charlie said hoarsely, "if I could only put you safe on shore!"

"Never mind," she answered, looking lovingly into his eyes, "if we die, we shall die together. And, Charlie, as we both trust in Jesus, it will only be going home together to 'forever with the Lord,' never, never to part again!"

"Yes, there's comfort in that," he said. "And if you are to go, I'm glad I'm here to go with you. But life is sweet, Amy, and we will not give up hope yet."

Mary and Edward had clasped hands, each gazing silently into the sad and anxious face of the other.

She was thinking of her invalid mother, her father, brothers, and sisters, and how they would miss her loving ministrations.

He, too, thought of his tender mother so lately widowed, her sorrow over the loss of her first-born son, and of other dear ones, especially Violet, away from the rest, the only one conscious of the danger. He was glad now that she had refused to come with them, but he knew the terrible anxiety she must feel, the almost heart-breaking sorrow his loss and the sight of their mother's grief would be to her.

"Mr. Tallis, I know we must be in great danger," Ella said, as he took her hand to help her to a seat. "Is there any hope at all?"

"Oh, surely, Miss Neff!" he replied. "We will not give up hope yet, though we are indeed in fearful peril. The greatest danger is that we shall be driven ashore. But we are still some distance off the coast, and the wind may change or lull sufficiently for an anchor to hold when we are in water shallow enough for trying that expedient. And even should we be wrecked, there will be still a chance for us in the good offices of the members of the life-saving service."

"Ah, yes," she said, a gleam of hope shining in her eyes, "the brave fellows will not leave us to perish if they can help us."

"And we will put our trust in God," added Mary.

What a day it was to them all, the storm raging throughout the whole of it with unabated fury, and their hope of escape from the dangers of the deep growing less and less.

The patrolmen were out, and toward sundown one of them saw the masts of a vessel far away in the distance. It was seen by others also, for all day long many glasses had been, at frequent intervals, sweeping the whole field of vision seaward.

The news spread like wildfire, creating a great excitement among the multitude of people gathering in the hotels and boarding houses, as well as among the dwellers by the sea, not excepting the brave surfmen whose aid was likely to be in speedy requisition.

Hundreds of pairs of eyes watched the vessel battling with the storm, yet in spite of every effort sweeping near and nearer the dreadful breakers. She seemed doomed to destruction, but darkness fell while yet she was too far away for any hope of recognition.

Violet and her companions had gazed upon her with fast beating hearts from the time of her appearance until they could no longer catch the faintest outline of her figure in the gathering gloom.

Donald had nearly satisfied himself of her identity, but would not for any consideration have had Violet know he believed her to be the *Curlew*. Even without that confirmation of her fears, the anxiety of the poor child was such that it was painful to witness.

It was indeed the *Curlew*. About the time she was seen by those on land, the captain remarked aside to her owner, "The Jersey shore is in sight, Mr. Tallis. And nothing short of a miracle can save us from wreck, for we are driving right on to it in spite of all that can be done. The *Curlew* is doomed. She has dragged her anchor, and we will be in the breakers before many hours."

"It will be a loss to me, captain," was the reply, "but if our lives are saved, I shall not grumble. I shall, on the contrary, be filled with thankfulness."

"Well, sir, we'll hope for the best," came his cheerful rejoinder.

Soon all on board knew the full extent of the danger, and the young friends gave themselves to solemn preparation for eternity. Also, in view of the possibility of some being saved while others were lost, made an exchange of parting messages to absent loved ones.

It was again a sleepless night for them—sleepless to their Ocean Beach friends at the cottage, also, and to many others whose hearts were filled with sympathy for those in the doomed vessel.

About midnight the report of a signal gun of distress sent all rushing to the beach. She had struck, not a quarter of a mile from the shore. As the clouds broke away the dark outline of her hull could be distinctly discerned among the foam-tipped breakers.

The rain had ceased, and there was a slight lull in the tempest of wind, so that it was possible to stand on the beach. But so furious still was the action of the waves, that the patrolman, having instantly answered the gun by burning his signal light, and now rushing in among his mates, reported that the surf boat could not be used.

So the mortar car was ordered out.

There was not an instant's delay. Gallantly the men bent into their work. They dragged the car tire-lessly over the low sand hills to a spot directly opposite the wreck, and by the light of a lantern placed it and every part of the apparatus — the shot-line box, hauling lines and hawser for running, with the breeches buoy attached — in position. They put the tackles in place, ready for hauling, and, with pick and spade, dug a trench for the sand anchor.

Each man having his particular part of the work assigned him, and knowing exactly what he was to do and how to do it, and all acting simultaneously, the whole thing was accomplished in a short space of time after reaching the desired spot.

An anxious, excited crowd was looking on. Apart from the throng and a little higher up the beach, were their friends — Fred in charge of his mother and Susie, Donald with Violet under his protection.

She had begged so hard to come "because it might be the *Curlew*." How could she stay away? He had no heart to resist her entreaties, and he felt that she would be safe in his care, while Mrs. Perkins' presence made it perfectly proper.

All being in readiness, the gun was fired and the shot flew through the rigging of the ill-fated vessel.

Edward, now standing on her deck, quickly grasped just what was to be done, and no time was lost. With a glad shout, heard by those on shore, the line was seized by the sailors and rapidly hauled in.

Ere long the hawser was stretched straight and taut between the beach and the wreck—the shore end being raised several feet in the air by the erection of a wooden crotch—and the breeches buoy was ready to be drawn to and fro upon it.

"Will you try it first, sir?" the captain of the *Curlew* said to Mr. Tallis.

"No, I should be the last man to leave the wreck."

"Go, go, Will!" cried Edward imperatively. "Go and tell them to send the life-car for there are ladies to be saved."

"Yes, go, sir. Don't waste precious time in disputing," cried the captain. And thus urged, the young man went.

He reached the shore in safety, was welcomed with a glad shout, and instantly the word circled among the crowd, "the owner of the *Curlew*. It is she wrecked there."

Violet had nearly fallen fainting to the ground, but Donald, supporting her with his arm said in her ear, "Courage, my brave lassie! They shall be saved."

"Take care of my mother and sister for a moment, Keith!" exclaimed Fred, and plunging into the crowd, he quickly made his way to the side of the rescued man.

"This way, if you please," he said, touching him on the shoulder. "A lady, Miss Travilla, would be glad to speak to you."

"Oh, yes! I know!" and all dripping and panting as he was, but having already delivered his message, and seen the men on the way for the safety-car, he went to her.

"It is Mr. Tallis," Fred said. "Miss Travilla, my mother and sister, and Mr. Keith," for it was too dark for a distinct view of each other's faces.

"My brother?" faltered Violet, holding out her hand in greeting.

"Is uninjured thus far, my dear young lady, and I trust will be with you in a few minutes. The vessel must, I presume, go to pieces finally, but will undoubtedly hold together long enough for all on board to be brought safely to shore."

Men from among the crowd had volunteered to assist in bringing the car, and while awaiting its coming, the breeches buoy traveled back and forth, bringing the sailors—for neither Edward nor Charlie would leave the ladies, and the captain insisted that he should be the last man rescued.

From the hour of their early morning meeting in the salon the *Curlew's* passengers were almost constantly together—a very sober, solemn, and nearly silent company. Mary, in speaking of it afterward, said she felt as if she were attending her own funeral and listening to the sighs and sobs of her bereaved friends.

"And yet," she added with a bright, glad smile, "it was not all sadness and gloom, for the consolations of God were not small with me. And the thought of soon being with Christ in glory was at times very sweet."

When the vessel struck, Charlie started up with a sharp cry, "We are lost!"

Then all immediately fell on their knees while Edward poured out a fervent prayer that they might be saved from a watery grave if such was the will of God; if not, prepared for death and a glorious immortality—adding a final petition for the dear ones who would grieve their loss.

Just as they rose from their knees, the signal gun was fired.

Then the captain came down the companionway and looking in upon them, said, "Don't despair ladies and gentlemen, things are not quite so bad as they might be. We have grounded very near the shore and a life-saving station. My signal gun was immediately replied to by the patrolman with his red signal light. So we may feel assured that prompt and efficient help is near at hand."

Hope revived in their hearts as they listened. Then, Will Tallis and Edward ventured up on deck, leaving the girls in Charlie's charge.

The warning lights on shore gave to the anxious watchers on the deck an inkling of what was being done for their relief, and when the shot was fired from the mortar and came whizzing through the rigging, Edward cried out in delight. "The line, the line! Now we shall be helped ashore!"

As the vessel was now without motion, save a shiver as now and again a great wave struck her, the girls were pretty comfortable and in no immediate danger, and as they urged it, Charlie, too, at length ventured upon the deck.

He soon returned with an encouraging report, the better understood by the girls because of their recent visit to the life-saving station. "The sailors were hauling in the line," he said, and soon the work of transporting them all to land would begin.

Amy shuddered at the thought of the ride in the life-car, yet, as the surfman had predicted, felt that even that would be far preferable to drowning.

The next report brought them was of Mr. Tallis's safe landing and the next that the life car waited for them.

Edward, the captain, and two sailors helped Mary and Ella across the wind-swept deck and into the car, Charlie and another sailor followed with Amy. They put her in after the other two and Charlie stepped in next, calling to Edward to come also.

"No," was the reply. "I go by the breeches buoy."

The sliding door was hastily shut, and Amy gasped for breath as she felt the car gliding swiftly along the hawser, while the great waves dashed over it, rocking it from side to side.

Charlie's arm was round her, holding her close, but she grew deathly sick and fainted quite away.

The minutes seemed hours, but at last they heard, above the thunder of the breaking waves, a great shout, and at the same instant felt the car grate upon the sand.

The door was pushed open. Charlie, the nearest to it stepped out, drew Amy after him, apparently more dead than alive, and leaving it to others to assist Mary and Ella, he bore her in his arms, in almost frantic haste, to the nearest house.

Mary was in Vi's arms almost before she knew that she had actually reached shore. Vi kissed her with tears and sobs, and crying, "Edward, Edward, where is he?"

"Coming," Mary said. "The brave, generous fellow would see us all safe first."

It was not long now till Violet's anxiety was fully relieved and her heart sending up glad thanksgivings as she found herself clasped to her brother, all dripping wet though he was.

And great was the joy of the young owner of the *Curlew* when he learned that though she was a total wreck, not a single soul had been lost in her.

CHAPTER
TWENTY-FIFTH

Those that he loved so long and sees no more,
Loved and still loves—not dead,
but gone before—He gathers round him.

—*R* OGERS

THE MORNING WAS BUT dull and dreary, for though the storm had spent itself, the sky was obscured with clouds and the sea still wrought tempestuously. But its sullen roar may, perchance, have been as favorable to the prolonged slumbers of the worn-out friends, whom the tempest had robbed of so many hours of their accustomed sleep, as the lack of brightness in the sky and atmosphere.

However that may have been, most of them, retiring about dawn of day, slept till noon, or near it.

In Mrs. Travilla's cottage the family gathered round the breakfast table at the usual hour.

The meal was nearly concluded when a servant brought in the morning paper and handed it to Mr. Dinsmore.

"I fear that brings news of many disasters caused by the storm, especially on the Atlantic seaboard," remarked his daughter as he took it up.

"Altogether likely," was his rejoinder. Then he ran his eye down the long list of casualties. "Why, what is this?" he exclaimed, and went on to read the article aloud.

"Went ashore last night at Ocean Beach, the *Curlew*, a pleasure yacht belonging to W. V. Tallis: Captain Collins. She is a total wreck, but no lives were lost, passengers and crew being taken off by the men of Life Saving Station No. 3. List of passengers: Mr. W. V. Tallis, Mr. Edward Travilla, Mr. Charles Perrine, Miss Mary Keith, Miss Amy Fletcher, and Miss Ella Neff. There was a moment of astonished silence, and then "Violet!" gasped the mother, turning deathly pale.

"She was evidently not on board," Mr. Dinsmore hastened to reply, "or else her name was carelessly omitted from the list, for it distinctly says, 'No lives were lost.'"

"I hope you are right, Horace," Mrs. Conly remarked, "but if she were my child I shouldn't have any peace till I knew all about it."

"There isn't the least probability that if a life had been lost, the reporter would have failed to say so," returned Mr. Dinsmore with some severity of tone.

"Of course, you are in the right, Horace, you always are," she said, bridling.

"Well," remarked Virginia, "I'm astonished, I must own, that such pattern good children should go off on such an expedition without so much as saying by your leave to either mother or guardian."

"I have just said that I am morally certain Violet did not go," said Mr. Dinsmore.

"And I do not blame Edward that he did," added the mother in her sweet, gentle tones. "He is old enough now to decide such matters for himself in the absence of his natural guardians. Also, he knows me well enough to judge pretty correctly whether I would approve or not, and I should not have objected had I been there."

"Shall we drive over and see about the children?" asked her father.

"Yes, papa, if you please. And let us start as soon as the necessary arrangements can be made."

Violet had scarcely completed her morning routine, though it was a little past noon, when glancing through the window, she saw a carriage at the gate and her grandfather in the act of assisting her mother to alight from it.

With a low, joyous exclamation, she flew to meet and welcome them.

"Mamma, mamma, I am so glad, so glad you have come!"

"My darling, my darling! Thank God that I have you safe in my arms!" the mother said, holding her close with kisses and tears. "What is this I hear of danger and shipwreck?"

"It is a long story, mamma; but we are all safe. Edward, Charlie, and the girls are still sleeping, I believe, for they were worn out with anxiety and the loss of two nights' rest."

"And you, dear child?"

"Was not with them, but of course slept but little last night—indeed not at all until after daybreak, when they were all safe on shore—and have only just risen."

"Then we will hear the story after you have breakfasted," her grandfather said.

They did not get the whole of it, however, until Edward joined them, an hour or two later. It was to them a deeply interesting and thrilling account that he gave. He had also much to say in Violet's praise, but was relieved and gratified to learn that neither mother nor grandfather blamed him for the course he had taken. He brought in his friend Tallis and introduced him, and was glad to see that the impression on both sides was favorable.

Edward had already urged Tallis to pay him a visit, and Mr. Dinsmore and Elsie repeated the invitation. But the young man declined it for the present, on the plea that the loss of his vessel made it necessary for him to give his attention to some pressing business matters.

Elsie proposed taking her son and daughter home with her, and they were not against it. She would have had all the rest of the young party come at once to her cottage and remain as long as they found it agreeable to do so, but all declined with thanks however, except Donald, Mary, and Charlie, who promised to come in a few days. Amy was not quite able to travel. They would stay with her until she was sufficiently recovered to undertake the journey to her home. Charlie would see her and Ella safely there, and follow Mary to the cottage home of the Travillas.

Before leaving Ocean Beach, Elsie and her father visited the life saving station, and the latter insisted upon bestowing a generous reward upon each of the brave surfmen. Also, he contributed largely to the making good their losses to the poor shipwrecked sailors.

Most joyously was the return of Edward and Violet welcomed by grandmother, brothers, and sisters. Edward was the hero of the hour, especially with Harold and Herbert, who in fact quite envied him his adventure now that it was safely over.

Violet found home and its beloved occupants dearer and more delightful than ever. The presence there of her aunt and cousin seemed the only drawback upon her felicity. Yet, that occasionally proved a serious one to both herself and "Cousin Donald," with whom Virginia was determined to get up a flirtation.

He did not admire her and would not fall in with her plans, perceiving which she turned against him, became his bitter foe, and made him and Violet both uncomfortable by sly hints that he was seeking her—and that simply because she was an heiress.

Old Mr. Dinsmore had gone to visit his daughter Adelaide and most sincerely did Violet wish that Aunt Louise and Virginia would follow.

Mrs. Travilla was living a retired life, not mingling in general society at all. An old friend of her husband and father, who had been a frequent and welcomed guest at the Oaks and Ion, had taken up his temporary residence at a hotel near by. And now and then he joined their party on the beach or dropped in at the cottage for a friendly chat with Mr. Dinsmore.

Sometimes Mrs. Travilla was present and took part in the conversation. Once or twice it had happened that they had been alone together for a few moments. She neither avoided conversation with the gentleman nor sought it, though he was a widower and much admired by many of her sex.

Perhaps Mrs. Conly and Virginia were the only persons who had sinister thoughts in connection with the matter; but they, after the manner of the human race, judged others by themselves.

One day Violet accidentally overheard a little talk between them that struck her first with indignation and astonishment, then grief and dismay.

"What brings Mr. Ford here, do you suppose, mamma?" inquired Virginia, in a sneering tone.

"What a question, Virginia, for a girl of your sense!" replied her mother. "He's courting Elsie, of course. Isn't she a rich and beautiful widow? I had almost added young, for she really looks hardly older than her eldest daughter."

"Well, do you think he'll succeed?"

"Yes, I do — sooner or later. He is certainly a very attractive man, and she can't be expected to live single all the rest of her days. But what a foolish will that was of Travilla's — leaving everything in her hands!"

"Why, mamma?"

"Because Ford may get it all into his possession and make way with it by some rash speculation. Men often do those things."

Violet was alone in a little summer house in the garden, back of the cottage, with a book. She had been very intent upon it until roused by the sound of the voices of her aunt and cousin, who had been pacing up and down the walk and now pausing for an instant close to her, though a thick growth of vines hid her from sight.

They moved on with Mrs. Conly's last word. And the young girl sprang to her feet, her cheeks aflame, her eyes glittering, her small hand clenched till the nails sank into the soft flesh. "How dare they talk so of mamma! And papa, too, dear, dear papa!" she exclaimed half aloud. Then her anger and grief found vent in a burst of bitter weeping as she cast herself down upon the seat from which she had risen, and bowed her head upon her hands.

The storm of feeling was so violent that she did not hear a light, approaching footstep. She did not know that anyone was near until she felt herself taken into loving arms that clasped her close, while her mamma's sweet voice asked in tenderest tones, "My poor darling, what ever can have caused you such distress?"

"Mamma, mamma, don't ask me! Please, don't ask me!" she cried, hiding her blushing, tearful face on her mother's shoulder.

"Has my dear, little Violet secrets from her very own mother?" Elsie asked in tones of half reproachful tenderness.

"Only because it would distress you to know, dearest mamma. Oh, I could not bear to hurt you so!" sobbed the poor girl.

"Still tell me, dearest," urged the mother. "Nothing could hurt me so sorely as the loss of my child's confidence."

"Then mamma, I will. But, oh, don't think that I believe one word of it all." Then with a little hesitation, "I think mamma, that I am not doing wrong to tell you, though the words were not meant for my ears."

"I think not, my dear child, since it seems it is something that concerns both you and me."

The short colloquy had burned itself into Violet's brain and she repeated it verbatim.

It caused her loved listener a sharper pang than she knew or supposed. Elsie was deeply hurt and for a moment her indignation waxed hot against her ungrateful, heartless relations.

Then her heart sent up a strong cry for help to forgive even as she would be forgiven.

But she must comfort Vi, and how vividly at this moment did memory recall a little scene in her early childhood when she was in like sore distress from a similar fear, roused in very nearly the same manner, and her father comforted her.

"Vi, darling," she said in quivering tones and with a tender caress, "it is altogether a mistake. And you need never fear anything of the kind. Your beloved father is no more dead to me than though he were but in the next room. His place is not now — can never be, vacant in either my home or my heart. We are separated for a time by 'the stream — the narrow stream of death,' but when I, too, have crossed it, we shall be together, never to part again."

The End